NEIGHBOURHOOD WATCH

Tom continued to watch, his gaze through the binoculars was constant and unwavering.

Jane flashed him a grin of conspiratorial amusement and then stroked the rounded head of the cigar tube between her breasts. The heat of her excitement grew. Teasing the tip against one nipple and then the other, daringly touching her tongue against the shiny end, as though she was about to fellate the tube, Jane threw herself into the erotic dance with fresh enthusiasm.

She knew Tom was watching and that was enough to allow her to continue with her eyes closed. The consideration that other neighbours might see was pushed aside as she lost herself in the realised fantasy of the exhibitionism. She licked the end of the cigar tube and then slid it down her bare body. The rounded end stroked between her bare breasts and over the flat expanse of her stomach. She continued to slide the glossy tube down, through the curls of her pubic bush, until it met the warm lips of her sex.

NEIGHBOURHOOD WATCH

Lisette Ashton

This book is a work of fiction.
In real life, make sure you practise safe, sane and consensual sex.

First published in 2008 by
Nexus
Thames Wharf Studios
Rainville Rd
London W6 9HA

Copyright © Lisette Ashton 2008

The right of Lisette Ashton to be identified as the Author of the
Work has been asserted in accordance with the Copyright,
Designs and Patents Act 1988.

A catalogue record for this book is available from the
British Library.

www.nexus-books.com

Typeset by TW Typesetting, Plymouth, Devon
Printed and bound in Great Britain by
CPI Bookmarque, Croydon, CR0 4TD

Distributed in the USA by Macmillan, 175 Fifth Avenue,
New York, NY 10010, USA

ISBN 978 0 352 34190 7

1 3 5 7 9 10 8 6 4 2

Symbols key

 Corporal Punishment

 Female Domination

 Institution

 Medical

 Period Setting

 Restraint/Bondage

 Rubber/Leather

 Spanking

 Transvestism

 Underwear

 Uniforms

Introduction

*An aerial photograph of Cedar View would show that the cul-de-sac looks like an enormous keyhole. The short, straight entrance to the road is lined by two houses on either side. The curve at the road's bulbous end, which isn't quite wide enough for a Mini Clubman to complete a full turning circle, looks like the hole where the barrel of the key would be inserted. Not that any of the residents know or care. They have more important things on their minds. Mostly SMANKers (**S**olvent **M**iddleclass **A**nd **N**o **K**ids), save for Tanya Maxwell at number two with her nasty cat and her tribe of squalling brats, the residents of Cedar View do share lots of similar passions, but I suspect that an interest in the local topography is not one of them. I only mention the distinctive shape because I have a penchant for looking through keyholes.*

Trees line the cul-de-sac, fledgling saps that are currently nothing more than caged twiglets and reflect the newbuild status of the surrounding houses. I don't know if they're going to grow into cedar trees, as would be appropriate for the street name, or some hardier variety better equipped for a life repressed by suburban paving stones. Again, I feel sure that no one else on Cedar View knows or cares. They're involved with more immediate pursuits.

1

Tom, the solitary occupant of number one, is a lifelong voyeur. Next door, at number three, the Smiths are both having affairs with other residents of Cedar View. Mr Smith frequently calls on Joanne Jackson at number five. Mrs Smith regularly visits Denise Shelby at number eight. Aside from the fact they have no morals, I also get the impression that Mrs Smith rules the roost at number three Cedar View. I don't think anyone has told Mr Smith about the dynamics of the arrangement. I've often seen him glumly smoking a cigar on the front doorstep, as though he and his tobacco have been banished from the picture-perfect interior of Mrs Smith's wonderful home. I believe the word I'm searching for is pussy-whipped. John Smith hasn't come across the term. But he will.

Joanne Jackson lives alone at number five. She has lots of visitors, if you know what I mean. She also has a water feature in her front garden: a small fountain over a pond that bubbles and trickles throughout the day. Her koi carp are large, colourful and pretty, although I think she spends an excessive amount of time tending to the damned things. It would certainly explain the wet patches on her clothing and the curious smell that surrounds her. Joanne is also pissed off because the cat from Tanya Maxwell's at number two keeps creeping around her ornamental pond, hungrily admiring the fish.

The Graftons live at number seven, and Denise and Derek Shelby next door at number eight. Denise and the Graftons frequently share a bed. They're like rutting rabbits. Derek doesn't seem particularly interested in the games they play. I've heard people say he gets more pleasure from polishing his car than from being intimate with his wife. But Denise doesn't let Derek's lack of interest interfere with her sex life. Denise and the Graftons are also regular attendees at the parties thrown by Ted and the beautiful Linda at number six. Special *parties, if you know what I mean. They're all hedonists. Libertines. Sex-mad immoral – amoral – bastards. Call them what you will.*

Ted and Linda have the only house on Cedar View that lays claim to a pool, at the rear of the property, inside the massive conservatory they erected two weeks after moving in. Personally I wouldn't see the point in spending so much money on something as frivolous as a pool. And it's not just the initial expense: there's the upkeep, making sure the temperature is correct, maintaining the balance of water and chloride or chlorine or chloroform or whatever it is they put in to stop algae forming. But Ted and Linda seem to enjoy the thing. The pool certainly fills up at their parties. Anyway, it's their house and their money.

A lot of people speculate about what goes on at number four. The McMurrays are a reclusive couple and spend so little time outside during daylight hours that some residents think they might be vampires. That would certainly account for the pale complexions, the gothic clothes and the midnight screams that sometimes issue from their cellar. But I know there's a rational reason for all those things and it has nothing to do with vampires. I know that Max McMurray is one of the most competent disciplinarians a servile woman could ever wish to encounter. And I know that's one of the reasons Megan keeps inviting her sister round to their house.

So, now you know the names of everyone on Cedar View, perhaps you'd like to meet the neighbours? They're just this way . . .

One

'He's at it again.'

'Who's at it again?'

'Tom. That pervy old twat from number one.'

'What do you mean, "He's at it again"? What's he doing?'

'What do you think he's doing? The same as he always does. He's *watching*.'

John stepped away from the bay window and glared at his wife. He was a tall, slender man with short blond hair and wire-rimmed spectacles. The white shirt and pale-grey pants gave him an insubstantial appearance, like a ghost. Most people described him as bookish. Neighbours, who had never thought to ask, assumed he worked in a dry, dull office and was probably some sort of accountant. Ironic, Jane thought, because her husband didn't work in anything remotely like accounting. Like her, he was in administration.

'I'm going out there,' John growled angrily. 'I'm going out there and I'm going to ram those binoculars up his arse.'

'Binoculars?' Jane's eyes opened wide.

She dropped her copy of *OK* to the floor and rushed to her husband's side at the window. She was shoeless – her sensible low black pumps were hidden discreetly

4

in the hall closet behind the front door – and her stockinged feet slipped dryly over the smooth, hard laminate. The TV played muted soaps in the background, and the remote lay on the polished glass surface of the TV stand, where it was always put, so that it couldn't be lost. The lounge looked as picturesque as an advert for furniture polish – and as antiseptic. A compact leather settee with matching armchairs dominated the floor space. The blandly tasteful walls were decorated with a triptych of blandly tasteful wedding photographs. The only clutter was the magazine Jane had just dropped on the floor.

'You're kidding me, aren't you? Has he really got binoculars?'

John shrugged, as if to say, 'Look for yourself.'

Jane twitched a corner of the net curtains to one side and squealed with a mixture of shock and delight. Tom was sitting on the low garden wall of number two. His face was half hidden behind a pair of glossy binoculars that wouldn't have looked out of place in a James Bond movie. The contrast of the modern equipment in the gnarled and nicotine-stained hands of their decrepit neighbour was jarring but, perversely, not unexpected.

'The brazen old bugger,' Jane gasped.

'I'm doing it,' John declared. He headed for the lounge door. 'I'm going out there, I'm going to snatch those binoculars out of his hands, and I'm going to ram them right up his –'

'No.'

Jane didn't shout the word. After seven years of marriage she had no need to shout any command she gave to her husband. There had been times when it was like training a dog – a tiresomely wilful dog like a Jack Russell or a particularly obstinate bull terrier. But now the hard work had been done. Jane knew she only had to speak to her husband in an appropriately stiff tone and his lapdog acquiescence, if not obedience, was instantly assured.

'You're not going anywhere.'

The idea came to her as though it was the fruition of a lifetime's planning. 'If Tom wants a show, that's what I'm going to give him. None of the other boring shits on this street will ever do anything to properly engage his interest.' A devilish smile lifted the corners of her mouth. Her china-blue eyes narrowed with merciless glee as she pulled the net curtains aside. 'Stick around, darling,' she suggested. 'You might see something new.'

'You're not serious.'

'Aren't I?'

With the curtains drawn back the lounge seemed an hour brighter. From the corner of her eye Jane saw Tom's binoculars twitch in her direction. A glint of sunlight on the lenses told her she had their neighbour's full attention. Glancing at John, she saw that his naked outrage had the same wide-eyed intensity as Tom's magnified gaze.

'You're joking, aren't you?'

Jane raised an eyebrow, knowing John would back down. She had made her decision and didn't care if he agreed or approved. More importantly, he had to *know* that she had made her decision and that she would never be swayed. It was one of the important lessons that she believed should be reinforced consistently throughout a good marriage. 'If you don't want to watch this, you can always go outside and have one of your damned cigars. No one's stopping you, darling.'

'What will the neighbours think?'

She regarded him coolly. 'Fuck the neighbours. Fuck the neighbours right up the arse. The self-obsessed shits round here wouldn't notice if I painted my backside bright blue and did cartwheels on the front lawn.' Turning away from her husband, smiling coquettishly towards the window, she shrugged off the cream cardigan that had been draped over her shoulders.

John released a sigh of protest. It sounded like a muted groan. He looked as if he was going to say something else. Defiance glimmered briefly in his eyes, then dwindled to a smoulder and disappeared. He marched to the DVD cabinet where he kept his tubes of cigars, took one and stormed from the room.

Ignoring her husband's departure, Jane began to pop the buttons on her cream blouse. She executed the striptease slowly, seductively, completely aware of her one-man audience. She was inspiring an excitement Tom had not felt in years. His binoculars remained fixed on her as she sashayed slowly around the room, his gaze intense and unwavering. From the little she could see of his face, he seemed to be wearing a huge, expectant grin. She knew she was thrilling him with the prospect of a private peepshow.

But it wasn't until she had removed her blouse that Jane found the striptease personally exciting. What had started as a malicious ploy to torment Tom and remind her husband of his place beneath her in the hierarchy of their home had unexpectedly become an epiphany. She was standing in an uncurtained window, showing her lace-trimmed bra to their curious neighbour. Yet when she caught a glimpse of her reflection in the glass, she felt a sudden sting of arousal.

A regime of sensible diet and occasional exercise had kept her looking trim. She was in her early thirties, but she realised that from where Tom was watching she could pass for much younger. Her hair was dark, shoulder length, and glistened like a shampoo advert. Her pale-blue eyes sparkled with mischievous excitement. Shadowed by the double glazing, her teasing smile seemed sultry, a far cry from her usual pale and pious prudishness. The ivory lace of her bra suggested more sumptuous breasts than she recognised, and she noticed, for the first time in ages, how sleek were the curves of her waist. She hadn't seen herself looking so desirable since the last time she called on Denise. The memory of that occasion was warming. Humming to herself, Jane began to dance.

She didn't know how good a view Tom had from his seat on the wall across the street, but she was no longer stripping for his entertainment: she was doing this for her own satisfaction. In an ideal world someone more attractive, available and able would saunter down Cedar View and glance through her open window. She fantasised briefly about a movie star or TV celebrity strolling down the cul-de-sac, glancing into her lounge and being won over by her exhibitionism. She dismissed the thought as silly and farfetched, but the idea added a licentious darkness to her mood and bathed her with warm perspiration.

Moving to the rhythm of her humming, she continued to strip, her hips swaying from side to side. She flicked a clasp and the pastel plaid skirt that matched her pastel plaid office jacket slipped smoothly from her hips and fell to the floor. She stepped away from it, glad she had elected to wear stockings that morning, hoping Tom was able to see the sheer cream denier clinging to her legs and the stark bands that encircled her coltish thighs. It would have been fun, she thought, if John could have seen how effortlessly she presented such an elegant yet saucy image. It might have rekindled a shared interest that had been waning over the years. But if he wanted to sulk childishly on the step with his smelly cigar, he was missing the show of a lifetime.

Deliberately, Jane turned a full circle, allowing Tom to see that a matching thong complemented her lacy bra and stockings. She kept her buttocks clenched, taut, envying their neighbour's enjoyment of the view of her neatly toned backside. When she turned to look out of the window again she saw the old man lecherously lick his lips.

Jane lifted her right bra strap and pulled it from her shoulder, then did the same with the left, leaving her slender biceps bound by the ribbon-thin strips of cream-coloured straps. Daringly, she pulled down the right cup of her bra and flashed a cherry-red nipple.

Even across the street she could see Tom's mouth shape the word 'Wow'. A glint of sunlight on the binoculars was like a blink of amazement.

Emboldened by his appreciation, Jane exposed her left nipple. That was as much as she was going to show him. Her striptease had already gone further than she had anticipated, and she was adamant he wouldn't see anything else. Her smile turned stony as she reached towards the curtains and prepared to draw them closed and end his view.

The pungent scent of cigar smoke touched her nostrils, reminding her that John was just outside. She was irritated by his insensitivity. She didn't approve of his smoking, but she allowed him to stand outside and have three cigars a day, though she found the smell nauseating. What she wanted was for him to come and help satisfy her, now that she was aroused by teasing Tom, but the thought of suffering his tobacco-flavoured kisses was repulsive.

Outraged that he had thwarted her plans, and determined to get satisfaction in one form or another, Jane shrugged the bra from her torso and continued dancing for Tom. Her breasts bobbed and swayed alluringly. She ran her splayed fingers over them, briefly concealing their plumpness from Tom's view, as she caressed the stiff buds of her nipples. The touch excited a tremor of sensation that was unexpectedly intense. Electric ripples spread from the sensitive tips, thrilling her with a rush of pleasure. She pinched lightly at the hardened beads of flesh, then tugged with more confidence. Gripping her nipples, drawing them away from her body, she basked in a glow of delicious discomfort. Spurred on by the mounting excitement, making sure Tom was still watching, she reached for the waistband of her thong.

It would have been satisfying to wrench it off with a single, swift gesture. It would have suited her mood of defiance to tear the thong from her hips and reveal her sex suddenly and brazenly bare. But even though her thoughts were smoky with excitement, they weren't so clouded that she was going to hurt herself and damage her underwear with such heedless hedonism. She turned her back on Tom and wriggled the rear strip of the thong down to the base of her buttocks. It was easy to picture the ribbon of fabric subtly underlining her backside. Bending forward, making her cheeks loom large for him, she slyly slid the thong over her thighs and down below her knees. When she stood up the flimsy garment fell to her ankles. And when she gracefully stepped out of the underwear and turned to face him, she was not surprised to see his leer broaden.

The excitement had been powerful before. Now it held her in a crushing embrace. The heat of her sex had been a minor distraction as she danced, stripped and showed herself topless. It had intensified as she played with her nipples. Yet, as soon as she showed her sex to Tom, her body temperature soared.

It crossed her mind that one of their other neighbours, their oh-so-respectable neighbours, might walk past the window and see what she was doing. She was a close friend of Denise Shelby at number eight but she didn't know any of the others beyond their surnames. They would surely be shocked by her outrageous display. Even that pair who were always throwing late-night parties, the ones with a pool whose names she couldn't remember, would be taken aback if they accidentally strolled past and saw her shamelessly displaying herself to the neighbourhood lech.

Her thoughts gave a keen edge to her arousal. She briefly wondered if John might be upset by the way she was performing for Tom. His outrage at the man's open voyeurism suggested he wouldn't wholly approve. She was momentarily tempted to stop herself and broach a reconciliation with her husband. But the idea of apologising, particularly when she was in the right, always made Jane defiant. 'Fuck them all,' she said to herself. Still dancing, still fixing her gaze on Tom as he continued to appraise her, no longer sparing a thought for her husband or the sensibilities of her neighbours, she whispered, 'Fuck them all right up the arse.'

The hazy reflection in the window showed a woman wearing only stockings. Her shape was sleek, surprisingly willowy, but made sexually exciting by the sway of her bare breasts and the sight of her exposed sex. If she had known she would be staging such a performance, Jane thought, she might have tidied the triangle of her pubic curls into something neater and more fashionable. But that was a minor consideration and didn't spoil the thrill of her mounting enjoyment.

As she executed a twirl she saw an open drawer spoiling the perfection of her flawless lounge. Her brow furrowed and the annoyance almost soured her mood. But when she realised it was the drawer of the DVD cabinet where John kept his filthy cigars, she had a wicked idea. She pulled out the glossy aluminium tube of a huge Cuban Presidente and rolled its fat girth

11

between her fingers. Continuing to sway her hips from side to side, enjoying the sensation of her unencumbered breasts rising and falling, she came to a quick decision before turning back to the window.

Tom continued to watch, his gaze through the binoculars constant and unwavering.

Jane flashed him a grin of conspiratorial amusement and then stroked the rounded head of the cigar tube between her breasts. The heat of her excitement grew. Teasing the cigar tip against one nipple and then the other, daringly touching her tongue to the shiny end as though she was about to fellate the tube, Jane threw herself into the erotic dance with fresh enthusiasm.

She knew Tom was watching and that was enough to allow her to continue with her eyes closed. The consideration that other neighbours might see was pushed aside as she lost herself in the realised fantasy of the exhibitionism. She licked the end of the tube and then slid it down her bare body. The rounded end stroked between her bare breasts and over the flat expanse of her stomach. She continued to slide the glossy tube down, through the curls of her pubic bush, until it met the warm lips of her sex.

Tom continued to stare, his jaw hanging wide open. Grinning at his obvious delight, and taking a malicious pleasure in the fact that he could only look and not touch, Jane allowed the cigar tube to rest against her pussy lips, on the brink of penetration. She continued to roll her hips, remembering techniques from a long-ago interest in belly-dancing that she had never bothered to pursue. The experience was no longer like being in her own home: it was like the thrill she felt when she was with Denise.

Jane pushed the cigar firmly between her legs. It didn't take much effort. Her sex was already warm and moist with excitement. She couldn't recall the last time her body had been so responsive while she was at home. But she wasn't in the mood for dwelling on such details, only for getting as much satisfaction as she could. Easing the cigar deeper, delighting in the way the thick tube pushed her sex wide, Jane threw back her head and let the rush of sensations flow through her body. Because she was standing, holding herself at an awkward angle, the tube slid against her clitoris as it slipped into her. Its slow caress and its warm smooth pressure against the centre of her sex were like a long, probing tongue.

She released a heavy sigh and then remembered her audience. Tom's pleasure was only a minor consideration; her own satisfaction was far more important. But because she wanted to do this properly and give him the greatest show he had ever seen, she forced herself to think from his perspective. She danced back to the centre of the room, dodging the furniture, keeping the cigar pressed inside her sex, enjoying the unusual sensations of the tube moving to and fro inside her body. Her stockinged feet slid on the floor like the smoothest of sexual caresses, the whisper of nylon against laminate a soft hiss of approval. When she reached the best position, centre-stage in Tom's view through the bay window, Jane deliberately turned around and bent over the back of the leather settee, her bare buttocks on full view for him.

She spread her legs slightly so he could see every naked millimetre of her exposed sex. It didn't matter that an untidy bristle of curls lined the pink labia, or that he could see the crinkled, mocha-coloured ring of her anus. Keeping her hand low so it didn't spoil Tom's view, working her wrist slowly back and forth, Jane wanked herself with the cigar tube.

It had gone from a performance to an experience. Her need for satisfaction was now more pressing than her need to show herself to the lecherous neighbour. Her priority was to squeeze a much-needed climax from her sex. Quickening her pace, thrusting the tube in and out with increased vigour, she teetered on the brink of orgasm. She bit her lower lip, savouring the mounting joy as it built in the pit of her stomach.

The idea of exposing herself so intimately had never crossed her mind before. But now, with the prospect of satisfaction only seconds away, Jane was amazed that she had never discovered this thrill. The seven years of her marriage seemed like a desert, barren of pleasure. Aside from her friendship with Denise Shelby it was a joyless existence that could have been spent far more productively. She felt a rush of anger that John had never helped her to uncover this part of her personality or to exploit its potential for pleasure.

And then the orgasm struck. The climax came with a fluid force. Her inner muscles contracted, expanded, quivered, relaxed. Wetness soaked her sex and daubed her upper thighs with a warm stickiness. The orgasm seared through her pussy with the heat and force of an exploding furnace. She had been sweat-swathed before but now she dripped with perspiration. Her naked stomach stuck to the leather of the settee. Between her thighs she was hot and sodden and desperate for more.

Greedily, she continued to slide the cigar back and forth. She briefly wondered if another contraction of her muscles might crush the fragile tube, but it slid so easily in and out that she decided not to worry about it. The second orgasm built swiftly inside her loins. She rubbed faster, desperate for another burst of satisfaction. Raising her head slightly, glancing over her shoulder and through the window, she saw Tom's gaze fixed unwaveringly on her naked backside. He grinned as she worked her hand more quickly back and forth.

14

The sight was enough to take her to the extremes of another climax. She howled with pleasure.

Her muscles clenched so tight they pushed the cigar tube from her sex. From a distance Jane heard it clatter and skid across the floor, as she soared over the highest plateau of satisfaction.

Her body trembled. Her fingers shook so much that she pushed them against her sex to still their tremors. She eventually caught her breath. She didn't bother searching for the fallen cigar tube. Her body demanded something more satisfying than a slender length of aluminium. Shivering with arousal, Jane magnanimously decided it was time to give her husband the benefits of her excitement. Even if he still stank of cigar smoke, she was desperate enough to let him take advantage of her desires. Anyway, there were places on her body where he could place his lips without causing too much offence. The thought made her grin lecherously. Hesitating for an instant, not sure if she should beckon him with a curt command or a sultry summons, Jane teased another eddy of pleasure from the open lips of her sex. Teetering on the brink of a third climax, and deciding this was probably the best time for John to become involved in the situation, Jane opened her mouth to call his name and allow him the privilege of her body.

'I've had enough of this,' John shouted from the hall. 'I'm going to the pub with my mates.'

Before she could respond the door slammed closed.

'Fuck him!' she murmured angrily. If he was happy to miss his chance with the horniest woman on Cedar View, then he could go and do whatever the hell pleased him. Angrily she hissed, 'Fuck him right up the arse.'

Two

5 Cedar View

If John Smith had been pressed to identify the horniest woman on the View, Jane Smith would have been the penultimate name on his list. Beneath his wife, a long way beneath his wife, he conceded in a spirit of grudging marital respect, was the shapeless, slovenly single mother at number two, Tanya Maxwell. He supposed it was unfair to dismiss her so abruptly. He didn't know her well enough to be sure if his low opinion of her was justified or simply based on a prejudice against her wash-weary pink sweat-suits and her dislocated air of inner-city poverty. He did know that it was always her children who were blamed for the occasional spurts of petty vandalism that struck the View. And he felt certain it was Tanya Maxwell's cat that kept digging shit-holes in his front lawn.

Above his wife he would have placed Denise Shelby and Rhona Grafton, as well as Ted's Linda from number six. There would have been no particular order or preference in his arrangement. Blonde, brunette and redhead, respectively, none was particularly glamorous but all were attractive in a soft-focus fashion. Denise Shelby usually looked as if someone else had selected her clothes, nevertheless, the woman inside the mismatched ensembles of pinks and blues or stripes and

16

paisleys was obviously attractive. When she wore her
biker gear – tight leather jeans, figure-hugging jacket
and a full-face helmet – he thought she looked like a
goddess. But then any woman on the View, even Tanya
Maxwell, would have looked desirable in such an outfit.

He considered this for an instant and then shook his
head to dismiss the idea. It seemed acceptable to argue
the sexual pros and cons of all the women on the View,
but Tanya Maxwell didn't belong in that grouping. He
wasn't even sure Denise, Rhona or Linda really
deserved his high estimation. He only believed they
were more sexually exciting than Jane because they
weren't domineering, ball-busting megabitches. Or, if
they were, they weren't domineering him or busting his
balls. And in his heart he knew that none of them was
sufficiently spectacular to earn first or second place on
his private list of the View's horniest women.

Across the road, the mysterious Ms McMurray
stepped from the door of number four, tossing a mane
of jet hair from her brow. Her head turned to the left,
then the right, as though she were looking for something or someone she wanted to avoid. Her eyes were
hidden by sunglasses as black as her hair, the lenses so
large they hid most of her alabaster face. When her
gaze swept in the direction of Tom from number one,
her retroussé nose wrinkled with disgust and she
quickly looked away.

Her body was draped with a long leather coat. Sleek,
sexy and shiny, it dusted the floor as she walked down
the path. Although the leather concealed most of her
slender figure, the slit up the front of the coat
occasionally parted to deliver a flash of fishnets and
ankle boots. In one porcelain-pale hand she held a torn
envelope and a small sheet of pink paper.

John blinked to make sure she wasn't a figment of
his imagination. He didn't think he had ever seen her

17

during daylight hours before. Ordinarily Ms McMurray was a creature of the night, a stranger he glimpsed in the glow of the View's two streetlights, a shadow from his wet dreams, an enigma from the realms of suburban legend. On his personal list of the cul-de-sac's most desirable women Ms McMurray competed for pole position with his darkly beautiful neighbour Joanne Jackson. The temptation to stop and stare, as Ms McMurray sauntered smoothly down the path, across the street and towards number seven, was almost irresistible.

But remembering his own outrage at the obvious voyeurism of Peeping Tom from number one – and the dirty old sod was still sitting there, one hand holding the binoculars to his eyes, the other thrust hard against his groin – John tore his gaze away and stepped through the gate of number five.

The sound of the water feature was with him immediately. The burble and glug of the fountain, splashing constantly and musically on to the ornamental pond, aroused him. It was the sound he always heard before he enjoyed the best sex of his life. A smile stretched across his face. He drew a deep breath, already aware of the stiffness in his pants, and pushed open her front door.

The scent of incense made his pulse quicken. The smoky floral perfume always reminded him of sexual satisfaction, punishing passion and glorious golden gratification. It was the fragrance he associated with visiting Joanne. He remembered an argument with Jane once, when she told him he had no interest in foreplay. Well, it hadn't been so much an argument as Jane shouting, 'Your idea of foreplay is to get an erection.' He hadn't said anything in response and had gone outside to have a cigar, but the harsh accusation had hurt, and he realised now that it was unfounded.

He did enjoy foreplay and always had. Leaving Jane at home, walking to Joanne's, hearing her fountain and inhaling the scent of the smouldering incense sticks: those were all elements of the foreplay rituals he enjoyed with his illicit lover. Quashing the urge to smile at this discovery of his sensitive side, enjoying the bowel-tingling thrill of being close to Joanne, and away from Jane, he closed the door gently behind himself.

'When will you ever learn to knock?'

'Joanne?'

'*Mistress Joanne.*'

He swallowed a nervous shriek and nodded.

She stood in the doorway of the kitchen at the far end of the hall, looking like the embodiment of his darkest desires. Thigh-high boots with eight-inch heels. A black corset compressed her full waist and made her plump breasts look even more generous. She had tied back her blonde hair so it looked viciously severe. In her left hand she held a riding crop, a quivering extension of her anger.

John's erection ached as though it was about to explode.

'*Mistress Joanne,*' he concurred.

'You're wearing shoes.'

He apologised and began to wrench them from his feet. At home, next door, *with Jane*, he despised the ritual of removing his shoes and placing them in the neat, tidy shoe cupboard behind the front door. His wife's insistence that he remove his shoes before entering his own home was a slight upon his masculinity and made him feel dominated, emasculated. But here, whenever Joanne demanded he remove his shoes, John found the act of going barefoot highly erotic. It was another element of the foreplay that Jane claimed he didn't understand.

'You're standing up.'

He knew what she expected and dutifully fell to his knees. She looked taller from this perspective, more commanding and more beautiful than ever.

He longed for her.

'How dare you walk in here unannounced,' she declared, striding towards him. 'Tanya spent the morning hoovering this house, cleaning from top to bottom. And you think you can simply march in here wearing your nasty shoes? Do you think that's acceptable behaviour?'

She was in front of him and towering over him. His face was on the level of the crotch of her panties. The familiar scent of her sex was warm, musty, musky and inviting. He inhaled deeply before dropping his gaze and mumbling another apology. His erection was a steel rod inside his pants. His balls strained for release.

'You stink of cigars. And you've only come here for one thing, haven't you? It's the same thing you come here for every Tuesday and Thursday night, isn't it?'

Blushing, he nodded.

She made no response and, as the silence stretched to breaking point, he knew she wanted him to say the words. Trying not to stammer, hoping she wouldn't berate him for not being worthy, he spluttered, 'Yes, Mistress Joanne.'

She shook her head and used the riding crop to slap him twice across the backside. His shorts and trousers cushioned the blows but he still felt twin stings of discomfort. Joanne used the tip of her crop to point at the toe of her boot.

'Only one person is allowed footwear in this house. Who is that?'

'You, Mistress Joanne.'

'And why am I allowed footwear?'

This was a new one. John hesitated. Was she allowed footwear because it was her house? Or was it

20

because she was the one in charge and he was merely her inferior? Maybe there was another reason he had missed? Knowing she despised lies and stupidity, aware that a wrong answer would earn him a punishment more severe than two stripes across the back of his trousers, John shook his head sorrowfully and lowered his gaze. His heart pounded with fresh enthusiasm and he savoured the sensation of bowing to her authority.

'I don't know why you're allowed footwear, Mistress Joanne.'

She sneered at him. Her maraschino lips wrinkled with disgust. Her teeth were as white and predatory as a shark's. 'I'm allowed to wear boots because I have slaves like you to keep them clean. Slaves like you to lick them clean.' She spat the words with obvious impatience. 'Stay down on your knees,' she said, stepping past him. The heels of her boots clicked hollow against the floor. 'Follow me into the front room. I want to see what's going on outside.'

'There's nothing going on out there,' John mumbled. 'Only that old pervert from number one spying on everyone with his binoculars.' She either didn't hear or she wasn't listening. She walked through to the front room. John, still on his knees, shuffled after her.

The layout of Joanne's house was identical to that of the home he shared next door with his wife. He supposed all the houses on Cedar View were virtually identical. The only difference he could see between Joanne's house and his own was that where he and Jane had a lounge, Joanne had a front room, and he wasn't sure if that counted as a real difference. When the buildings had been completed the designers had installed laminate flooring throughout all the properties and finished off their work with the same fixtures, fittings and colour

21

schemes. Joanne's choice in furniture, however, stretched to a darker shade of leather than the suite Jane had installed in number three.

Joanne walked to the bay window and rested her elbows on its sill. Like a well-trained dog, John followed at her heel. Because she was bending slightly he was able to admire the rounded curves of her backside. Joanne had no time for thongs, dismissing them as uncomfortable and unflattering. Staring at the panel of black fabric that concealed her broad rear, John thought she was probably right not to compromise her principles for the sake of fashion. But he still wished he could take a good look at her bare bottom. The unspoken desire filled him with a mixture of longing and frustration.

'Was that the McMurray woman I just saw? Going over to the Graftons? What the hell is she doing out before nightfall?'

John said nothing. He had been present during conversations like this before and knew he was not expected to contribute or participate. As soon as he was close enough to Joanne's backside she extended a foot and presented him with her boot. It was his job to hold her shin and then lick the sole of her boot, kiss the toe and the heel, while he worshipped her superiority. The bent leather behind her knee squeaked softly as he held her leg. His erection ached and throbbed with the urgent need for release.

'I didn't think she ever went out during daylight,' Joanne murmured. There was a trace of irritation in her tone, as if a secret had been kept from her. 'And what's she doing at the Graftons? Rhona and Charlie have never mentioned that they know her.'

John stroked his tongue against the sole of Joanne's boot. The taste of house dust and grit from her front path was unexciting but, as with most things at

Joanne's house, it was a flavour he associated with arousal. Not that he thought of the task as tasting house dust or grit. He was being allowed to worship at Joanne's feet, kiss her boots and pay homage to her superiority. Moving his lips to the toe, kissing the leather with genuine passion and adoration, he longed for her to notice his enthusiasm and effort. When he slipped his mouth to the rear of her foot, taking the eight-inch heel between his lips and sucking on the length, he wished she would glance down at him and congratulate him for doing such a thorough job.

'You were right about *Peeping Tom*,' Joanne said with a sigh. 'The seedy old bastard is out there with his binoculars. They're pointed in this direction now. Although I doubt he can see anything through these nets. Is he playing with himself?' She laughed, a shrill, nasal sound, etched with disgust. 'I can't abide men who play with themselves,' she muttered. 'I despise them. They're weak and despicable fools. It always makes me think of gruesome little boys playing with worms. Puerile. Vulgar. Contemptible.'

She turned her head and stared down at him. John still had her heel in his mouth. His lips sucked hungrily on the eight-inch spike. One hand was pressed hard against his groin, squeezing, stroking.

'Are you going to play with your worm, little boy?' she sneered.

The disdain in her voice was crushing. He almost came in his pants. Breathing deeply, trying to find the internal reserves to stave off his climax, he took his lips away from the heel and shook his head. 'I'll only play with my worm when you've given permission, *Mistress Joanne*.'

She glowered at him. 'You're a snivelling puddle of piss.'

He grinned at her insult as though she had awarded him the highest praise. Her scorn was a spur to his excitement. Her contempt was one of the most powerful aphrodisiacs he had ever encountered. He abruptly stopped rubbing at his lap, fearful he would bring himself to climax before she had granted permission.

Joanne tore the boot from his grasp and readjusted her position. She continued watching through the window but lowered herself to squat on her haunches. If Tom's binoculars had been able to penetrate the veil of the nets he would have seen only her head bobbing over the bay's windowsill. Her backside, large before, now seemed swollen to an immense and glorious size. John knew what she expected from him but he prudently waited for her command.

'Lie down on the floor,' Joanne barked. She tilted her head in his direction so there was no chance of him missing the command. 'Face up. Head beneath my ass. I want you to sniff me and tell me how good I smell.'

Beaming with gratitude, John did as she demanded. He adored being beneath her. From the moment he had left the front door of number three, from the instant he had manfully told Jane he was going to the pub, he had been waiting for Joanne to deliver this revered instruction.

Ignoring him, Joanne turned her attention back to the world beyond the window. 'I wonder why there are so many cars this evening? Oh! Wait. That's right. Ted and Linda are throwing another party tonight, aren't they? I'm surprised her fanny isn't worn out.'

The comment went over John's head. He hadn't noticed any more cars than usual when he walked from number three to number five, although admittedly his attention had been divided between his anger at Jane, his outrage about Tom, his impending visit to Joanne and the unexpected glimpse of the mysterious Ms McMurray. From his position on the floor, basking in the broad shadow of Joanne's backside, he couldn't see enough of the View to confirm or argue the point.

Not that he was bothered about cars, parties, or the curious comment about Linda's fanny. His world was currently darkened by the glory of Joanne's panty-covered buttocks and nothing else mattered. With his nose only an inch from her crotch, he drew a slow breath and savoured the sultry tang of her sex. Being so close to her and drinking in the intimate flavour of her perspiration, his erection bulged at the front of his pants with ardent enthusiasm. The need to climax struck him with a debilitating force but he resisted the impulse. Willing himself not to try and touch her, remembering that she had only asked him to sniff, he whispered lovingly, 'You smell divine, *Mistress Joanne.*'

She ignored him for a while and then asked, 'Where the hell is your wife going?' Her question almost broke the thrall of his arousal. The urge to get up and see what Jane was doing and what Joanne was seeing was almost irresistible. He suddenly wanted to push the woman's vast buttocks away from his face, move Joanne from the window and find out where his wife was going. But he knew better than to show Mistress Joanne such bursts of insurrection. Reminding himself that he wasn't supposed to be involved in the conversation, John remained beneath her buttocks and daringly stroked his tongue against her crotch.

Joanne shivered and John allowed himself a moment to enjoy the rich flavour of her gusset. The musky taste that filled his mouth was somewhere between noisome and nirvana. His erection pressed harder against the front of his pants. He made a renewed effort not to spoil the moment by ejaculating before she had given permission. More firmly this time, he pushed his tongue against the gusset-sheathed centre of her sex.

She sighed. For an instant he was euphoric, believing he had elicited a response from her. It was only when she began to talk that he realised she had simply been drawing breath before speaking. The disappointment was crushing.

'Now this is unexpected,' Joanne murmured. 'I think your wife's coming here.'

He gasped. The impulse to get up had been strong before. Now it was a compulsion. He didn't know if he was more horrified by the prospect of being caught with another woman or frightened that Jane's presence in Joanne's home would defile something special in his life. The most important thing in his mind was the absolute certainty that Joanne and Jane must never meet. Not while he was at Joanne's. Not while he was lying on his back worshipping her gusset. He braced himself to suffer Joanne's wrath as he tried to work out the best way to slide from beneath her.

'No,' said Joanne, laughing cruelly, 'I was wrong. She's gone past here. She's headed further up the road.'

He released a trembling sigh and realised the instant's panic had left him dizzy. Taking a moment to catch his breath, trying to convince himself that the prospect of his wife finding him had not engendered a rush of cold, black fear, John stared at the broad expanse of Joanne's gusset and willed his arousal to return.

Joanne glanced back over her shoulder, shifting her buttocks so she could glare down at him. 'Weren't you supposed to be sniffing my hole?'

'Yes, Mistress Joanne. Sorry, Mistress Joanne. You smell divine.'

She ignored his apologies and sycophancy, putting her rear back over his face and returning her attention to the street outside. 'I do hope you're thirsty down there,' she muttered absently. 'I think it's time for me to be a good hostess and offer you a drink.'

He held his breath and gripped his hands into fists. Her words suggested she was about to indulge him with one of his favourite fantasies. His ultimate fantasy. Mounting excitement made him tremble and vacillate between the choices of drawing his tongue against her gusset or lying with his jaws expectantly open. The hope that she might deign to piss in his mouth was more thrilling than he could properly explain. It was a treat she had allowed him only twice before but on both occasions he had been elated to bask in the shower of her golden spray. Anticipating that dark and deviant thrill, John squirmed against the discomfort of the hard floor. He silently admired her rear and tried to detect the subtle change in Joanne's scent that would indicate she was about to relieve herself on his face.

'No,' Joanne muttered. 'It looks like she's going to the Graftons'. Maybe I was wrong about Ted and Linda's party being tonight.'

She managed to sound completely distant, uninterested in him and his efforts to please her, concerned only with the mundane events occurring outside the window on Cedar View. John marvelled at the way she was able to feign such cool impartiality when he felt sure she shared his intense arousal.

'What with the McMurray woman going over there before,' Joanne continued, 'maybe it's Charlie and Rhona who are throwing a party tonight?'

John didn't respond. In truth, he wasn't listening. He stared up at the black fabric covering Joanne's buttocks and sex and privately beseeched her to release her hold on her bladder. The scent of something briny touched his nostrils but he wasn't sure if that came from his anticipation, imagination or a genuine change in the air of the room. He was so close to the thinly sheathed centre of her sex, he knew he would detect any difference before she did let go. He felt certain she was just about to do it and the thought made his erection throb with painful force.

'No. I was wrong again,' Joanne said distractedly. 'I guess Ted and Linda's party is still on. Your wife's going to the Shelbys'. She's probably off to see Denise. Again.'

With his concentration fixed on the crotch of Joanne's panties, John didn't want to question her about that statement. He wanted to lose himself in the black vision of loveliness that was Joanne's panty-clad buttocks. But she had said his wife was going to see Denise Shelby, and she had made it sound as though Jane regularly visited the woman, although John wasn't aware of a friendship between them.

Why would Jane be visiting Denise Shelby? he wondered. Why would she have a friendship with the woman? And why had she kept it secret from him? His brows knitted and he prepared to voice his questions. Even though he knew it would disturb his arousal, and Joanne would chastise him for his impertinence, he had to have an answer.

'Open your mouth,' Joanne snapped.

His questions were suddenly forgotten. He could sense the change in the air and knew what was about to come. His erection strained for release but, more than that, he physically craved the decadent humiliation of what was about to happen. His nostrils caught the pastel scent that always presaged the delivery of her pee. His chest tightened as he watched Joanne's buttocks clench. The crotch of her black panties grew darker. Blacker. And then they were glossy. As he watched the magical transformation, and revelled in the display, his erection throbbed with a tense and agonising need.

28

The first tentative droplets of piss spattered loosely on his forehead. Then they turned into a downpour, scalding hot, gushing over his face, sluicing across his spectacles. The downpour was so heavy it trickled underneath the lenses, dripping into his eyes, nostrils and hair. Her water seemed to go everywhere except his mouth and he wriggled and writhed beneath her as he tried to catch some of the flow. He was suddenly soaked by the rush of her hot golden shower. Spluttering for breath, trying to grin with his mouth open, he extended his tongue in the hope of catching a stray droplet.

'Drink it all,' Joanne said softly. Her tone was matter-of-fact, not harsh as it had been when she insisted he remove his shoes. It was the closest she ever came to sounding affectionate. 'Drink every drop and I'll let the little boy play with his little worm.'

The promise was unnecessary, for he had come. He revelled in the climactic pulse of his erection spurting into his shorts. The shock of release was powerful enough to leave him breathless and gasping. But his own pleasure was nowhere near as important as his need to do as Joanne had asked.

When he pushed his mouth up, closing his lips around the sodden, sagging crotch of her panties, he came close to choking on the rush of too-hot piss that streamed from her sex. Swallowing greedily, wishing there was time to taste her flavour, wishing there was time to breathe, John basked in the absolute delight of being Mistress Joanne's toilet.

She finished without ceremony. The Niagara-like stream tapered to a rush, then a trickle, then stopped. He kept his mouth pressed against the crotch of her panties, enjoying the shape of the labia beneath as they met his lips, delighting in the nearness of simply suckling against the cloth over her wet hole.

29

'That was . . .'

She shifted position.

His voice trailed off. There weren't words to describe the experience. There never had been and there never could be. He stared meekly up at her and tried to charm her with a piss-wet smile.

'That was . . .'

Looking down on him she said, 'That was *a relief*?'

He laughed more loudly than the joke deserved.

Ignoring him, Joanne stood up. The sodden crotch of the panties clung to the outline of her sex lips. Stray dribbles of pee trickled down her thighs, painting glossy lines that disappeared inside the neck of her boots. Mesmerised, John stared at the vision of the sodden fabric coating her crotch.

She stared down at him with an expression that lacked her usual disdain. John didn't know her well enough to be sure but he thought there was something contemplative about the way she was considering him. He braced himself for the indignity of whatever else it was she might now need from him. The spent and sticky length of his flaccid penis began to stir with the promise of a fresh erection.

'Since your wife's gone out, I guess that means you're mine for the rest of this evening,' Joanne observed. She retrieved her riding crop from the windowsill and flexed it between both fists. 'That's right, isn't it?'

John considered this for a moment and then nodded. There was no need for him to go back to an empty house. No reason for him to spend his time in solitude when he could be serving Joanne.

'I'm yours,' he agreed. Easing himself from the floor, remembering to get to his knees and not upset her by standing upright, he was still unable to drag his gaze away from the sopping crotch of her panties. Addressing the question directly to her sex, John asked, 'What did you have in mind?'

She placed a boot in front of his mouth, silently encouraging him to lick away the spatters of pee that had fallen on the leather. As soon as his mouth began to work against the toe, she said, 'I'll fetch you a mop and bucket so you can clean up in here before we leave. Then we'll get you dressed and you'll accompany me over the road to Ted and Linda's party.'

With his tongue still working against her shoe, John could only nod by way of reply. Even though Joanne bullied him with her insults and commands, pissed in his mouth, threatened him with a riding crop and was now telling him how they would spend their evening, he didn't think she was as domineering as his bitch of a wife.

Three

7 Cedar View

'Was this your idea?' Megan McMurray demanded. 'Or do I blame your bitch of a wife?'

Charlie, still dressed as though he was ready to browbeat his minions on the board of directors, considered the sheet of pink vellum in silence. Dark, commanding yet ominously affable, he looked like a man who always got his own way and never backed down from a challenge. Megan had passed his BMW as she walked up the driveway and she thought the sleek yet functional vehicle was strongly reminiscent of the attractive and imposing Mr Grafton.

Beside the sink, coolly preparing vegetables for their dinner, Rhona Grafton turned to face their visitor. Her shoulders stiffened. The tension briefly turned her model good looks into something stilted and unnatural. With the back of her hand she wiped a stray brunette curl from her forehead. It immediately returned to her brow but she pretended not to notice. The razor-sharp paring knife remained in her clenched fist, like an unvoiced threat. Her ice-blue eyes regarded Megan with frosty hostility. 'That's a bit harsh, isn't it? You don't know me well enough to know whether I'm a bitch or not. I'll thank you for an apology unless you can justify that accusation.'

Megan fixed her with a withering glare. Because she still wore her raven sunglasses she doubted Mrs Grafton got the full impact of the expression. But it gave Megan some small satisfaction to scowl at the picture-perfect vision of Rhona Grafton.

'You want me to justify the accusation?'

Rhona nodded.

Megan's lips broke into a leer. Parodying Rhona's clipped pronunciation she said, 'Charles, I simply have to have that McMurray girl. I know you've said you fancied riding her, but I think I want her now. I want to eat her pussy and have the pasty little slut begging for more. Do you think that would be possible, Charles? How do you think we could organise such an event?'

If Rhona Grafton was embarrassed by Megan's words she kept her emotions contained. Her colour didn't change and her expression remained poker-faced. Brushing the stray curl from her forehead again, smiling tightly as though she was pleased to be discussing the matter, she said, 'I had no idea you were an eavesdropper. I think that aspect of your character makes you even more desirable.' She placed the knife with the vegetables beside the sink and walked to her husband's side.

'Cock-up,' Charlie said simply. He flexed a terse smile and handed the sheet of paper to his wife. 'Your writing, Ronnie. My mistake. I delivered it to the wrong address.' Glancing at Megan he said, 'This was supposed to go to that fat lass. The one with all the kids and those fuck-awful pink tracksuits.'

'The Maxwell girl,' Rhona elaborated.

'Tanya,' Megan added, supplying her neighbour's name. 'Tanya Maxwell.'

Charlie nodded. 'I must have shoved it through the wrong letterbox.' Looking vaguely contrite, but only vaguely, he flashed Megan another smile and said, 'Sorry. I guess I wasn't cut out to be a postman. I suppose it's fortunate I made up my mind to work for a living.'

Uninvited, Megan took one of the captain's chairs and sat down facing him. She pulled a pack of tobacco and some papers from inside her coat and began to roll a cigarette. The kitchen was a haven of cleanliness and perfection. One window stared out on to the Graftons' rear garden, a modest stretch of neatly manicured lawn. Another window overlooked the driveway at the side of the house and Charlie's BMW. The décor inside was spotless. The surfaces were polished and the fixtures and fittings were hidden behind discreet doors that looked like the other cupboards. Sprinkling curls of tobacco dust on the spotless linen cloth that covered the kitchen table, Megan ignored the room and the Graftons and glowered at the cigarette she was making.

'Well,' she murmured dryly. 'That certainly puts a different spin on things, doesn't it?'

Rhona took the letter from her husband and read it slowly. The pink paper looked as if it belonged in her slender, attractive hand. 'I honestly don't understand what the problem is,' she said eventually. 'Why would this letter make you call round here in such an angry mood? I can't see anything in it that would be offensive.'

With her cigarette rolled, Megan snatched the sheet from Rhona's hand. Charlie was watching her with the intensity of a hawk pursuing a fieldmouse. Not for the first time in her life Megan was thankful that she concealed her eyes with the impenetrable dark glasses. Max, her husband and master, exuded the strongest air of authority she had ever encountered in any man. He doled out discipline with a mastery that was breathtaking and delightful. But Charlie Grafton seemed to have a similar aura of power and control. As she snapped her cigarette lighter aflame, Megan glanced again at the letter.

Dear Ms M,

We would be interested in employing your services for a couple of evenings each week. Please let us know if you are able to accommodate us and we can then get together and negotiate the terms and conditions most satisfying to all our mutual needs.

Yours sincerely,

Charles & Rhona Grafton

The misunderstanding was now so obvious she wondered how she had been so careless as to make the mistake. Because she had heard Rhona and Charlie discussing her – *'Charles, I simply have to have that McMurray girl . . .'* – and knew the swinging couple shared a desire to get her into bed, she had assumed the letter was a bold offer proposing payment for sex.

The connection had seemed obvious when she read the letter. Now Megan was amazed that she could have been so self-centred and stupid as to make such an erroneous assumption. 'I read it the wrong way,' she mumbled. Raising her gaze to meet Charlie's she added defiantly, 'But it was your fault for delivering it to the wrong house.'

He held up his hands. His smile was genial, forgivable. 'My bad,' he admitted. 'I'm sorry for causing you any upset. It was strictly unintentional and, even though I don't know how I offended you, I'm genuinely sorry for doing it.'

He was on his feet a moment later, opening the fridge door and plucking out a bottle of white wine. Rhona had put three glasses down on the table before Megan realised the woman had moved. The couple worked with the sort of close-knit choreography she knew she would never have with Max, regardless of how many times he striped her backside.

Before she had a chance to tell the couple she didn't drink wine, Charlie was pouring a conciliatory measure into the glass nearest to her and then filling one for himself and another for Rhona.

Realising a refusal would offend, and deciding she had already risked enough upset with the neighbours, Megan picked up the glass and took a tentative sip. The drink wasn't as vinegar-like as most of the wines she had tried before but, although it had a pleasantly fruity flavour, she realised it was dangerously potent.

'Why did it upset you so much?' Rhona asked, sliding into the chair next to Megan's and inching the seat closer. 'Are you that much of a snob that cleaning is beneath you?'

'I guess I must be,' Megan agreed. 'Why do you want someone cleaning house for you?'

'Touché.' Rhona grinned and gave Megan's arm a lingering, if platonic, squeeze. 'I'm a snob and cleaning is beneath me. I've been telling Charles that I'm not the only woman on this street who feels that way.' She slipped her fingers away from Megan's arm and sipped her wine. 'I'm glad we're of a like mind.'

The conversation developed easily. Although Megan knew the couple by sight and the occasional nod of curt greeting, she had never spoken to either Grafton for such an extended period. Sipping her wine, and not complaining when Charlie 'filled her up', she found the pair were engaging, witty and nowhere near as pompous as she had expected.

It was quickly obvious that Rhona Grafton was an out-and-out snob. She spoke with disdain about most of their neighbours, particularly Tanya Maxwell at number two and Tom at number one. But her bigotry was so constant and convicted that it came across as amusing rather than offensive.

'I'm surprised no one's reported him to the police,' she said with a sniff as they talked about Tom. 'I've seen him out there today, peering through his binoculars and rubbing at his lap. It's absolutely obscene. His crotch must smell like a fisherman's farts.'

Megan almost choked as she tried not to splutter a mouthful of wine across the table. She appreciated Rhona's genuine apology and the comfort of the woman's hand on her back as she caught her breath and resumed her composure.

Charlie didn't voice the same superiority that dripped from his wife's venomous tongue, but Megan soon understood he had a firm belief in his own authority. While he let his wife do the majority of the talking and appear to make decisions, Charlie was clearly the driving force behind the marriage.

'You still haven't explained why the letter caused you so much upset,' Charlie said as he poured a third glass of wine.

Although she could feel her good judgement clouding over, Megan didn't believe she was out of her depth. The couple were unexpectedly warm and interesting. Not what she'd expected. After the amusing anecdotes and confidences they had already shared with her, she felt it was right to explain the nature of the misunderstanding that had led her to their door.

'I thought you were propositioning me,' she admitted.

The couple were silent for an instant, then they began to laugh. 'I told you I should have written that letter,' Charlie declared.

'You can't write letters for shit,' Rhona returned. 'Your handwriting is appalling.'

'I don't write letters that sound like sexual propositions.'

'Well, I didn't think I did.' Rhona clapped a hand over her mouth and stared at her husband. 'My God! What if you'd had brains and delivered it to the right address? You don't think we'd have Tanya Maxwell opposite us now, do you? Can you picture her, sitting there in one of her ghastly tracksuits and thinking we were up for a threeway?'

Megan heard herself laugh but she wasn't sure whether it was with amusement or horror. The conversation was more explicit than she would have expected of her prim and proper neighbours, and skated way beyond decency and her own sympathetic appraisal of poor Tanya. Megan had always considered herself fairly unshockable, but she realised she simply wasn't used to discussing acquaintances in such brutal and uncompromising terms.

Charlie considered his wife's remark for an instant and then shuddered as he drained his glass. 'A threeway with Tanya Maxwell? That's the scariest suggestion I've heard in years.'

Rhona snorted. 'Like you're fussy about where you stick it.'

Megan managed to avoid another choking session in response to Rhona's outrageous remark.

'I draw a line at Tanya Maxwell,' Charlie grunted. He glanced at Megan and said, 'But if Rhona's letter upset you so much, if you thought she was propositioning you, why did you bother to come round here? Why not just tear up the letter and glare at us menacingly each time we passed on the street? Wouldn't that have been the more sensible thing to do? Wouldn't that have been the *Cedar View* thing to do?'

She hesitated between the truth and an excuse. He had left her the ideal opportunity to say that she didn't hold with petty bickering and childlike glaring contests on street corners. She could offer the lie and come out of the conversation sounding noble and proud. But Megan thought the unexpectedly likeable couple deserved more honesty than that.

'I was considering the offer,' she admitted.

She had intended to make the remark in a light-hearted tone that matched the mood of their conversation, but instead it came out sounding more serious than she meant, and a thick silence fell. The air in the kitchen hummed with taut sexual tension. If her words had been written for a soap opera, Megan thought, that would have been the final line before the scene cut to a commercial break.

Four

A commercial break played in the background from an unseen TV set outside the room, probably downstairs. But Jane Smith wasn't listening. With Denise's tongue pressed firmly against her sex, sliding against the labia and occasionally punching between the lips of her pussy, Jane told herself the only thing she was aware of was the pleasure.

But that wasn't strictly true. She could hear the advertisements, cheerful, brash and louder than the regular TV programmes. Chocolate, dishwasher tablets and car insurance were briefly elevated to a euphoric status that her mere orgasms would never attain. Determinedly, she tried to shut the sounds out and concentrate only on the slurp of Denise's mouth against her sex.

Above, in the newly installed mirrored ceiling over the bed, her reflection stared curiously down. Lying on the black satin sheets, with Denise's bowed figure kneeling between her thighs, Jane thought that sight more than anything else should give her the thrill she needed to push John from her thoughts and bring her mind back to the more immediate pleasures of her arousal. She still wore her stockings, their cream bands cutting tight into her thighs and the sheer denier making her legs look slender and desirable. With the rest of her body bare she had to admit that her reflection looked sultry, glamorous and exciting. She could understand why Denise wanted her so badly, why she so urgently desired to inflict such a rigorous and thorough tongue-fucking. Yet, as much as Jane tried to lose herself in the pleasure of having Denise lap and lick at her sex, she couldn't stop brooding over her argument with John.

'He's such a selfish bastard,' she complained, spreading her legs a little and urging Denise to lick higher. 'I hate that part of him. Why does it always have to be about him? Why can't he ever be like the rest of us and think about others for a change?' Her fingers caught a fistful of stray blonde curls and she tugged and guided her friend's head until her tongue was probing Jane's sex and striking sparks from her clitoris.

'He just walked out?' Denise glanced up from her homage to Jane's pussy. Her mouth dripped with her own saliva and Jane's musk. Her chin looked glossy, wet and kissable. 'Where did he go?'

'Fuck knows.' Jane tried to say the words as though she didn't care. 'He said he was off to the pub again. But he never says which pub.'

'Do you think he's seeing someone else?'

'John?' Jane laughed at the idea. 'He wouldn't dare.' A flicker of doubt crossed her mind. She glanced sharply at Denise. 'You don't think he'd dare, do you?'

Denise shrugged and lowered her head back to the gaping wetness of Jane's pussy. She pressed a couple of gentle kisses on the bare flesh above the tops of Jane's stockings and then ran her tongue up to the pouting labia. 'He's *your* husband, Janey,' she murmured. 'I wouldn't know whether he'd dare or not.' There was a long, sultry silence as Denise's tongue pushed into Jane's sex and struggled against the clenching muscles. Her upper lip pressed heavily against Jane's clitoris.

'Do you know something I don't?' Jane pulled her sex away from Denise's mouth and sat upright on the bed. Panic clutched her chest like a large and powerful fist. 'Have you heard something? Or has John been round here and –'

'Jesus, Janey.' Denise stared at her with disbelief. 'You're blowing this out of proportion. You and John have had a row. He's probably back home now, sulking and wondering where the hell you are.' She sighed and leered hungrily at the slit of Jane's sex. She stretched out her fingers and touched the tip of one against Jane's labia. The contact sent a velvet thrill of excitement through her.

'John's a dull and boring bloke,' Denise continued. 'He doesn't fulfil your needs. You've told me that before. You've said he doesn't even *try* to fulfil your needs. What would another woman want with him?'

Jane considered this solemnly. The words contained a grain of truth, but she wondered if Denise was missing something. She supposed that was unlikely. When it came to knowing about husbands who could be described as 'dull and boring', Denise was already an expert. Without thinking that the free association might cause offence, Jane asked, 'Where's Derek this evening?'

'He's gone round to his mother's. He never takes his car when he goes round there. He doesn't trust the neighbourhood kids near hers not to run a coin down the side. I usually send him out of the house when I go round to Ted and Linda's. It makes it easier for me to enjoy my night.'

Jane digested this and tried not to squirm on the black satin sheets. Denise and Derek had an unusual relationship. Denise's sexual appetites were voracious in the extreme. Conversely, Derek's sole interest in life seemed to be a pathological obsession with polishing his car. They each enjoyed their pastime. Yet they remained together as man and wife, as though there was nothing untoward in the way they conducted their social lives.

Jane wasn't sure if Derek knew about Denise's frequent and fantastic infidelities, but she sorely envied the woman her freedom to enjoy the fruits of an adventurous private life. The only drawback to this arrangement – the only drawback that Denise had ever mentioned – was that Derek seemed reluctant to give Denise the pregnancy that her body clock currently craved. It was a sensitive topic, a subject that invariably made Denise's mood plummet, and because it didn't really concern her, Jane didn't want to broach the issue this evening.

'You're going to Ted and Linda's?'

'They're having one of their parties.'

Denise always used the same expression when talking about Ted and Linda's parties. It was never 'a party' or 'the party', it was always 'one of their parties', as though it differed from every other type of party in the world. And, while Jane had never been to 'one of their parties', she had heard enough from Denise to know that the events merited such a distinction.

Her evening had already been powerfully exciting. From the moment she decided to strip for the entertainment of Tom, through to turning up at Denise's door and explaining she was horny and not completely satisfied, the gnawing, nagging remainder of an unspent orgasm had lingered in her loins like a tightly bound knot. There had been lots of sexual stimulation and a couple of enjoyable bursts of pleasure, but she hadn't yet satisfied her need for a phenomenal climax.

After an age of Denise's tongue at her sex, as well as the delicious pleasure of having her friend's fingers glide softly in and out of her hole, Jane still felt frustrated and in need of something more. But she also felt sure Ted and Linda's party wasn't the place where she would find that something more. Parties like the ones thrown by Ted and Linda weren't for people like her. Parties like those were for sexual daredevils like Denise. Glumly, Jane climbed from the bed, reached for her coat and gave her friend an apologetic smile.

'If John's at home now, I'd better go back and talk to him.'

Denise stopped her putting on the coat and, with more force than Jane would have expected, pushed her back onto the bed. The silky satin sheets caressed her buttocks. Denise's naked body pressed smoothly against hers. The swell of her breasts was only a light, rounded pressure but Jane could feel the thrust of stiff nipples against her ribs. Fresh tingles of arousal flurried through Jane's sex.

'I've had a lousy day so far today,' Denise murmured. She pressed gentle kisses upon Jane's body between each word. 'I overslept. The office was a bitch. Traffic was a nightmare. I dropped my bike when I was putting it in the garage this evening. It fell against Derek's car, and I've put a huge gash in the door panel. He's going to go ballistic when he gets back from his mother's and sees it. Everything that could go wrong has gone wrong. The only good thing to happen today has been you turning up naked and horny, so I'm not letting you go until we're both satisfied that the crappiness of this day is finished.'

Denise continued to smother Jane with kisses, pressing them against her cheeks, jaw and lips. Her fingertips trailed over Jane's nipples. Her breath was tinged with the scent of pussy.

'If John's sitting at home now,' she continued, 'if he's there alone and worried, you should let him stew. I think you should do something for yourself this evening. I think you should do something that helps you let off some steam.'

Jane tried to remain rigid beneath her. The temptation was to caress the naked flesh that pressed against her. She could feel Denise sliding over her body, exciting urges that Jane seldom encountered at home. Not wanting to be so easily swayed, Jane kept her hands away from her, and allowed Denise's kisses to remain unreciprocated. She told herself she could control her base desires and resist the temptation, so long as she didn't touch Denise.

Sweat-slick fingers stroked her waist. Denise moved her caresses downwards, reaching for the slit of Jane's sex. With a forceful thrust she pushed a thumb between the folds of her labia. The penetration was swift and easy. Jane's inner muscles clenched treacherously around the warm intruder. She bit back a sigh and struggled to remain distant for a moment longer. Even when Denise curled her thumb upwards, pressing the tip against the spongy swelling of her G-spot, Jane clung to the belief that she could still show some resistance.

Denise lowered her mouth to Jane's and delivered a slow, sultry kiss. Her tongue slipped between Jane's lips as her thumb probed more deeply. When Denise's knuckles rubbed over the ball of her clitoris, the rush of raw excitement banished the last of Jane's willpower.

'What do you want me to do?'

'I think you should do something for yourself this evening.'

'What are you suggesting?'

Denise moved her head until her mouth was poised over one stiff nipple. Jane watched as the woman

45

sucked the stiff bud of flesh and then pulled her head back slightly, the nipple caught between her lightly clenched teeth. When Denise finally released her hold, Jane knew she was ready to go along with whatever her friend had planned.

'What are you suggesting?' she repeated.

Denise raised her head, looked towards the open bedroom window and tilted her head towards the ostentatious front garden of Ted and Linda's. 'I'm suggesting you should come with me. I'm going to Ted and Linda's party tonight. I'm sure everyone there would make you feel welcome. And I'm sure you'd enjoy yourself sufficiently to forget all about John for the evening.'

As Jane considered the invitation, the tingling sensation in her sex lips suggested that her body had already made the decision.

Five

6 Cedar View

Despite the tingling sensation in her sex lips, Linda had one last chore to perform before the party was ready to begin. There was a garden seat at the rear of the house, standing on the decking and facing the brightly lit conservatory. On the table beside the seat she placed four tins of lager and a plate of cellophane-covered sandwiches. Next to the lager and sandwiches she added a small box of tissues. She thought the food and drink should have looked sad and pathetic as they sat on the garden table, but they caught enough of the day's fading light to glimmer with expectant hope. Smiling tightly to herself, proud of her altruistic gift to those less fortunate, Linda stepped back into the warmth of the conservatory.

The lapping of the pool, accentuated by the hollow acoustics of the conservatory, was always a stark contrast after the tranquillity of the garden at dusk. The air smelled of chlorine and the light was unbearably bright. But it was her pool and, although it seemed large, empty and desolate, she knew that in less than an hour it would be the scene of laughter, passion and a dozen or more naked bodies writhing and jostling. She sniffed twice, trying to decide if the air was too chemical for guests to enjoy themselves, and then walked through to the adjacent kitchen.

'Is anyone here yet?'

'Only Phil. He's been helping with the snacks.'

Linda nodded a polite greeting to Phil. In dark pants
and a plain white shirt he looked understatedly digni-
fied and attractive. Ted wore a similar outfit, making
the two men look more than ever like brothers. The
similarity was apparent in their rounded faces, full-
lipped grins and the identical wrinkles that creased the
corners of their eyes. The only difference between them
was that Ted's hands were as spotlessly clean as any
hospital worker's while Phil's bore the ingrained grime
of a lifelong mechanic.

Ted glanced at her and, before he spoke, Linda
knew what he was going to say. It was part of an
empathetic understanding she often encountered in
long-term relationships. With Ted that telepathy
seemed stronger than anything she had met before,
and she didn't know if that was because they shared
something particularly special or because he was ten
years older than her and therefore ten years wiser.

'Have you been leaving beer for the garden gnomes?'
he asked.

Linda blushed softly at Ted's question, as though
embarrassed that he had discovered a guilty secret.
'I'm just giving a little something back to the commu-
nity,' she explained. 'Don't you feel sorry for Peeping
Tom? His life must be pretty empty if he can only get
his thrills from watching other people. And, on a dry
and passionless street like this one, don't you think his
viewing pleasure must be severely limited?'

Phil grinned and sipped his wine. Ted laughed and
shook his head. 'Dry and passionless? This street? You're
having a laugh, aren't you? Denise lives next door and
the Graftons are only over the road at number seven.'

Linda shrugged. She was content with her own sex
life but aware it was more varied and colourful than

most. Although Ted made a valid point in referring to Denise and the Graftons, she couldn't imagine many of their other neighbours enjoying a passion for anything other than pristine properties, conservative cars and tasteless TV. Mention sex to any of them and Linda felt certain they would flush like the primmest of maiden aunts. Not wanting to disagree with Ted, especially with the party so close, she snatched his wine glass and took a quick sip. With the Bordeaux still dripping from her lips she pushed the glass back towards Ted and pressed a kiss upon Phil's mouth.

His tongue slipped through the wine-flavoured moisture of her smile. She stroked the firm roundness of his biceps. He moved his hands over her hips, then one arm was around her waist, and his mouth devoured hers. His erection thrust against the front of her skirt.

'Phil,' she demurred, easing herself from his embrace. Her mouth tingled from the intrusion of his tongue. She wiped the back of her hand against her lips to dab away a droplet of wine. 'You really shouldn't do things like that in front of Ted. He can get very jealous.'

Ted, looking anything but jealous, continued to sip his wine as Linda and his brother exchanged smouldering stares. 'That's me,' Ted agreed. 'I'm Mr Jealousy.'

Linda gave him a wink then turned her smile back to Phil. 'Although,' she began, 'I think you're just the right person to give me some advice before the party begins. Would you mind?'

Phil sipped his drink as he studied her. 'Advice?'

Linda reached for the hem of her dress and teased it coyly between her fingers. 'I've been preparing my pussy,' she explained. 'In readiness for the party,' she added quickly, scared he might think she was some sort of pervert. 'Would you tell me if it looks OK?'

Slyly, she waited for his nod of approval. Ted continued to watch, his wine forgotten, his expression inscrutable.

Linda went to the breakfast bar, sat on the counter and placed one shoe on the seat of a stool. Appraising Phil coolly, absorbed in the part she was playing, she said, 'Are you sure you don't mind checking this out for me?'

'Stop teasing the poor bastard,' Ted grumbled.

Phil waved him silent. 'I don't mind checking you out,' he assured Linda. 'And if you want an honest opinion, I'll be happy to give you one.'

All three struggled to suppress their smiles at his *double entendre*. The air between them was thickening with the expectation of sex. Linda could feel her body focusing on the need that throbbed between her legs. It was always exciting preparing for a party; the knowledge that her libido was about to enjoy a smorgasbord of potential pleasures never failed to set her pulse racing. But this was a different and more specific kind of anticipation, the kind she felt when she knew she was on the verge of doing something pleasurable that fulfilled a personal ambition. Savouring the moment, pausing for a beat to ensure both men were watching, she began to raise the hem of her dress.

Her legs were bare, smooth, shaved, shapely. She lifted the hem higher to reveal the milky flesh of her inner thighs. Ted gazed at her over the rim of his glass. Phil's eyes grew wider. Linda parted her legs and pulled the dress so it no longer obliterated their view. She was delighted to hear both men gasp with awe.

'Bloody hell,' Phil marvelled.

Ted gave a soft laugh of appreciation. 'I see you did it.' His voice was rich with wonder and disbelief. 'I wondered why you were so long getting ready. I can understand now. You went and did it.'

'What the hell have you done?' Phil asked.

Linda's cheeks blushed with pride and accomplishment. She was thrilled by their approving gazes, delighted that her efforts had been able to provoke such enthusiastic responses.

'Does it look OK?'

'OK?' Ted was shaking his head incredulously. 'It looks beautiful.'

She beamed at him.

For the last two hours Linda had been playing with a pussy pump. The suction device cupped her vagina and, when she activated the pump, held her labia in a relentless vacuum. The edge of the cup had easily clung to the smooth, waxed flesh of her sex. The seal between her pussy and the mechanical device hadn't been broken through the long glorious hours she'd spent in preparation. As the vacuum continued to suck against her labia, the lips of her pussy had stretched and swollen, until they were rounded, puffy and grossly engorged. Checking her appearance in the mirror before going into the back garden and leaving Tom his lager and sandwiches, Linda had thought her sex had never looked so full, flushed or painfully exotic. Now, seeing the reactions from Ted and Phil, she felt sure she had made the right decision in preparing her labia for the party in such a unique way. Her sex looked so obscenely engorged she knew she would be the centre of attention.

'Christ! Linda! That looks sensational.'

She grinned, not surprised that Ted had lost his usual sangfroid.

Phil gaped. His eyes were wide. His jaw hung open.

Ted stared at her with an expression of approving bewilderment. His gaze repeatedly flicked from her face to the bulbous, bulging explosion of her sex lips.

'Do they hurt?'

'They're sensitive,' she answered carefully. Hurt was not the right word to describe the way her pussy currently felt, but she had to say something about its heightened responsiveness. The gentlest movement of air was like a skilled lover's tongue kissing and probing deeply. 'But that's the whole point of pumping them up big, isn't it? I wanted to make them more sensitive.'

Phil's fingers moved towards her.

She didn't flinch at the prospect of his touch but she was pleased when he remembered his manners and refrained from caressing her without permission. Even though they'd known each other for the best part of a year, even though Phil and Ted were brothers, even though Phil regularly attended Ted and Linda's parties and sometimes organised private get-togethers of his own, there were still protocols that needed to be observed.

'Sorry,' Phil mumbled, withdrawing his hand. He flashed a sheepish grin and said, 'They just look so damned irresistible.'

'He's right,' Ted agreed, putting down his wine glass and stepping closer to Linda. He lightly touched the top of her inner thigh, adding fuel to the smouldering heat of her arousal. 'I can understand Phil wanting to touch those puffed-up lips of yours. I'm aching to get at them myself.'

She pressed a hand against his chest, dizzied by the rush of adrenalin. Her heart pounded. The tingling in her sex felt more acute than normal. During the first few parties they had organised, Linda had felt similar thrills as she looked forward to the evening and anticipated all the fun that was likely to be had. In the hours beforehand she had felt this same poignant rush – almost like a drug high, only natural – and she had savoured the pleasure it always gave. But the parties themselves had been disappointing, and that anticipatory thrill had waned and then disappeared. Now, revelling in the honest approval of her partner and his brother, Linda realised she was reliving that glorious natural high. Her body trembled with a surge of sudden excitement. 'I've got no objection to Phil touching,' she said. Laughing at the idea, she added, 'The whole point of doing this was to make myself look irresistible. So I've got no objection to anyone touching.'

Both men moved in on her.

Phil pressed a kiss against her mouth, one hand going behind her back, the other sliding up the inside of her left thigh. Ted approached from the right; he stroked her breast through the flimsy top of her dress while his other hand stole to her right thigh. Simultaneously, both men reached the swollen flesh of her labia.

Linda gasped. As the shiver of pleasure struck her body she arched her back.

When she admitted her labia were sensitive it hadn't been a lie, but it hadn't been the whole truth either. Her honest response should have been to admit that the swelling was fantastically tender. The slightest caress inspired a rush of stimulation that left her breathless and gasping. Even a change in the temperature could provide so much sensory overload that she was pushed close to the point of climax. The sensation of fingers against her flesh was almost instantaneously orgasmic.

'Are you sure we've got time for this?' Ted asked. 'The party's due to start any minute. The first guests will be here soon.'

'No one's here yet,' Linda replied. Giving him her sultriest pout she added, 'From what I can see, the three of us are alone right now.' She could have gone on to say that none of the guests would be upset to find their hosts fucking as they arrived.

Ted nodded with a seriousness that matched her own lustful need. 'You want us here?' he asked. 'In the kitchen?'

'Of course not,' she panted. Although her need for satisfaction was intense, it wasn't so severe that she was going to get down and dirty in the kitchen. Aching with frustration and desire, she rocked her hips back and forth, and with the movement her labia rubbed against their fingers and knuckles. She chewed on her lower lip as the waves of pleasure rolled over her.

'The pool?' Phil suggested.

His hand was upon her thigh, holding her firmly, so tightly that her skin dimpled beneath his touch. Ted had her in a similar grip, with one hand pressed against her back. The knowledge that two strong men held her, both of them wanting her and preparing to have her, added an extra frisson to Linda's excitement.

'The hall,' she hissed. 'Take me in the hall.'

They carried her swiftly out of the kitchen and into the ornate charm of the hall. For once Linda paid no attention to the classical features of the décor or the architecture. In the mirror that faced the porch she caught a brief glimpse of her scantily clad body being carried by two men, a redhead trapped between two burly brothers, an image that made her think of fantasy heroines being kidnapped by romantic heroes. It was enough to add a fresh surge of desire to her need.

And then she was laid on the floor, her dress pulled over her shoulders in one easy sweep, and she was left naked and ready for them.

There was no need for conversation. Linda had played with Ted and Phil often enough to know how they would want to work together and she wasn't going to argue with a winning formula. As Phil knelt between her legs, lowering his head to her pussy and moving his mouth close to the engorged flesh of her sex, Ted unzipped his trousers and brandished his erection in her face. He knelt above her head, grinning down at her naked figure and watching his brother prepare to lick her hole.

She reached for the length with one hand and hungrily guided it towards her mouth. He was thick, hard and slick with pre-come. The flavour was the delicious aphrodisiac she most appreciated as an aperitif before a party. Something about the taste of cock in her mouth always quickened her pulse and made her sex clench. Taking him into her mouth, growing giddy on the cloying taste of his shaft, Linda sucked and licked as though devouring his flesh.

Phil stroked his tongue against her hole.

The shock of pleasure was enormous. The light pressure of their fingers had been incredible, but as soon as Phil's tongue touched her bulging lips Linda was transformed into a seething mass of feeling that demanded satisfaction. Everything else was forgotten: the forthcoming party, the imminent guests, Ted, even the politeness of protocols and permission. All of those considerations were pushed from her thoughts as the urgent need in her loins became a furious demand.

Her hands went from Ted's erection and grabbed hold of Phil's head. Pulling him hard against her sex, she thrust her pelvis up to meet him. She sensed the briefest hesitation as he stiffened. She was vaguely aware that she was ignoring her husband. But she forgot all that as soon as she felt her sex being squashed against Phil's mouth.

Ordinarily Linda was used to the pleasure of an orgasm building slowly through her body. As she became more aroused she usually enjoyed a rush of anticipation and the thrill of knowing that the pleasure was about to burst through her body.

This was nothing like those previous experiences.

Her body exploded as soon as Phil's tongue slipped between her flushed lips. The waves of pleasure continued to batter her flesh as she rocked her pelvis and slid her sex against his face. His fingers bruised her thighs, pushing them apart as he struggled to get his head closer to her wetness. His tongue repeatedly lapped, probed, kissed and caressed. Linda groaned and tried to urge him on with guttural instructions but the words made no sense. There was nothing Phil could have done to make her satisfaction more complete. There was no instruction she could have given that would direct him to do anything better.

'They feel as good as they look?' Ted said with a laugh.

Through a haze, she smiled for him, and then urged her pelvis back up to meet Phil's tongue. Another surge of pleasure rippled through her body.

She believed the need inside her clenching pussy should have been sated by the first orgasm. The pleasure was long, full of marvellous peaks. But she needed to know how her sex would feel with a cock buried between the bulging pussy lips. She yearned to feel a thick shaft, or maybe two, plunging between her overblown labia. The idea of being penetrated by both cocks was exciting enough to encourage another explosion to burst from her loins. She pulled Phil closer as she prepared to tell him that she wanted to be fucked.

Instead, a different word came from her mouth. 'Party,' she gasped. Reality came back in trickles. She was supposed to be having fun this evening. But she was also supposed to be a good hostess. As much as she craved her own satisfaction, Linda had to make sure that her guests were catered for and enjoying themselves. The whim of 'testing' her swollen labia was now out of her system and she needed to think about the others who would soon be arriving. 'The party's due to start any minute,' she panted. Pushing Phil's face away from her sex, sorry to be denying herself the glorious pleasure of his tongue against her lips, she said, 'The first guests will be here soon.'

'Wise words,' Ted muttered, stuffing his stiff cock back inside his pants and standing up. 'Why didn't I think to say that earlier?'

Phil gallantly helped Linda to her feet and then both men were touching her and treating her to a light, tender embrace.

Linda slipped from their arms and rushed to the mirror. Her body was swathed with perspiration. Her hair was dishevelled and her smile broad with satisfaction. 'I think I should put something on,' she decided. 'I want to look my best for the party. I want to look *the* best.'

Ted joined her and pressed a hand against her flat stomach, one finger pointing downwards towards the flushed and bulging slit of her pussy lips. He planted a kiss upon her throat and said, 'I can't imagine anyone at the party is going to be more distinctive than you.'

'Really?'

He grinned and shook his head. 'What could anyone possibly do tonight that would make them stand out more than you and your pumped-up pussy?'

Linda considered this and realised he was probably right. She was about to kiss him with renewed gratitude when a voice behind her cut into the exchange.

'Are we the first to arrive?'

Joanne stood in the open front doorway dressed like a model for leatherwear. Her black leather boots were complemented by a leather basque that cinched her waist and made her breasts look large and inviting.

With her blonde hair tied back and a riding crop in her hand she would have looked formidable. But the fact that she held the leash of a pathetically anonymous gimp kneeling by her feet made Linda sure that the woman would be the most commanding presence at the party.

She glanced at Ted but his interest was already caught by the dominatrix in the doorway. And when she remembered his question ('What could anyone possibly do tonight that would make them stand out more than your pumped-up pussy?') she realised she only needed to nod in Joanne's direction to provide an answer.

Adopting her most diplomatic smile, reminding herself the party was for everyone's pleasure and not just to show off her own attributes as a hostess, Linda greeted Joanne with a warm kiss and asked Phil to show her round the house. She struggled to hide her disappointment when Joanne and her gimp stepped quietly past her. Wearing her most tactful expression she asked, 'Are Charlie and Rhona coming?'

Ted shrugged. 'They said they'd be here tonight. Ronnie mentioned something about trying to get her hands on the McMurray girl, and we all know they've both got designs on her, but I can't imagine that would be happening tonight.'

Linda sucked her teeth. 'I hope you're wrong. I don't think it would be wise for them to do anything with Megan McMurray.'

'Why?'

'The McMurray girl?' She shook her head, suddenly solemn. The thrill of her stretched pussy lips and the nuisance of Joanne's appearance were forgotten. 'Megan McMurray is a tempting package. But she's tied to some pretty serious baggage.' Instinctively her gaze went to the side of the house adjacent to number four. She believed, for an instant, she could see through the walls and glimpse the dark and sinister figure that resided there. 'The McMurray girl is tied to some very serious baggage,' she repeated. 'I wouldn't want to see Ronnie or Charlie get on the wrong side of Mr McMurray.'

Six

4 Cedar View

'You're baggage,' he declared.

The cellar was lit only by a scarlet bulb. The glow turned pale flesh bloody, and darkened the darkest recesses. The room should have been spacious but the lack of light made it claustrophobic, gloomy and foreboding. Strengthening beams had lowered the ceiling. Thick chains dangled from them like remnants of the world's largest cobweb.

Caught in the spider web of chains was a near-naked woman. Her hands were tied behind her back, secured by leather cuffs. Her legs were bound at the ankles by thick black straps. Loops of leather, taut around her chest, made her modest breasts bulge in an explosion of trapped flesh. A tight-fitting mask hid the upper half of her face, while the lower half was distorted beyond recognition by a ball-gag that stretched her mouth open in a silent scream. A leather thong exposed her backside but kept her sex a thinly veiled secret. Chains beneath her shoulders and hips suspended her above the floor.

Max studied her without speaking. His brow was wrinkled by a solemn frown. The cane in his hand twitched as though he longed to use it but hadn't yet decided how. He was tall, broad and powerfully commanding; his shaved head almost touched the lowest of the beams. Black tattoos, in Celtic and tribal designs, covered his muscular biceps. His jeans were tight and faded. His crisp white wife-beater, bloody in the crimson light, was stretched across a broad and manly chest.

He stood motionless, admiring her and her initiative at having prepared herself in this way for his return home. He doubted there were many wives so thoughtful as to make themselves available to their husbands in such a unique and exciting way.

But something was amiss. He had been about to regale Megan with a litany of her favourite insults, the words that always made her nipples stiffen and her pussy moist and her body hot and receptive for him. The familiar opening phrase in this game, telling her she was baggage, was usually enough to make her moan. But this evening Megan remained silent. Not that she could moan properly with the gag in her mouth, admittedly. But she usually let out a muffled sigh to indicate that they were operating on the same wavelength and playing the same game.

They had devised it together. He began by calling her baggage and then went on to berate her for being a wayward, cock-hungry slut. He tempered the expletives with bland words that wouldn't have suggested sexual chemistry to anyone else. When he called her a filthy little harlot, she responded as he would have expected of any woman with a fondness for humiliation. But when he used choice phrases from their personal dictionary of dirty words, calling her baggage, trash or 'the bucket', Megan always responded with a distinctive and eager enthusiasm.

This evening she simply remained still, silent and unmoved.

'You're baggage,' he said again.

Nothing. He sliced his crop across her backside. The blow was delivered with consummate skill. He struck in a swift arc that avoided the chains and landed directly on his intended target. There was a metallic shudder as the links stretched taut, his victim stiffening in silent protest. A slender line of red crept across her porcelain-pale buttocks.

She made no sound.

He studied the red line: it curved round one buttock, vanished and returned to curve round the other. It was a perfectly delivered slash, a testament to his artistry as a disciplinarian. Her buttocks shook slightly in response to the punishment, then her entire frame shuddered as the raw hurt of the blow spread through every pore.

But her response wasn't what he had expected.

Wondering why there should be a difference, Max raised his cane and slashed a second blow across the tops of her thighs. Before he returned to the list of insults he wanted to see some evidence of normality in Megan's reactions. The air was broken by a whistle. The sound of the crop on her skin was like the snapping of an icy, brittle twig. Her backside shook with the force of the impact, and again she stiffened.

The cellar was momentarily filled with the hiss of her escaping breath. The ball-gag didn't allow her the opportunity to scream. It kept her mouth wide open but muted every sound she might make. Max was used to cries of muffled suffering, but this evening there were none. His frown deepened.

A second red line crept along her flesh beneath the first. The rounded cheeks were tense and trembling. The obvious pain of the stripes was enough to make his arousal harden into an urgent, obsessive demand. Her buttocks quivered and the sounds of the chains creaking told him that his victim was shivering in her bondage.

He circled her slowly, his eyes narrowing to slits as he studied her body. Her biceps were taut and well defined. The familiar curve of her back echoed every other time he had caned her bound and suspended body in this fashion. The roundness of her rear, the way the stripes on her cheeks slowly blossomed to red and painful welts: these were all sights he had seen and enjoyed before. And yet . . .

He spun round, marched to the wall of the cellar and snatched a pair of nipple clamps from a shelf. He returned to her and fixed one in place and then the other. The jaws bit hard into her bound breasts. He watched the soft bulb of each nipple yield to the powerful force of the rubber-edged clamps. The outer edges were crushed to a white and bloodless agony. Her position looked unbearable, insufferable. He heard her breath deepen in a series of agonised gasps. Yet it still wasn't quite right.

Whirling from her side, returning to the shelves that lined the cellar walls, he grabbed a pair of weights and attached them to her clamps. They tugged the chains down, dragging at her flesh, punishing her skin mercilessly. The sight was excruciatingly exciting. Her breasts had been tightly bound. The modest mounds of flesh had been transformed into painful, unsightly tubes, the skin that bulged from the top a dusky grey, darkened by trapped blood. Her areolae and nipples were flushed to the lush purple of an angry sunset. When he added the extra weights, her torment looked complete. The weights dragged her breasts downwards, tearing at her nipples and tugging on her sensitive flesh. The torture looked exquisitely arousing.

Determined to know what was wrong, Max tore the mask from her face – and immediately understood why he had perceived a difference. He unfastened the ball-gag from her mouth, tossed it into a corner and said simply, 'Hello, Aliceon.'

'Max.' She smiled weakly. 'How are you?'

'Puzzled,' he admitted honestly. 'I thought you were Megan.'

'That happens a lot,' Aliceon admitted. Garrulous by nature, she continued: 'Because we're twins people often mistake us for each other. I've had that happen so many times where people have come up to me, thinking I was Megan and saying, "Hi, Megan", and I have to say, "I'm not Megan. I'm her twin sister Aliceon."'

Max said nothing.

Aliceon's smile turned conciliatory. Whatever torment she was suffering from the two stripes on her backside and the weight of the punishing clamps, she chose not to show her discomfort in her voice or her expression. It reminded Max that, aside from her propensity to talk too much, his wife's twin shared a lot more with her sister than physical similarity. The two women had an identical appetite for pain and punishment.

'Megan had an errand to run,' Aliceon explained nonchalantly. 'She asked me to take her place in the cellar this evening. She was the one who tied me up like this. We both know you like your women bound and helpless. Neither of us thought you would mind.'

Max chewed thoughtfully on his lower lip. He didn't particularly mind that Aliceon had replaced Megan for this evening's escapade in the cellar. He appreciated the fact that his wife and her sister were equally happy to cater for his need to dominate and humiliate. On those occasions when he had been given the opportunity to punish both sisters simultaneously, Max had enjoyed some of the most memorable sex of his life. But he wasn't comfortable with the idea that Megan and Aliceon had worked together to deceive him. The fact that Megan had tried to hide her absence suggested she was doing something of which he wouldn't approve.

'Where is she?'

'I expect she'll be back soon enough. She told me it would only take a couple of hours and –'

'Where is she?'

'And she was thinking of you and knowing you have a lot on your mind and didn't want to trouble you by begging for permission or –'

'WHERE THE HELL IS SHE?'

As he roared the question Max slashed his crop against Aliceon's exposed rear. His aim was true and the crop sliced against both ruddy cheeks. There was no artistry in it: he had only struck her to stop her prevaricating and elicit the answer he wanted.

Aliceon gave a gasp of outraged surprise. Then, quickly, clearly anxious to avoid further punishment, she gasped, 'Megan went to see a neighbour. She got a letter. She didn't tell me which neighbour. She only said she was going over the road.'

'Insurrection?' he muttered. The word echoed like a hollow death knell in the blood-red nightmare of the cellar. He reached for his mobile phone and dialled a number.

Seven

2 Cedar View

The telephone chirruped noisily in the background but Tanya Maxwell ignored its shrill call. She pressed her face against her front window and sneered.

That dirty old bastard Tom was still ogling everyone on the View – and it looked as though this evening everyone on the View was giving him something to watch. His huge binoculars had done a complete circuit of the cul-de-sac from number three all the way round to her neighbours at number four. She watched the grizzled figure ease himself from her garden wall where he had been sitting and straighten his pants. From where she was standing it looked as if the dirty old bastard was sporting an erection. Her upper lip curled with disgust.

Tom brushed at his pants and then took a glance at his own house. For a moment Tanya thought he was going to head back to his home and treat himself to a tin of catfood and a night in front of a one-bar electric fire, or do whatever else it was that old people did when they closed the doors of their nasty little houses. But, to her surprise, Tom headed in the other direction, trudging deeper into the View. She strained to see where he was going but her window wouldn't allow her to see any further on her own side of the road than number four. Quietly cursing him she scoured the opposite side of the street in search of something interesting to watch, anything that would take her thoughts away from the grim calculations she had made on the notepad by her armchair.

The telephone continued to ring.

Before moving to Cedar View, Tanya had spent her evenings in front of the TV set, watching the soaps and greedily devouring other people's lives. The fact that her own life lacked the excitement of television drama was not something she often dwelt on. But she had regularly wondered why, if the soaps were supposed to reflect some sort of reality, they never showed someone like herself, sitting in front of a TV and living her life vicariously through a series of poorly scripted programmes.

Not that she watched soaps any more. Now that she lived on Cedar View there was always something more interesting to see than there had ever been on the most entertaining of soap operas. Her gaze flashed across the road to number three.

She scowled at the pristine front of the Smiths' house, despising the couple even though she barely knew them. Mrs Smith had a snooty way about her that made Tanya feel instantly inferior. She supposed the woman was probably that way with everyone but for some reason she suspected that Jane Smith was particularly aloof towards her. Her scowl deepened as she remembered Mr Smith, perpetually standing on the front doorstep with his high-and-mighty cigars, occasionally glancing in her direction, never once bothering to give her a smile. She could feel her mood darkening as she glared at the neighbours' unlit house. Quickly, she switched her gaze further up the street to number five.

A light shone in the front room of Joanne's house, as well as in the hall. Knowing her neighbours, Tanya realised this was a sign that Joanne was out for the evening. She sniffed with disdain at the transparency of those who lived on Cedar View. Her contempt escalated as she stared at the water feature over the koi carp pond in front of number five.

Joanne was a bitch to work for. Tanya cleaned the woman's house twice a week, polishing the stupid laminate floor, squirting polish on the pretentious leather settee and getting her bottom spanked every time Joanne found something out of place. Tanya's hands went to the substantial flesh of her backside and rubbed the memory of the most recent sting, sure that the punishment had been undeserved. A mantelpiece ornament had been put back facing the wrong way. Joanne had got out her crop, Tanya had been commanded to bend over and show her bare backside, and Joanne had administered six swift and punishing stripes, giggling as she delivered the blows. Tanya, as usual, had been confused by the thrill of pain and pleasure. Being spanked or striped was a disconcerting experience. Her body invariably reacted to the punishment with a rush of sexual anticipation. Every time her bare backside was caned she could feel her sex growing wetter and her nipples turning hard and needy. She had been surprised to discover that even being spanked by a woman inspired those responses, and she had been frustrated to find that Joanne had no interest in helping her explore further the urges she awoke. After each punishment session at number five, Joanne instructed her to finish the cleaning properly and then disappeared for half an hour to the sanctuary of her bedroom.

It didn't help that Joanne was a demanding employer who wanted her house transformed into a show home. Yet, no matter how much polish and spray Tanya put down, there was always a strange smell lingering around the woman's house. Tanya thought the odour was reminiscent of something she knew, but she couldn't quite place it. It might have been the koi carp in the front garden pond, but Tanya didn't think so.

She wrestled the waistband of her pink tracksuit higher around her stout midriff and shifted her gaze away from Joanne's. Joanne's name was on the notepad next to some of the grim calculations and she didn't want to think about the bleak picture that those figures painted.

Her scowl deepened as she stared at the Graftons' property. Not for the first time she wondered why she was living on a street that was filled with so many snobs and snooty bastards. Not bothering to conceal her disgust, showing her teeth in a snarl of disapproval, she glowered at the Graftons' house and the Graftons' car and wished one of them would come to the window so she could scowl at them. Her cat, Mr Tiddles, black and sleek, leapt on to the sill beside her. Absently, Tanya reached out and stroked his ears. And still the telephone continued to ring.

Sighing with frustration, knowing who her caller would be, Tanya grudgingly gave up her place by the window and walked towards the telephone. She picked up the handset and held it to her ear without speaking.

'Tanya?'

She recognised Max's voice immediately. Breathing deeply, determined not to be controlled by his casual authority, she waited coolly for a moment before grunting, 'Yeah?'

'Megan's gone missing.'

'So?'

'She's in one of the houses on this street.'

'So?'

'So you clean half the houses on this street, don't you?'

'I don't think it's that many.'

Max sighed.

The obvious exasperation in his tone was amusing on this occasion but Tanya knew better than to test his patience too far. He was her neighbour and landlord and a year ago, prior to her moving into the house on Cedar View, they had enjoyed a brief and wholly disconcerting fling. Tanya believed herself to be a strong woman, the equal of every man she had ever met, yet Max McMurray had filled her with a need to be servile that was so powerful it had been frightening. He had been the first to teach her the pleasure of being disciplined. Unlike Joanne, Max was also happy to show Tanya that she could enjoy a supreme satisfaction after being aroused by such punishing foreplay. He had made her want to suffer the cruelty of his crop and, for a while, she had dreamt of being regularly and repeatedly disciplined by him. But, because he was married to Megan and involved with Megan's sister, Tanya thought it would be sensible to end the relationship before it became any more perverse. She had been shocked to find herself subordinate to a man, uncomfortable that she was thrilled by his despicable punishments. She had ended their affair a month after Max secured her rental of the Cedar View property. Thinking back to that time, she supposed she should have ended the affair before Max introduced her to Joanne Jackson.

'You know everyone on the damned street,' Max hissed impatiently. 'And you clean for half of them. You've got a potential excuse to visit each person on Cedar View and try to find out where Megan might be.'

Tanya scoffed. 'What? You're expecting me to knock on everyone's door and say, "Excuse me, have you got Megan here?"'

'I'm sure you can do it more subtly than that.'

'What's in it for me?'

'You can forget about next week's rent if you find her.'

The words made her stomach lurch with excitement. She glanced at her notepad and then looked around the room, wondering if Max had some way of seeing what she had been writing. She had been glumly calculating her finances. Money was tight but she didn't want to continue cleaning for Joanne Jackson. She had worked out that a week's reprieve from her rent would give her the opportunity to leave that job and look for a different cleaning position. Max's offer was a chance to attain her most heartfelt desire.

Tanya considered it for an instant before saying, 'No.'

Max said nothing.

She wondered if she might have pushed him too far. When it came to negotiating finances, Tanya didn't think she had ever misjudged her mark. Max clearly needed this favour from her and, if he needed it so badly that he was willing to forgo a week's rent, he could be urged to part with more if she negotiated properly.

'If I go and look for her I'll get the next week rent-free,' Tanya told him. 'If I find her I'll get the next month rent-free.'

There was silence at the other end of the telephone. Tanya heard a crop slicing through the air and then the muffled gasp of someone in pain. She crushed her thighs together, silently envying the victim of Max's anger. Obviously it wasn't Megan who had just suffered the blow – Max had told her that Megan wasn't there – but the punished woman sounded very much like her. She guessed Aliceon was looking after Max. Images of the woman's striped backside and wet pussy lips made Tanya's crotch grow damp.

'You drive a hard bargain,' Max growled.

'You can always get the View's other resident cleaner to search for your missing wife,' Tanya suggested. She paused, grinned and said, 'Oh! Wait! The View doesn't have another resident cleaner, does it?'

'One month rent-free if you find her,' Max hissed. 'One week if you look. But just hurry up and damned well do it. I don't have all night.'

The connection was severed.

Tanya was quietly pleased that she had managed to negotiate such a good deal and proud that she had annoyed Max so much. If she annoyed him sufficiently, the next time she was cleaning his home Max might take it upon himself to treat her to the spanking she clearly craved.

She walked through to the kitchen and found a tin of lager in the fridge. The thought that she might be able to stop working for Joanne Jackson was enough to make her smile big and broad. Flopping lazily down on the settee she decided she might go out and look for Megan McMurray later. Even if she simply sat on the settee she could still pretend she had been looking for her and claim a week's free rent. But the idea of taking Max for a month's rent, knowing the money would provide a very comfortable safety net once she quit working for Joanne, was far more tempting. And, because she had seen Megan McMurray crossing the road earlier in the evening and going into the Graftons' house, Tanya didn't think she would have to search very hard.

Eight

3 Cedar View

They waited at the front of Denise's house, watching the street to make sure it was empty. Tom had vacated his spot outside Tanya Maxwell's, walked past the McMurrays' and disappeared into the front garden of Ted and Linda's. Twilight had darkened into early evening. A spattering of stars twinkled in the dark blue canopy above them and the View's two streetlamps already blazed bright. Denise took a moment to lead Jane into the garage and show the huge scar she had accidentally inflicted on the door panel of Derek's Rover. In the dim light it looked like a gaping wound in the otherwise unblemished polish of the white paintwork.

'He's going to go ballistic,' Jane muttered.

'He's going to make me pay for it,' Denise sighed. 'And I can't afford to cover the cost of a respray. Not even a partial.' Her frown lines deepened as she added, 'And I'm not looking forward to coming home from Ted and Linda's to face an argument with Derek about his stupid car. That's really going to spoil my night.'

Jane looked away, not really concerned about Denise's carelessness, Derek's milquetoast tyranny or the inevitable conflict the pair would endure. It seemed obvious to Jane that the main source of Denise and

Derek's problems was Denise's desire to have a baby and Derek's reluctance to address or even acknowledge it. In previous conversations Denise had admitted that Derek showed no sexual interest in her and, while Denise's lifestyle compensated for the frustration of being in a sexless marriage, Jane could see that her friend's strong desire to have a child was eventually going to split the couple apart. But she didn't think this was the time for such a gloomy, if honest, observation. It certainly wouldn't make Denise feel any better about the damage she had inflicted to Derek's car.

She studied the rest of the street and puzzled over a less contentious part of Denise's statement. 'Do you mean Derek would make you pay for it *with money*?'

'He's let the last couple of incidents pass.' Denise's tone trembled with distress. 'But he said I've got to cover the full cost if it happens again.'

Jane chose not to notice that Denise was close to tears. She would never have let John dictate how she was supposed to spend her money, but she didn't think Denise wanted to hear her thoughts on successful husband control. Denise was clearly content to be subjugated by Derek, even if his authority didn't include the sexual domination she would have appreciated.

But then, Jane reflected, not all marriages were the same.

'When I grazed the damned thing last week, he said the next time it happens, I'm going to have to pay for the respray out of my own money,' Denise babbled. 'And I just can't afford to do that. I'm going to have to sell my bike to cover the cost. And I don't want to sell my bike. It's my baby.'

Jane was about to make some sort of sympathetic noise, a clucking sound or a 'there, there', when she

74

remembered something more important. Silencing Denise with a hand on her arm, she asked, 'Did I just see Tom going into Ted and Linda's?'

Denise nodded. She sniffed back the threat of tears and said, 'Linda lets him watch their parties. You know what Linda's like about older blokes. She has a real soft spot for geriatrics. It's the same soft spot she keeps in the crotch of her knickers.'

Jane didn't know Linda well enough to be aware that she had a soft spot for older men or that she kept it in her knickers. In fact, earlier in the evening she hadn't been able to remember the woman's name. Now, hearing Denise talk about Linda's interest in Tom, she didn't know whether to think of it as decadent, daring or depraved. Realising this wasn't the time to consider it, and aware that the diversion she had suggested might put an end to Denise's plan for the rest of the evening and make all this conversation about Linda, Ted and Tom immaterial, Jane waited as another car swept into Cedar View.

The Audi parked outside Ted and Linda's and the occupants climbed unhurriedly out and walked towards number six. They were a smartly dressed couple: attractive, from the little Jane could see, and affluent enough to make them desirable. His jeans had a designer label. The twinkle of eighteen-carat gold sparked from his knuckles and his ear. She was wearing a micro-mini, too small to accommodate even the most succinct of designer labels. But her top was obviously Chanel and her four-inch heels were clearly Prada. Jane didn't know if that made them genuinely affluent but she was sufficiently impressed to conclude they had enough money to be classy. Her stomach tightened with conflicting thrills of twisted excitement.

The classy couple were visiting Ted and Linda's for the sex party. If events panned out the way Denise wanted, Jane realised there would be a chance to have sex with them. The prospect made her wet between her thighs. She wondered if she should just go along with Denise's plan and head straight to the party. Her own idea, to take Denise home with her, hopefully encounter John and then have an argument, seemed unlikely to end the day with an orgiastic climax. And, while the satisfaction of a blazing row had earlier held a lot of appeal, Jane now wondered if Denise's plan might ultimately prove more satisfying.

For an instant she was torn between equally tempting options. Denise and a sex party sounded as much fun as John and an argument and she was held in the sway of uncharacteristic indecision. Battle or bonk? Row or rut? Fight or fuck? It was, she thought, the toughest of tough calls.

But Jane made her choice as soon as the classy couple were safely behind Ted and Linda's front door. She placed a hand on Denise's arm and said, 'Let's go.'

Denise grinned and nodded. The lilt of her smile made Jane hungry for them to kiss again. She knew there would be a chance to do that, and maybe more, if they went to the party. But that wasn't where Jane was leading them. She had told Denise she wanted to go home and get clothes that were appropriate for Ted and Linda's. She had said she would collect them without disturbing John – without letting him know she was there or where they were going for the evening – but she knew John wouldn't allow her to steal through the house so effortlessly. Knowing that the evening was certain to end with a huge argument made the heat surge in her loins. She pulled on Denise's hand and they ran quickly together down Cedar View, their heels clicking loudly against the paving stones.

'That's strange,' Denise murmured.

'What's strange?'

Denise nodded at number seven. 'Charlie and Rhona. Their lights are still on. I thought they would have been at Ted and Linda's by now.'

Jane glanced at the house. 'Maybe they've left a light on to deter burglars?'

'They do that,' Denise agreed. 'But they leave the front room light and the hall light on, like everyone else on this street. That's just the kitchen light you can see. It means Charlie and Rhona are still at home.'

Jane shrugged and urged Denise to hurry with her. Whatever anomaly was happening at the Grafton house, it had nothing to do with her plans for the evening. Urging Denise to run by her side, anxious to get home, Jane rushed past Joanne's house and up the path of number three.

'There are no lights on,' Denise observed.

Jane shrugged. Either John had gone to bed early or he was sulking with the lights off. She hoped it was the former because the thought of John being asleep in bed gave her a wicked idea. Trying not to splutter with laughter at her own deviousness, she quickly shushed Denise as she opened the door and let them both inside.

'Where is he?' Denise asked. 'Are we alone?'

Her voice was lowered to a whisper that was deliciously conspiratorial. The inner muscles of Jane's sex trembled as she heard the undercurrent of naughtiness in Denise's tone. She had planned to spend the evening arguing with John but, hearing the suggestiveness in Denise's voice, Jane wondered if there would be a chance to do something more.

'He'll be in bed,' Jane hissed. In the darkness of the unlit hall she pulled Denise closer. Ordinarily she insisted that guests remove their shoes when they came into her home but, with her thoughts distracted by licentious ideas, she was beyond telling Denise to take off her shoes or bothering to remove her own. It was much easier to insist on having Denise's arms round her so they could share the passion of a daring embrace.

Their lips met. In the darkness of the hall, sure John was somewhere in the house and that she was going to be caught in the arms of her lesbian lover, Jane felt her arousal shifting into overdrive. Denise was an eager partner. Her slender body was firm against Jane's, her hands inquisitive. Fingers slipped over Jane's waist and hips. Their breasts squashed together. As Denise hungrily explored Jane's mouth with her tongue, she daringly wrapped one leg around Jane's thigh.

'Are you sure he's in bed?' Denise asked. 'Are you sure he's asleep?'

'I guess,' Jane shrugged, trying to sound as though she didn't care.

'Isn't there a danger of him finding us?'

The thought sent a shiver down Jane's spine. Denise's kisses and caresses were exciting, but they were nowhere near as thrilling as the prospect of being caught by her husband as she boldly embraced Denise. She could picture the raw excitement of telling John that Denise was a far more proficient lover than he had ever proved. She could imagine his humiliation as she told him that he was incompetent in bed and that she visited Denise to satisfy the urges he had never been able to satiate. Imagining the conversation, Jane felt her labia grow dewy.

'Tongue me,' she murmured.

'Now?'

'Yes.'

'Here?'

'On the stairs.' Jane dragged Denise with her as she climbed the first couple of stairs and then sat down. Stretching herself over the treads, burying her heels into the bottom riser, she opened the belt on her coat and urged her pelvis up to meet Denise's face. 'Tongue my pussy,' she hissed. 'Make me come.'

Denise's grin was visible even in the darkness of the unlit hall. Jane watched her smile grow closer as Denise lowered herself between her legs.

It had always been exciting visiting her friend and enjoying an hour or two of naked intimacy. From the moment they had first become lovers Jane had discovered a new facet to her sexuality and had shared it fully with Denise. Starting off with exploratory kisses, moving on to undressing each other and then discovering the joys of another woman's body, Jane had been thrilled to realise her sex life had not died as a result of marrying the unexciting John Smith. But, although she and Denise had indulged a few unusual fantasies, Jane had never expected the sex could be as arousing as what she was now enjoying in her own home. The growing danger that John might see what she was doing, the certainty that he would be upset and angry, her confidence that she would still be able to control him – they all added to the mounting thrill.

Denise's tongue slipped against her cleft.

They had left number eight dressed only in heels and matching macs. Beneath the clothes they were both naked. Jane's cool body basked in the pleasure of Denise's warm mouth touching her sex. There was none of the lingering foreplay that usually preceded their lovemaking. Instead of placing gentle kisses on her upper thighs and teasing her to a fury of anticipation, Denise applied herself to satisfying Jane's need. Her tongue was pressed flat against Jane's labia. She nuzzled Jane's clitoris and then plunged her tongue between the pouting pussy lips.

Jane groaned.

The sound echoed loudly through the empty house. She wondered if the inadvertent moan might be enough to disturb John from his slumber and make him come into the hall and see what was happening. The idea of being caught in such a compromising position and knowing she would be able to triumph from the situation sent another bolt of pleasure through her body.

'You're wet,' Denise giggled. She slurped her tongue hungrily against Jane's sex as proof. Jane stiffened, feeling the flow of raw arousal course through her. When John did find her – and she intended to gasp so loudly that he was certain to make a curious inspection of the hall – Jane wondered how she should treat him. She supposed it would be polite to let Denise go back home, or on to the party, and avoid the upset of witnessing a major confrontation. But a devilish part of her wanted to insist that Denise remain and finish what she had started, while John was banished to the front step with one of his lousy cigars. The idea of dismissing him so cruelly, making him stand outside while his wife and her female lover moaned and screamed through multiple orgasms, was so twisted and diabolical she couldn't shake it from her thoughts. When John found them, that was how she would react. The decision sent another dark pulse through her clitoris.

Denise continued to suckle the bead of flesh, filling Jane with so many marvellous urges that the prospect of climax drew wonderfully close. She wished there were more lights in the hall, so she could see the pretty woman between her thighs and appreciate the smile she knew Denise would be wearing as the climax inched closer. She also wished there was enough light for her to see John when he eventually appeared and stared at them both in slack-jawed amazement.

'Fuck! Yes!' Jane gasped.

'Jesus, Janey,' Denise murmured. 'You're going to wake your hubby.'

'Fuck him,' Jane grunted. 'Fuck him right up the arse.'

She giggled at the idea of using her husband the way she had suggested. The thought was sufficiently exciting to spark another thrill in her loins. When Denise's tongue pressed more forcefully against her hole, slipping between the moist lips and teasing the muscles inside, her giggles turned to a throaty groan.

'Do you want him to catch you?' Denise whispered.

'I don't fucking care.'

And, as the pleasure began to build, she told herself those words were fairly close to the truth. She writhed on the stairs, pushing her sex against Denise's face and wallowing in the delight of having her labia and clitoris properly pleasured by her lover's mouth. Her sex felt wet and warm and she craved the release of orgasm.

Dancing for Tom had been exciting. The hour she had spent earlier with Denise had been good. But she now needed to exorcise the maddening knot of arousal from the pit of her stomach, and she knew it would be dispersed only if she did something outrageously different from anything she had done before. Humiliating her husband and revealing the secret of her relationship with Denise might create that extra rush her body needed. The only other way she could imagine achieving satisfaction was going with Denise to Ted and Linda's party.

Denise's fingers stroked her upper thighs, then her hips, before moving onwards and upwards to her breasts. Jane's nipples were caught between teasing fingernails, gripped, tugged, rolled and teased. She squirmed against the stairs, wishing her body would give in and release a flood of satisfying sensations. Her heart hammered at a quickening pace and for a moment she thought the climactic urge within her was going to peak. Not bothering to mute her voice, not caring if she made a sound that was loud enough to draw the attention of her husband, she urged Denise to kiss her. 'Harder! Deeper! Get your tongue all the way in there. Drink my pussy dry.'

Dutifully, Denise obeyed. She pressed her mouth hard against Jane's sex and thrust her tongue between the sopping folds of flesh. Jane gasped with growing pleasure and squirmed as Denise took her close to the brink of orgasm. Jane's cries were no longer instructions but wordless sighs of approval. She put extra effort into making sure John heard that she was back in the house and enjoying an excessive degree of sexual stimulation.

But still it wasn't enough.

Opening her eyes, Jane stared up the empty stairway and realised she and Denise were still alone. She groaned with frustration and pulled herself away.

'Bastard,' she hissed, starting up the stairs.

Denise stared after her. She blinked when Jane switched on the lights. Her eyes were wide open when Jane came out of the bedroom.

She had changed into black stockings, heels, a lacy thong and a matching bra. In one hand she clutched a black sequined eye-mask. Her scowl was a picture of unconcealed fury.

'What's wrong, Janey?'

'The bastard's not here.'

To confirm the statement, Jane disappeared into the spare bedroom and reappeared looking even more ferocious. She glowered down the stairs at Denise and then marched into the house's third bedroom. When she returned she slammed the door angrily closed.

'The bastard's definitely not here.'

'Where do you think he is?'

Jane thundered down the stairs. 'Don't know. Don't care.' She pushed past Denise and turned on the lounge light. Walking to the front door, grinding her teeth, she motioned to Denise to hurry up and come with her.

'You're not going to leave him a note?' Denise asked.

Jane shook her head. 'Fuck him,' she hissed. 'I'm going to go with you to Ted and Linda's party this evening. I'm going to do whatever the hell I please while I'm there. And when I do get home and I find John curled up in bed, I'm going to wake the fucker up and tell him everything I've done tonight.'

Denise laughed. 'Excellent. If that's the case, you only need one more thing to make your outfit complete.'

Puzzled, Jane glanced at her. She held up the eye-mask and said, 'I got this. What else do I need?'

Denise took her hand and urged her towards the door. 'It's back at my house,' she said. 'Come with me. It will only take two minutes and then we can go to Ted and Linda's.'

Nine

Tanya paused outside number five, glancing over the road to number four and waving to Max. She didn't know if he was at the window of his cellar, watching and making sure she did as he had asked, but it didn't hurt to let him see that she was earning her rent-free week. Knowing Joanne was out and not bothering with the pretence of knocking, she slipped her key into the lock and stepped inside. Megan still hadn't come out of number seven and Tanya didn't think she would be appearing any time soon. Knowing she had all the time she wanted, she headed straight for Joanne's fridge and found herself a lager. She popped the tin, downed a satisfying mouthful, stepped through to the lounge and went straight to the drawers behind the door, which Joanne would always remind her were off limits.

'The content of those drawers doesn't concern you,' she would say with a sniff. Her haughty tone made Tanya cringe. Standing alone in the empty house, Tanya could almost hear that superior voice sniping at her. 'While you polish the surface of those drawers, I'll be in the room watching to make sure you don't look inside.'

Tanya had never had any desire to look inside the drawers. She cared nothing for Joanne or her property.

But, having been repeatedly told not to look into them, and having been punished twice because she had been polishing the drawers' handles while Joanne was out of the room, Tanya realised this was the perfect opportunity to find out what it was that Joanne didn't want her to see.

She took another swig at her lager, then opened the top drawer. A clutter of photographs stared back at her. Tanya could see pictures of men and women – most of them naked, some of them vaguely familiar – caught in embarrassing and revealing poses. She rummaged through the pictures, her eyes growing wide. She recognised John Smith from number three, and Max and Megan and Megan's sister Aliceon. The pictures showed bare backsides, mostly lined with stripes. There were some Polaroids that revealed objects penetrating anuses or pussies.

And then Tanya saw the pictures of herself. She didn't know when Joanne had taken them. Perhaps every time Joanne punished her for a mistake with the cleaning? Appalled that the photographs existed, and determined that Joanne wasn't going to get away with holding on to such incriminating evidence of her servility, Tanya began to snatch the pictures from the drawer. She had to put her lager down, leaving a ring on the perfectly polished top of the drawers, but that didn't concern her as she filled her pockets with the entire collection.

Ten

7 Cedar View

'You were considering the offer,' Charlie repeated.

Rhona shifted forwards in her seat. Her smile was broad and predatory.

Megan fumbled with her tobacco pouch and tried to steady her nerves by rolling another cigarette. Her hands shook but she paid no attention to the signs of her unease and tilted her head arrogantly to regard Charlie and Rhona. 'Was that wrong of me?'

'Hell! No!' Charlie laughed.

'How much would you have made us pay?' Rhona asked eagerly.

Megan squirmed uncomfortably on her seat.

Her hostility towards the Graftons had disappeared when she realised she had misjudged them. The letter she had received had not been intended as a proposition and, as the three of them laughed at her silliness, she had found it easy to like the couple and feel relaxed in their company. Admittedly Rhona was more tactile than Megan was used to in her women friends. Her reassuring fingers continually touched Megan's hand, arm or shoulder. Charlie, too, had been studying her with an obvious sexual interest, but he was a handsome and authoritative man and three glasses of wine had made it easier to endure his attention.

Yet now, with them both eager to know the answer to this question, Megan could feel the atmosphere in the room changing again. Whereas before it had been cool and relaxed, now the air vibrated with the hum of sexual tension. She was aware that both Rhona and Charlie desired her and, riding high on the suggestion of their lust, she could feel her own arousal growing. After what seemed like an age, Megan found her voice.

'Yeah. I was thinking about it.'

'I bet you'd have priced yourself beyond what we could afford,' Charlie said with a grin. Without asking he replenished her glass. If she hadn't been rolling a cigarette Megan would have placed a protective hand over her drink and prevented him. But by the time she was able to say, 'No more, thank you,' a fourth glass of the potent white wine was waiting for her.

'Don't be so parsimonious,' Rhona chastised her husband. She placed a reassuring hand on Megan's arm and said, 'He can be a cheap shit at times. You're a very attractive girl. I bet you'd have named a price that *I* wouldn't think was too high.'

Megan finished rolling her cigarette and tucked it in the corner of her mouth. The shape was bizarre: her hands had been too unsteady to form a proper tube and the result looked like a lollipop stick designed by Salvador Dali. She hesitated before lighting it, sure most of it would incinerate as soon as she touched a flame to its end.

'How much would you have asked?' Charlie enquired.

'Does it matter? Isn't it a moot point now?'

'It's a moot point,' Rhona agreed. 'But it would be interesting to know.'

Taking a deep breath, Megan wondered whether she should admit her plan. Deciding it would be rude to deny them the information, she laughed nervously and said, 'I'd come here with the idea of haggling. I was going to wait to hear how much you offered, and then insist I wanted double the amount. I came here prepared to screw you physically *and* financially.'

Rhona chuckled enthusiastically and clutched Megan's arm. 'You are so much a girl after my own heart.'

'You don't have a heart,' Charlie grunted.

'I might not have a heart,' Rhona agreed, 'but I'm not a cheap shit and I can post letters through the right doors.'

Charlie turned his attention away from his wife and studied Megan. 'So,' he began slowly, 'if I'd offered you five hundred pounds to play with Rhona and me for the night, you'd have demanded a grand? Is that what you're saying?'

Megan considered this and nodded. 'Yeah. I might have settled on a grand.'

'A grand,' Rhona reflected. The hand on Megan's arm gripped tight. 'What would you have done for a grand?'

Megan blushed. She was about to explain that she hadn't given much thought to what she was likely to do, but that wasn't entirely true. Before she could wave the question away, or try to divert the subject to something less embarrassing, Rhona was pressing her face close to Megan's cheek and whispering in her ear.

'What would you have done?' she breathed.

The question, caressing the lower lobe of her ear and kissing the side of her neck, fired a sultry warmth in Megan's loins. Deciding honesty was probably the best way to respond, Megan turned her face to Rhona's. They were so close their lips almost touched. She scanned Rhona's picture-perfect beauty at such close range that she could just see the tiny imperfections left by her cosmetic surgery: a nearly imperceptible pair of white dots at the corners of her eyes, a hair-thin scar that followed the angle of her kissable jaw, tiny puncture marks along the line of her lips. Megan marvelled at the perfect thickness and distribution of Rhona's lashes. The woman's large sapphire eyes appraised her with frank eagerness. Her skilfully sculpted cheeks were high with colour.

'What would you have done?' Rhona insisted.

'I'd have made you come your brains out,' Megan murmured.

Rhona grinned. Her smile was polished white perfection.

'I'd have opened my coat, shown you that I was naked underneath, except for a pair of hold-up fishnets and my ankle boots, and then I'd have screwed Charlie first, and then you.' Keeping her voice low, making sure every word struck Rhona with the full force of the passion she wanted to invoke, Megan said, 'Then, once you and I'd both got Charlie hard again, I'd have fucked both of you at the same time.' She paused, licked her lips and then said softly, 'That's what I would have done.'

Rhona trembled. 'You'd really have done all those things?'

'I even brought condoms,' Megan whispered.

Rhona's grin inched wider. 'And you're really naked beneath that leather?' Her gaze dropped to the open neck of Megan's coat and her smile grew broader as she noted Megan's bare décolletage, with no suggestion of blouse, bra or top. 'Did you mean that? Or were you joking?'

Megan lit her cigarette. Coolly, she sat back in her chair and nodded. 'But –' she spoke through a mouthful of smoke '– like we agreed before, it's a moot point. The letter was a mistake. You'd never intended to pay me for those kind of services. I'd got the wrong end of the stick.' She took another drag from her badly rolled cigarette and realised it had already burnt down to a stub. 'I can't even see why we're discussing it.'

Charlie dropped a handful of notes on the kitchen table.

Megan studied them and saw there were twenty fifty-pound notes. Her stomach churned. She stubbed out the remainder of her cigarette in the ashtray Rhona had provided and tore her gaze from the money to study Charlie.

'What's that?'

'It's a grand.'

'I can see that it's a grand. Why is it there?'

He flashed a broad grin. 'You came here expecting to earn some money,' he said slowly. 'I'm just being a good host and doing what I can.' Raising his eyebrows as he studied her, Charlie said, 'You never answered Ronnie's question and I'm dying to know: are you really naked underneath that coat?'

Nausea twisted Megan's stomach. She glanced from Charlie to Rhona and realised she had talked herself into an inescapable corner. Quite when the dynamics had changed was a mystery to her, but she suddenly realised that it would be impossible to refuse the money and remain on good terms with her new friends. She wasn't sure she did want to be friends with them, but the confusion of the moment swayed her decision.

Charlie was right to point out that she had come to their house with the purpose of earning some money. And Rhona's lascivious interest had inspired a slick warmth between Megan's legs. Studying the pair, trying to remember how she had intended handling the situation, Megan realised that she could only go along with whatever the couple wanted.

She snatched the notes from the kitchen table and stuffed them in her coat pocket. Trying to remain nonchalant, hoping the couple couldn't see that she suddenly felt fearfully out of her depth, she sat back in her chair and began to roll another cigarette. This time it was properly made. By the time she had finished and had tucked it into the corner of her mouth, the anticipation around the table had turned as thick as treacle.

Megan snorted twin plumes from her nostrils and studied Charlie from across the table. Reaching for the top button of her leather, plucking it open with an arrogant flick of her wrist, she said, 'Yes. I'm naked underneath this coat.' Not allowing herself to think about what she was doing, certain that a moment's thought would bring her to her senses and drive her from the Graftons' house, she pulled open another button and said, 'Do you really want to see?'

Charlie laughed. 'You wouldn't believe how badly I want that.'

Rhona clutched Megan's arm with renewed force. When Megan glanced into her face she could see the earnest appreciation and genuine enthusiasm in the woman's large sapphire eyes. The discovery that she was so ardently desired made the inner muscles of her sex clench with fresh excitement.

'You wouldn't believe how badly we both want that,' Rhona whispered.

Megan pulled open another button. The flick of her wrist briefly exposed one small, pert breast. Rhona gasped and Charlie made a startled sound of approval.

Megan covered the breast again, then reached down for the final button. Before going to the Graftons' she hadn't been entirely sure how the evening would work out. She had intended to put on a display of outrage and disgust, and then give them what they wanted once a decent price was negotiated. Thoughts of Max had been easy to push aside. With Aliceon taking her place

91

in the cellar, Megan knew her husband would be having adulterous fun with her sister while she fucked the neighbours.

It was an arrangement that met the conditions Max had set for their relationship. At drunken parties, and when they were entertaining friends, he claimed they shared a tacit agreement that allowed some degree of infidelity. 'There are only two conditions,' Max always said. 'If one of us is screwing someone else, we owe it to our partner to try and get them laid. And, while we don't have to tell each other everything that we do with other people, we never have anyone at home on the sly.'

Megan had never tested whether Max really wanted to live by this credo. It wasn't a topic that lent itself to regular conversations. Because their sex life often involved either her sister or one or more of their friends, Megan had never thought it was something they would need to nail down in such fixed terms. But, now that this opportunity had presented itself, she felt sure she had met both her husband's conditions. She had arranged for Aliceon to satisfy him while she was out of the house, and she was making sure her liaison with the Graftons didn't happen in the home she shared with Max.

And yet, the worry that Max might be upset by what she was doing made her wonder if she should rethink the situation. In the past they had played some sexual games with other couples. Aliceon occasionally joined them in their marital bed, always making herself available on Max's birthday. There had been a few Christmas parties where Megan publicly demonstrated her skills in Shibari, the Japanese art of bondage, much to the satisfaction of one or more of their naked female friends. There had also been a handful of evenings throughout their marriage when Megan had found herself being spit-roasted by Max and his best friend Daniel: Daniel's cock in her mouth, Max's length sliding into her pussy. But those events had always happened while they were together, as a couple, and she felt certain she was breaching some unwritten protocol by not having mentioned anything to her husband before leaving the house. Troubling her conscience even more was the niggling suspicion that Max knew she wasn't with him and was worried about her and trying to find her.

Drawing again on her cigarette, deciding there was no time to fret about such considerations now, she pulled open her coat and shrugged it from her shoulders. Rhona gasped and Charlie raised his glass in silent salute.

Megan sat back in her chair, allowing the couple to admire her nudity. She raised one booted heel and placed it on the edge of the kitchen table. The change in posture meant she was showing off the length of one fishnet-covered leg and concealing her pussy from Rhona's view.

She felt exposed. Rhona and Charlie both remained dressed.

Megan couldn't breathe for the charge of sexual electricity that crackled in the kitchen. The sensation of being the focus of their attention brought a prickle of gooseflesh to her forearms. She wanted to squirm on the chair but she knew that would make her look like a woman who didn't have full control of the situation. Knowing the couple wouldn't notice if she was discreet, Megan clenched the inner muscles of her pussy to try and vent some of the arousal that had built in her loins.

Rhona leaned close and reached out a hand to Megan's breast. As her fingers cupped the orb, squeezed and kneaded bare flesh, she moved her mouth closer. Her lips met Megan's. The kiss was warm and intrusive. A tongue slipped between her lips, shocking Megan with its swift intimacy. Her excitement grew more profound. She couldn't tell if it was the sensation of Rhona's tongue sliding into her mouth, or the weight of her fingers squeezing her nipple, but, whatever the cause, a surge of fluid urgency rushed through her body.

Without thinking, not allowing herself to consider her actions, Megan gave into the kiss. She stubbed out her cigarette and moved against Rhona's lips. The pleasure of meeting her mouth was sensational.

Hesitant at first, then with a little more confidence, Megan found the shape of Rhona's breast. A thin layer of silk covered the flesh. Her thumb slipped against the pliant swell until it touched Rhona's nipple. Teasing it until it became hard, delighting in the way the stiff bud responded to her caress, Megan sighed against Rhona's kiss.

'Are you going to take off your sunglasses?'

'No.'

'I'll bet you've got beautiful eyes.'

Megan laughed. Feeling suddenly charged by the control she had over the couple she said, 'Neither you nor Charlie are interested in looking at my eyes. Not now my tits and my pussy are visible.'

'She's got a point,' Charlie grunted.

Megan glanced up and saw he had risen from his seat on the opposite side of the table. An erection pushed at the front of his trousers and, although he was trying to look as though his arousal wasn't an issue, Megan could see that every step was causing him some discomfort. She smiled as she leaned back towards Rhona and extracted another long, lingering kiss.

Rhona's fingers slid over Megan's breast. The light tease of her caress was so delicate it made Megan catch her breath. When the woman's hand slipped from her chest and began to glide down her stomach, Megan stiffened with the prospect of greater excitement. She allowed Rhona's tongue to slip back between her lips. A thrill built in her stomach as the woman's hand crept closer to her cleft.

'You look as good as I'd hoped,' Rhona breathed.

'I'm flattered you had a mental picture,' Megan replied.

Her heart raced. Charlie had stepped closer and, even though she wasn't looking in his direction, she could sense that he was smiling greedily. Still savouring the pleasure of Rhona's kisses and caresses, she decided to ignore him. She even managed to feign uninterest as Charlie unzipped his trousers and extracted a large, meaty erection.

'I thought your plan involved servicing me first?'

'It did,' Megan admitted, breaking away from Rhona and shifting her pelvis so the woman's fingers could delve deeper. Rhona was on the brink of touching the trimmed thatch of curls that led down to her pussy. Speaking without a stutter was almost more than Megan could manage. She regarded Charlie through the comforting darkness of her shades and grinned at him. 'My plan *was* to service you first. But I never suspected your wife could be such a great kisser.'

She lowered her gaze to Charlie's cock. It was on the same level as her mouth and she could have kissed it without shifting position. The bulbous end was so close to her face she could catch the scent of pre-come as it leaked from the open eye of his shaft. Her appetite for arousal peaked with fresh fury. She reached out and held him between two fingers, as though his cock was a cigarette. Lowering her head, she paused with her lips apart and ready for him, then glanced back up at his face.

'Surely we're not just going to spend this evening sticking to my loose plans, are we?'

Charlie was surprisingly cool in his reaction. 'What else did you have in mind?' His erection trembled between her fingers with every word. 'I'm sure we can accommodate any particular interests you have. There's not much that we won't try.'

Megan smiled at him. 'There are so many things the three of us could do together.' Glancing at Rhona she said, 'I once made a woman come with my Shibari.'

Charlie said, 'That's the Japanese art of –'

'I know what Shibari is,' Rhona interrupted. 'You're not the only one in this house who's ever had sex.'

Megan continued to study Charlie's face. His cock remained between her fingers and she longed to encircle the glans with her lips. 'I've made men come with my bondage too,' she admitted coyly. Flicking her tongue against his flesh, she saw him flinch with pleasure. 'But I also like to have my backside spanked, and I can endure so much nipple torture you'd come your brains out just watching me.'

'I'm on the verge of coming my brains out just hearing about it,' Charlie confessed.

Megan laughed. Bobbing her head close to him, opening her mouth and taking his glans between her lips, she sucked gently on his length before moving back to receive another kiss from Rhona.

'I can taste Charlie's cock on your lips,' Rhona told her.

'You don't sound like you object.'

They giggled together as Rhona's kiss became more intrusive and her fingers found their way to the lips of Megan's sex. Her hands were warm, oily with perspiration and deliciously gentle. As one finger and then another slid against the moist folds of her pussy lips, Megan shook with mounting desire.

Although she was trying to remain in control of the situation, Megan quickly perceived that Charlie and Rhona were adept at working together. Rhona's teasing was a maddening distraction. Charlie's looming presence made Megan hungry to do more than simply kiss his cock. Telling herself she needed to distance herself from the pair for a moment, collect her thoughts and decide how the evening was going to progress, Megan pulled herself from Rhona's kisses and reluctantly eased Rhona's hand from her pussy lips.

'I need to pee before we carry on doing what we're doing,' she said. She slid out of the chair, leaving her coat, and glanced towards the kitchen door. 'Does your loo face the top of the stairs? The same as at my house?'

Rhona nodded. Charlie opened the door for her.

'Are you two going to get undressed for when I get back?' Megan asked. She grinned to show it was a question and not a command.

'Maybe we want you to undress us?' Rhona suggested.

The idea triggered another burst of horny need deep in Megan's loins. She drew a faltering breath and then turned away from the couple. The kitchen door closed softly behind her but, rather than heading across the hall and up the stairs, she lingered for a moment to catch her breath and get her bearings. Because she stood so close to the kitchen door she could hear the conversation inside the room.

'Didn't I tell you this would work?' Charlie asked Rhona. 'Didn't I say that this level of cunning was needed for us to have a proper chance at getting to grips with the delightful Megan McMurray?'

'You were right,' Rhona agreed. Her voice was lowered: not whispering – Megan didn't think Rhona was capable of whispering – but it was soft enough to imply discretion. 'My idea to simply approach her wouldn't have worked,' Rhona continued.

Megan strained to hear more.

'But your devious plan, making her think she'd been propositioned with that silly letter for the fat girl at number two, and then pretending it was all a big misunderstanding: it's worked like a charm. You really are a master of the Machiavellian.'

Listening to them, Megan quietly seethed. And plotted her revenge.

Eleven

8 Cedar View

Jane waited outside while Denise opened the door of
her house. Denise had insisted that Jane needed one
more thing to complete her outfit but she refused to
say anything more.

'What is it?' Jane pressed.

Denise shook her head. Her grin was broad and
curled with the prospect of mischief. 'I'm not going to
tell you. I'm going to show you. You'd say no if I just
told you, but you won't be able to refuse if you see it,
I promise you that.'

Jane stared at her, mystified. She adjusted the eye-
mask she had decided to wear to the party, in case her
identity needed preserving, and gestured to Denise to
hurry up.

Glancing at the closed garage door, she remembered
Denise's concern about the scratched paintwork on
Derek's car. Shaking her head slightly, amazed that
Denise should be so upset over such a trifling matter,
she wondered if she should offer some advice for a
solution. The problem would never have arisen in her
house. She would have simply declared it was John's
fault. She didn't know why Denise couldn't employ the
same strategy on Derek. If she had damaged John's
vehicle in any way, even if she had done it deliberately

by scraping an awl across the bonnet to gouge the words BORING FUCKER, she would have still argued that it was his fault. And it was an argument she knew she would have won.

All Denise needed to do was tell Derek he had parked his car in the wrong spot or at an awkward or inconvenient angle. If he demanded compensation, she would counterclaim for the scratched handlebar and any other damage to her bike. To Jane's mind, there would be no way for Derek to win the argument. And, if Denise really did want Derek to provide her with a baby, she could use the argument to make her demands known and negotiate his co-operation. If the couple were having a volatile row concerning a scratch on his car, Denise could use the momentum of the argument to tell Derek that he should either do his duty as a husband or pack his bags and piss off. Looking away from the garage door, Jane made a mental note to mention those points to Denise when she returned. She expected her friend would be pleased to have all her marriage problems resolved with the single, easy solution of browbeating her husband into submission.

The usually quiet Cedar View was surprisingly busy this evening. Cars she didn't recognise lined the kerb. She suspected the majority of them had arrived with guests for the party at Ted and Linda's. There was an unreasonable amount of noise coming from number six and, if she hadn't been planning to attend the party, Jane would have considered phoning the local police station to register a complaint. But that wasn't something to worry about this evening. She heard Denise's footsteps and Jane turned to smile at her friend as she stepped out of the house and offered the fruit of her search.

'You're kidding,' Jane marvelled.

'Wear it,' Denise insisted. 'You know you want to.'

'I thought you'd gone back to get condoms,' Jane muttered.

Denise laughed and pushed a fistful of condoms into Jane's hand. 'I brought some for you,' she said. 'I'm thinking I might do this party bareback.' Her eyes softened with a moment's sadness as she added, 'Derek isn't giving me what I want on the baby front. Maybe someone at tonight's party could oblige.' She shook her head suddenly and smiled to show she wasn't trying to be maudlin. 'But here,' she said, pushing her main gift towards Jane. 'You've got to wear this. You've got to put it on now. This is just what you need for the party.'

She could have declined, Jane thought, or pretended it wasn't something she would have the courage to wear, but she couldn't bring herself to show any modesty or hesitation. Snatching the gift from Denise's hand she said, 'Help me put it on. I'm going to love wearing this.'

Giggling and doing as she had been asked, Denise said, 'Do you know, I think this is going to be one hell of a party.'

Twelve

6 Cedar View

It was proving to be a hell of a party, Linda thought, the best she had ever hosted. Passion and promiscuity filled every niche of the house. Since her sandwich experience with Ted and Phil and discovering Joanne had acquired a gimp, the night had become an extravaganza of sexy fun, shocks and revelations. It didn't matter that her preciously pumped lips had quickly deflated: they had impressed Ted and Phil and the heightened sensitivity had made for a memorable beginning to the evening. Consoling herself that she could pump them up again whenever she wanted to enjoy the same effect, Linda threw herself into the role of a good hostess.

Connie and Corrine, two of her work colleagues, had arrived from the office. They surprised Linda with the announcement that they had been swinging for years and expressed incredulity at not having previously bumped into her 'through the scene'. She welcomed the pair enthusiastically and introduced them to a handful of other guests as the party began to swell. Attractive women, dark-skinned, exotic and exciting, they hugged each other intimately as they mingled. Linda wondered whether it was sensible to have sex with colleagues or if that would have repercussions in the arena of office politics, but before she could make up her mind she lost track of them as they paired off with another couple. It was a temporary solution to her dilemma, but Linda felt sure the issue would resurface before the night was ended.

Passing the pool she watched Joanne cane the backside of her gimp as the submissive male was forced to lick pussy after pussy after pussy. Joanne looked resplendent in her thigh-high boots and dominatrix outfit. Linda had thought the woman didn't have the cruelty to be a proper disciplinarian, but now, seeing how Joanne mistreated her subordinate, she wondered if she should revise that opinion. She toyed with the idea of how much fun she could have on the suffering end of Joanne's crop, but quickly put the thought aside as it filled her with a rush of conflicting urges.

Linda had no idea who Joanne's gimp might be, but she couldn't ever recall seeing a man so aroused by such humiliation. A huge length protruded from one of the zippered slits at the front of his gimp suit. His flesh strained with obvious urgency each time he was presented with a fresh cleft to devour. A string of pre-come trailed from the end of his shaft but Joanne offered him no opportunity for release or relief.

Unable to draw her gaze away, Linda continued to watch the gimp, envying his predicament. Joanne didn't show any signs of approval of her subordinate's behaviour: she simply insulted him and threatened to remove his mask and expose him. Linda stayed long enough to watch Joanne push her buttocks into the gimp's face while a cheering crowd urged him to lick her anus. Linda wondered if Ted would ever allow her to wear a gimp suit and let her be used with such cruel disregard. The thought made her stomach churn with sudden longing. For an instant she was so jealous of the gimp she simply wanted to push him away and take over his role as the party's toy. The idea sent fresh warmth coursing through her pussy muscles. It was time to take a break from the intensity of the party and get a breath of fresh air.

Ordinarily Ted and Linda's parties seldom saw more than a dozen couples, and usually Linda had to field calls throughout the evening from guests apologising for their absence. But this evening it seemed that everyone they had invited had arrived, many of them bringing unexpected extras. Singles, couples and triples barred her way and she had to weave through an undulating orgy of bodies and decline several suggestive propositions.

Thanks to the hectic pace of the evening, Linda hadn't been able to remember everyone's name. It was one of her personal rules that she never did anything with anyone unless she knew their full name. It crossed her mind that the rule would have to be revised if she ever took the gimp's position, and the thought almost paralysed her with the rush of lust it inspired. She fought her way outside into the cool air of the back garden.

Night had taken hold of Cedar View. The chill breeze was welcome on her bare body. Not caring that she was naked and outdoors, only relieved to be away from the claustrophobic atmosphere of the party, she took a deep breath and closed the conservatory door. Glancing around the still garden she spotted a solitary figure at the barbecue table and smiled apologetically. Hesitating, she asked, 'Is it OK to join you out here?'

'It's your garden.'

'I didn't want to intrude.'

'Are you the lady who left me the sandwiches and the beer?'

Lowering her gaze, she nodded.

'Are you the same lady who always leaves me sandwiches and beer?'

'And tissues,' she said, nodding at the box beside the plate. FOR MEN was written across the side of the box and for some reason the words made her smile. Tom thanked her for her kindness and assured her she wasn't intruding. Linda took a seat next to his and glanced up at the stars above. The wooden slats were chilly against her bare buttocks but she didn't mind. After the insane heat of the party the coolness of the night was a balm to her sweaty skin. The music remained loud enough to be irritating but, away from its immediate bellow, she felt as though her senses were being allowed a brief but much needed respite.

Looking at Tom she asked, 'How's the view been this evening?' The concern that he might have been masturbating, and that he could be embarrassed by her nearness, made her determined to show some consideration. Hoping he wasn't uncomfortable with her nudity, she studied his shaded gaze for a moment longer, trying to work out if he was looking at her eyes or her bare breasts. But Tom was only a shadow, darker than those that surrounded him. The deepening night made it impossible for her to see what he was looking at.

'It's been entertaining,' Tom told her. 'You certainly know how to throw a good party.'

She sniffed. 'Ted organises the invites. I just greet the guests and point them towards the canapés.' Glancing through the window of the conservatory, admiring the brightly lit alternate reality where the pool was populated with naked and near-naked couples, she asked, 'What have you seen so far?'

'I've seen enough to make my hair curl,' he grunted. Pointing, he asked, 'Who's that fellow in the leather body suit? The one Joanne is dragging round on a lead like he's her shiny pet mongrel?'

105

Linda laughed. The sound surprised her. During the evening she had heard herself sigh with gratitude, moan with satisfaction and scream with orgasm. But this was the first time she had heard herself laugh. She felt warmer towards Tom. Rather than wondering whether he had noticed her nakedness, she needed to know that he had and that she excited him. Restraining herself from asking the question outright, she forced her thoughts back to the conversation and glanced at Joanne's guest.

'I don't know who he is. Jo said he was her gimp and –'

'Gimp?'

Linda shrugged. 'It's an American term, I think. It's their word for someone who's sexually submissive and gets pleasure from being an anonymous plaything to anyone and everyone.'

'Gimp.' Tom turned the word over as though savouring it. 'And no one knows who he is?'

'I guess Jo might know,' Linda admitted. 'But I think she's the only one.'

'Joanne's gimp should give disguise lessons to that silly cow with the eye-mask and the false cock.'

Again, Linda heard herself laugh. Tom's frank appraisal of the situation mirrored so many of her own thoughts that she wouldn't have been surprised to learn he was a mindreader.

'If Jane Smith thinks she's fooling anyone with that disguise, let's hope she never decides to rob a bank or do something where she really needs to hide her identity.'

Linda laughed so hard that tears began to stream down her face. The image of Jane Smith robbing a bank in her stockings, suspenders, silly eye-mask and strap-on cock was thoroughly absurd. Almost as absurd as Jane's evident conviction that no one at the party knew who she was. Linda wiped the back of her hand delicately against her eyes, trying not to smudge her mascara as she brushed the tears away. It wasn't nice to bitch about her neighbours and party guests, but some of them asked to be criticised.

'Why are you out here?' Tom asked.

'I needed a break,' Linda said eventually. 'Don't get me wrong. I love everything that's happening in there. I love the excitement and the thrill and the daring.' She fanned her bare breasts with one hand and wondered if he was going to shift his position and give her an indication that he was moved by her nudity. To her frustration, Tom remained maddeningly still. 'I just needed to spend ten minutes away from the excitement to catch my breath.'

They remained in silence for a moment. Tom munched a sandwich and took a swig of beer. Glancing at his lap Linda realised with annoyance that shadows from the night and the table made it impossible for her to see if he was touching himself. The idea that he might be masturbating had stirred a small thrill in her loins. Now, realising she wasn't going to find out one way or the other, she felt as though she had been cheated of a rare and special treat.

'You were watching Joanne's gimp quite intensely,' Tom observed.

'Was I?'

He chuckled. 'There were so many things you could have been watching around the pool. That blonde with the big chest was sucking two men without protection. Those gorgeous black lasses were going at each other. Joanne herself looks quite resplendent in her costume. And there was a woman in the kitchen doorway being sandwiched between two men. Yet you weren't watching any of those events. You couldn't tear your gaze from Joanne's gimp.'

'You must have been watching me quite intently,' Linda muttered.

He took another swig of beer and tilted his head. She still couldn't read his eyes, but she had the impression Tom was looking only at her face and was not interested in her naked form. The thought was crushing.

'You could never be a gimp,' he told her. 'Not an anonymous one.'

If the remark had come as a shock she would have asked him why he thought she wanted to be a gimp and then denied his assumption. But, because it was so in keeping with her thoughts, she couldn't control her automatic reaction.

'Why on earth not?' She heard her voice ring with indignation. 'I could gimp as well as Joanne's shiny pet mongrel. I'd be obedient and I'd eat pussy and suck cock and I'd take whatever anyone wanted to –'

'You couldn't be anonymous,' Tom broke in gently. 'I saw your quim at the start of the evening. The lips were so full and ripe and appetising I'd recognise them anywhere. I'm sure any man with a passing interest would spot you straightaway and know who you were.'

She shivered in the darkness. Ted and Phil had both been amazed by the sight of her pumped-up pussy lips, but, as soon as the party began, they had gone in separate directions and not mentioned the temporary modification. Tom's obvious appreciation was made more remarkable by the simple fact that he had noticed. In that moment, she realised, if he had suggested they do anything – absolutely anything – she would have happily obliged.

'You'd best be getting back inside,' Tom said, nodding towards the conservatory. 'You'll catch a chill out here.'

Linda wanted to argue, tell him she was enjoying his company, but she suspected Tom would rather watch than interact. And, even though she now longed for him, she didn't want to make him uncomfortable or act against his wishes. Squaring her shoulders, pushing her chest forward and breathing in so her waist narrowed, she allowed him a moment to appreciate her body while it was tangibly close.

'I'm glad you liked my pumped-up pussy lips.'

'I still like the way they look,' he admitted, 'even though the swelling has subsided a little.'

She trembled, delighted by the idea that he might now be looking directly at her cleft. Not wanting to leave him, feeling the need to say something else, she added, 'I think I could play the role of a gimp if I really wanted. I could take the punishment and the humiliation. And I don't think anyone would ever know it was me.'

His head moved slowly from side to side. It wasn't a firm denial, she thought, only a gentle assertion of disagreement. 'If you want to try the gimp experience you'd be better off making contact with McMurray at number four. I don't know much about him, but I hear he knows how to properly punish and humiliate a woman. If you really want to try that sort of experience, I'd suggest you meet up with him first.'

Shocked by the excitement that Tom's suggestion inspired, Linda thanked him and then stepped back inside to the party.

It was proving to be a hell of a party, John thought, the best he had ever attended. When Joanne suggested he should wear the gimp suit his initial reservations had vanished beneath her insistent scowl. Slipping into the tight-fitting costume as she assailed him with a barrage of insults and abuse, he had found his spent length quickly growing hard again.

109

It helped that his identity was concealed beneath the gimp suit's mask. Even though no one knew who he was, it had still been humiliating walking at Joanne's side as she strode across the street to the party. When they entered Ted and Linda's house and Joanne commanded him to crawl on his knees, John thought his degradation could never be more complete. And yet, as the evening progressed, Joanne had thoughtfully taught him that there were still fresh depths for him to plumb.

He had never known such a thing as a gimp suit existed until Joanne threw the leather at him. Now, wrapped inside its tight confines, aware that everyone could see the inadequacy of his physique and that they could use him however they saw fit, he wondered why the existence of such a treasure had been hidden from him. He had already decided that, regardless of what happened at the party, he wanted to wear Joanne's gimp suit again and again and again. If it had been possible to give up his job, and dedicate his life to wearing the suit and serving his mistress, he would have happily thrown himself into the new lifestyle without a thought for all that he was leaving behind.

The leather was tight across his crotch. It had remained tight until Joanne unfastened the zip there and allowed his erection to burst into view. A few people had snickered at his length but the majority had simply ignored his arousal. Each time he was presented with a new pussy to lick – and there had been so many of those delicious folds of labia pushed in front of his face he could no longer be sure of the number – his erection had twitched into fresh life and come close to the point of climax.

'Aren't you doing well?' Joanne murmured.

Her praise warmed him. He would have felt a genuine affection for her if Joanne hadn't chosen that moment to slice her crop across his rear. Even though leather covered his backside, she still wielded the blow with enough efficiency to make it smart. A blazing line raged across his buttocks. Tears of raw anguish blurred his vision. He teetered on the brink of ejaculating.

She had commanded him to lick her. She had insisted he bury his nose into every woman who consented to be serviced by her gimp. She had even laughed at him as a group of her friends watched and he was forced to slide his tongue through the puckered ring of her anus. Her control had been divine, his submission exhilarating.

'Joanne?' John didn't bother to look up. Joanne had already informed him that he was not expected to interact with any of the guests at the party. He tried to work out what was happening by studying the dark trousers that moved into his range of vision. It was impossible to tell who the man was but he could see from the way Joanne turned and enthusiastically greeted the stranger that it was someone she considered an equal.

'Darling,' Joanne purred. 'How are you tonight?'

'All the better for seeing you in that outfit.'

She laughed demurely.

John instantly loathed the man. He had been in Joanne's company as her gimp throughout the evening and hadn't managed to make her respond with so much enthusiasm. He despised the confident authority of the man who now embraced her and pressed a hand against her barely covered buttock. Raising his gaze slightly, not wanting to see but desperate to know what was happening, John saw the man draw a finger along the slit of Joanne's sex.

She had discarded her panties earlier in the evening. The sight of her bare sex was nothing new to him. But this was the first time he had seen another man's hand touch the flushed folds of her labia, another man's finger slide inside Joanne's warm, wet hole.

John's erection throbbed urgently as Joanne flicked her cane against his rear. He flinched and glanced up at her.

'Stay here,' she growled. 'I'm going to get myself laid now. I expect you to be waiting in this position when I get back. Move and the punishment will be far more severe than you could possibly imagine.' Her tone was so severe he almost climaxed. Watching her stride away on the arm of the man, wishing he could be by her side and able to watch as she had sex with someone – even if he wasn't allowed to physically participate – John squirmed miserably on all fours and quietly cursed the torment of his agony and ecstasy.

A glance in the mirrored surface of the conservatory windows showed that he had become a ridiculous spectacle. He was a shiny figure on all fours, a black-swathed intruder in a sea of naked pink flesh. He sported an erection that no one wanted. He was an undesired sex toy. It was a new level of humiliation that he yearned to enjoy but, without Joanne's guidance and control, he couldn't take pleasure from it.

A hand slapped his rear. The pain was short, sharp and deliciously condescending. John turned to see who had struck him and stopped, mesmerised. There was something familiar about the woman but he couldn't place her. Her hair was dark, shoulder length, and glistened like a shampoo advert. Her china-blue eyes, shadowed by the eye-mask, sparkled with mischievous excitement. Glancing down her body, marvelling at the lacy dark bra hugging her breasts and the jet stockings that clung to her thighs, he gazed reverentially at the large black strap-on protruding from her loins. The shaft was a good twelve inches long and as thick as his wrist, the bulbous end huge and rounded. It had obviously been modelled on some heroically equipped giant.

John swallowed.

'Stay down on your knees, gimp,' she sneered.

John did as she commanded. He had thought Joanne was a commanding authority figure, but this woman was far more menacing. Staring up at her with the respect she deserved, he contemplated stammering an apology and then remembered it was not a gimp's place to speak.

She knelt by his side and reached beneath him. Her wrist brushed against his erection and he stifled the urge to moan. Not daring to look at what she was doing, reminding himself he was there as a gimp and simply had to suffer whatever any of the guests wanted to do with him, John remained rigid as she fumbled with the zipper on his suit. He had assumed Joanne had opened it to its full length when she tugged its teeth apart and allowed his erection to tumble free. But, when the masked stranger pulled more fiercely on the zip, and his balls were released from their confines, he realised the design of the suit was not as simple as he had first imagined.

She tugged the tab of the zipper hard underneath him and then yanked it up between his buttocks. John hadn't expected the costume to open in such a fashion and was disquieted by the idea that so much of his body was now visible and accessible.

'Don't move away,' she muttered. 'I've been wanting to play with you since I first came to this party.'

He nodded and remained still. Her hand encircled his length and squeezed with more force than he thought necessary. She stroked his shaft and then cupped his scrotum. Her hand was cool against the sticky, sweaty flesh of his sac. He stiffened, sure she was going to squeeze, not knowing whether he wanted that level of punishment or if it would prove more than he could tolerate. Holding his breath, trying not to sigh with relief when she lightly kneaded his balls and then moved her hand away, he resisted the urge to glance at her and try to work out who she might be.

A finger brushed against his anus. The sensation was almost too much. He had spent an evening as the plaything to a dozen or more unknown partygoers. His backside had been repeatedly cropped and caned. He had enjoyed the humiliation of Joanne's cruel, scathing insults. But he had never known pleasure like this.

'Don't move,' the woman beside him hissed. 'Just let me get you lubricated so I can ride this tight little arse of yours.'

It was all the warning she gave before sliding a finger into his rectum. The muscle of his anus yielded to her. The slender girth of her finger slipped easily inside. His erection hardened with such force that he wondered if his body was already in the throes of climax. As her cool finger slipped deeper, gliding easily on a greasy layer of lubrication and shocking him with undiscovered sensations, John lowered his head and released a soft moan of satisfaction.

'If you're going to speak at all you'll call me Goddess,' she said firmly.

'Goddess,' he murmured.

The name suited her. He was about to tell her as much when she dragged her finger from his backside. The muscle clenched tight and a spasm of obscene pleasure rippled through his rear, bringing him to the verge of orgasm. He resisted the impulse with superhuman force and a frantic gasp.

'Don't even think about coming yet,' she hissed.

Again, his rectum was caressed. This time, instead of a single finger threatening to penetrate him, John could feel the pressure of two slick digits on the muscle. He forced himself to relax as she pushed them forward. He wondered why she was taking so much time and pleasure in stretching him. It was only when he remembered her gargantuan strap-on that the truth of his predicament struck home. As her fingers delved deeper, forcing his anus wide and teasing previously undiscovered pleasures from his body, John clenched his teeth and whispered, 'Goddess.'

There were four of them on the bed, lying in a loose square so they could touch hand to thigh, head to groin, mouth to crotch. Ted's face was buried between Denise's thighs. Denise had her lips wrapped around Phil's erection. Phil slurped at the split of Joanne's pussy while Joanne sucked Ted's cock.

They were all naked. The excess of nudity, sweaty flesh and saliva-silvered genitals made Linda shiver. She wasn't sure if her reaction came from revulsion or fascination. It was certainly exciting to see so many of her friends involved in such explicit intimacy, but she felt slightly miffed that none of them had thought to invite her to join the game. Pushing the jealous thoughts from her mind, recognising them for what they were and realising they weren't appropriate at a party like this, she joined the quartet on the bed and stroked Ted's chest.

He grinned at her, moved his mouth from Denise's sex, and gave Linda a chaste kiss on the cheek. His breath was flavoured with the perfume of Denise's pussy, his lips moist with the rich juice that glistened on their neighbour's cleft. When he moved his face away from hers, Linda could feel the sticky gloss of Denise's wetness upon her cheek.

Denise, noticing that Ted had moved away from her, glanced at Linda and then grinned. 'Hell of a party.'

'Thanks.'

Linda would have said more but she could feel hands moving against the insides of her thighs and heading towards her crotch. Thrilled by the casual caresses, she saw that both Phil and Joanne were trying to touch her pussy as they continued sucking and fucking the others on the bed. Linda's thoughts of being ignored and unwanted were cast aside as she revelled in the sensual seduction of her neighbours. When Ted returned his mouth to Denise's pussy, and Denise settled back contentedly, Linda couldn't recall why she had felt she wasn't being included in the evening's activities.

Phil slipped a moist finger inside her sex. The smooth friction was delicious.

Joanne stroked the ball of her thumb against Linda's clitoris. The pressure was exhilarating. Linda gave a sigh and wondered how long it would take the pair to have her gasping with satisfaction. She bit her lower lip, trying to remember something that had seemed important just before she entered the room.

Denise's hand clutched Linda's left breast. Ted grabbed her right. They both kneaded and stroked, Ted paying more attention to her nipple, Denise concentrating on exciting whorls of pleasure by teasing her areola. Linda's worries were forgotten. The familiar excitement of being with naked friends, enjoying their bodies as they teased and toyed with her, thrust every other consideration aside. She shivered as a dozen different sensations reminded her she was in the company of likeminded hedonists who shared her devotion to sensual pleasure.

'Someone should get Charlie and Rhona in here,' Denise mumbled. 'Have they arrived yet?' She spoke with her lips around Phil's erection, tucking the length into the corner of her mouth so that she could articulate the words. The suggestion made, she returned to sucking and licking him, devouring his cock as though it was a seldom enjoyed delicacy.

'I haven't seen Rhona or Charlie this evening,' Linda responded. 'And they both said they would be here.' Her earlier worries about the couple from number seven returned with enough force to distract her from the thrill of being with Denise, Phil, Ted and Joanne. 'I've not had a call from them and I'm getting a bit concerned.'

'Maybe they just decided to stay home this evening,' Denise suggested, briefly removing her mouth from Phil's cock. 'It wouldn't be the first time they'd bailed because they'd got caught up in a private game.'

Linda considered this and then shrugged. She didn't know Rhona and Charlie as well as Denise clearly did, but she thought the idea was unlikely. Both of them had seemed enthusiastic about the idea of attending the party. According to Ted, Rhona had said the only thing she could imagine that would stop them being there was if she and Charlie got a chance to play with Megan McMurray.

'Maybe they're here already?' Phil suggested. He continued to kiss Joanne's wet pussy as he made the comment; his interest in the topic was obviously no more than casual.

'One of us would have seen them if they were already here,' Ted grunted.

'Maybe not,' Phil argued. He dragged his mouth from Joanne's hole. She gasped and glared at him but he was oblivious to her anger or her needs. 'There are so many people here Charlie and Rhona could have easily got lost in the crowd. That could even be Charlie in the gimp suit.'

'It's not Charlie,' Joanne told him. 'If you don't believe me, I'll take you downstairs now and unmask him so I can prove it.'

'I believe you,' Phil assured her.

'I mean it. I will. I'll unmask him.'

Linda glanced at Phil and could see he was puzzled by Joanne's sudden insistence on unmasking and exposing her gimp. He carefully returned his mouth to Joanne's sex.

'Let's just get back to enjoying the evening,' he murmured, lapping at the moist folds.

Joanne sighed and nodded. 'I can unmask the little fucker later,' she decided. She was about to wrap her mouth around Ted's cock when a thought occurred to her.

'I saw the McMurray girl headed towards theirs earlier this evening,' she said. 'If she'd turned up at my house I wouldn't have come to this party.' She gave a salacious chuckle that made Linda feel ill. 'If she'd turned up at my house I'd be riding that little bitch until she screamed for me to stop.'

'You're sure it was her?'

Joanne nodded. 'I'd recognise the McMurray girl anywhere. I've had her so many times in my imagination I know her better than I know my own reflection.'

Denise and Phil shifted positions. They started to mumble something about Megan McMurray being one of the most desirable women on the street. Then, as the four of them resumed their head-to-crotch daisy-chain, Linda realised none of them was concerned about the safety of their friends from across the road. Climbing off the bed, she thought it was time to take matters into her own hands.

It was proving to be a hell of a party, Jane thought, the best she had ever attended. Hiding behind the eye-mask, amazed that such a simple little device could keep her identity a secret from everyone around her,

she could enjoy the evening without fear of repercussions.

She eased a third finger inside the gimp and paused
until his muscles had clenched tight. Either Ted or
Linda had made sure there was lubricant available
throughout the house in tubes, tubs and jars. Jane had
never used it before. She'd always thought that if a
woman needed lubricant she had some sort of problem,
and if a man needed it he was some sort of pervert. Yet,
scooping the glistening jelly into her palm, then sliding
her fingers into the gimp's slowly widening anus, she
had decided that lubricant was neither an aid to
perversion nor the last resort for those who should
have given up. Lubricant was wonderful. Her hands
were sticky with the viscous fluid. The tactile thrill was
another delicious memory she intended to take from
this evening. Her fingers were crushed by the gimp's
sphincter clenching against her. She had never realised
such marvellous pleasure could be had from sexually
dominating a man. Her pussy tingled with the rush of
warm arousal. Because the lips of her sex were pressed
tight against the heel of the strap-on, it was like being
deftly teased by a talented lover. That thought added
fresh wetness to her excitement and she threw herself
into the pleasure of being a dominatrix for the evening.

'How does that feel?'

'That feels wonderful, Goddess.'

'Do you feel stretched?' She kept her fingers inside
him, twisting them against the pressure of his muscles
and enjoying the warm velvet throb of his flesh against
her hand. She lowered her mouth to the side of his face
and spoke where the mask covered his ear. 'Do you
feel full and really stretched?'

'Yes, Goddess.' He panted the words as though
trying to bite back an ejaculation. 'Yes. I feel
stretched.'

'Fully stretched?'

'Yes, Goddess.'

'Good.' She slipped her fingers from him and stood up. Towering over him so that her strap-on waved in front of his face, she said, 'Then you may now suck my cock. You may suck my cock so it's wet and ready to slide inside you.'

'Where the hell did Linda go?'

Denise had been teetering at the more pleasurable end of the satisfaction spectrum. Someone – Ted, she believed – had been lapping at the moist flesh between her legs. The scents of cock and pussy, a cocktail of carnal perfumes, tainted every breath. Phil's erection was in her mouth, stretching her lips and making her tremble each time she drew her tongue against his tightly stretched skin. But, when Ted sat up to ask the question, the pleasure was abruptly brought to an end.

'Where the hell is she?' he demanded.

'She was here a minute ago.'

'Didn't she say she was going to check on Charlie and Ronnie?'

Neither of the answers seemed to satisfy Ted. Perplexed, he glowered around the room. 'Well, if she's gone across the road to get those two, who's hosting our party?'

Joanne sighed. Denise tightened her jaw, not wanting to complain but bitterly frustrated that the passion and intensity of the group dynamic were evaporating. She had to clench her teeth when Ted climbed off the bed and said, 'I'd best go downstairs and be a good host.' He grabbed a towel to put round his waist and left the room without another word.

'I'll join you,' Joanne called after him. She made the bed tremble and squeak as she pulled herself away from Denise and Phil. 'I think it's about time I went

downstairs and tormented my gimp a little bit more.'
There was a vicious smile on her lips. Her eyes were
bereft of amusement or good humour. 'It's probably
about time I tore the mask from his face so everyone
can see who he is.' She hastily got back into her boots
and leathers, then disappeared from the room in Ted's
wake.

'And then there were two,' Denise mumbled. She
stopped Phil leaving the bed, holding him tight to her
naked body. 'What's your hurry? Where are you
wanting to go?'

He shrugged but made no attempt to distance
himself from her. Turning slightly, resting one broad
thigh between her legs and using his free hand to
tease her bare torso, he said, 'I'm in no hurry to
go anywhere. I'm just trying to enjoy the party, the
same as you.' He grinned and added, 'Unless you want
us to have our own little party in here now we're
alone?'

She squirmed against his thigh, pressing the wet flesh
of her pussy lips against his flesh. She felt the
scratching of wiry leg hair. After the gentle stimulation
of a warm wet tongue upon her sex, the brutal caress
of his thigh was exhilarating. She wondered if Ted's
brother might be the man she needed to ride her
bareback. Common sense told her it was irresponsible.
She had never considered having anybody at one of
Ted and Linda's parties without making sure they
wore proper protection. But she felt as though she
knew Phil, and the idea that he might impregnate her
made the prospect incredibly tempting. Even if he wore
a rubber, she thought bitterly, he was more likely to
get her pregnant than Derek and his current perform-
ance in the bedroom.

He sucked her breast, teasing her nipple between his
teeth. She shivered.

Reaching down to stroke his thick wet cock, Denise contemplated just guiding his length into her hole and squeezing until he came. It would be so easy: Phil would be inside her before he remembered he was unsheathed. And she so needed to feel a man ejaculate inside her. The urge was so strong it took the strongest effort of will to pull herself out of his arms.

'I should really go and make sure Jane is OK on her own,' Denise told him. It was an excuse: she didn't want to leave him, and she didn't doubt Jane would be enjoying herself without an escort. She desperately wanted to feel him inside her, without any protection, but she knew that wouldn't be sensible. Trying not to think about her sudden craving for Phil's bare length and his seed, she said, 'It was naughty of me to leave Jane to her own devices but –'

'Jane's here? Jane Smith from number three?'

Denise remembered that, as Ted's brother, Phil knew most of the residents on Cedar View. His garage regularly serviced and repaired a lot of the cars on the View and Phil was sufficiently conscientious to remember most of his customers by sight.

'Jane's here,' she assured him. 'You must have seen her. She came in with me.'

Phil shook his head. 'I haven't seen Jane. I would have remembered.'

'She's wearing an eye-mask and a –'

'Dear God! Is that Jane?' Phil sounded surprised. Denise studied his face, not sure if he was joking. She had thought Jane's disguise was completely inadequate and had expected everyone to recognise her. Yet Phil seemed genuinely amazed to learn it was Jane behind the mask. He was climbing off the bed and she had to grab hold of his wrist to stop him leaving her side.

His brow furrowed. 'What's the matter?' He glanced briefly towards the door and she could see that he was anxious to hurry back to the party and try to negotiate an intimate encounter with Jane.

'I've been wanting to ask you a favour.'

His hesitation lasted only a second, and he fell back to her side on the bed. Teasing her breasts with casual caresses and placing his thigh back between her spread legs, he said, 'You know I'd be happy to do you any favour. What do you want?'

She giggled and moved her mouth up to meet his lips. Phil's kisses tasted of Joanne's pussy. It was a flavour Denise knew intimately and she savoured the sweet perfume in a rush of giddy excitement. Although Ted's swift departure had tempered the mood of the room, she was pleased to note that the excitement hadn't completely vanished. The thickness of Phil's erection, still sticky with her saliva, nudged at her labia.

'How long has it been since this cock was inside a woman?'

Phil raised a questioning eyebrow. 'You were sucking it a minute ago,' he reminded her. 'So I think the honest answer is: not that long.'

Denise shook her head and eased herself closer. The thought of thrusting her hips down and being impaled on his unsheathed shaft was almost too tempting. With a huge effort of restraint she remained on the brink of penetration. Holding her breath, resisting the urge to slide on to him, she asked, 'How long since it was *inside* a woman?'

'I screwed Linda just before the party began.'

Still toying with his length, stroking it slowly against her sex, Denise stiffened herself in anticipation of his rebuke and asked, 'How long since it's been inside a woman without a rubber?'

He studied her in stunned silence. Denise held her breath, ready for a blunt refusal.

Phil licked his lips. 'Bareback?' he muttered. The end of his cock trembled against her sex. 'Are you serious?'

'Why not?' To pique his interest, Denise rubbed the slit of her sex more forcefully against him. He was hard, naked and ready to slide inside her pussy, and she was desperate to feel him. It was increasingly difficult to appear cool about this conversation. 'You haven't ridden anyone unsheathed for ages, have you? I'll bet you're ready to slip inside me now and feel my wet pussy gripping your cock.'

The shaft in her hand twitched.

'Is that what you want?' Phil asked. He started to raise himself on the bed, urging his shaft closer to the point of penetration.

Denise stayed him one hand. 'That's what I'm offering,' she said carefully. 'But I'll want you to do something for me first. It's something that needs doing urgently – tonight. And it's something that only you have the skill to do.'

Phil seemed genuinely puzzled. His erection started to wane. 'What do you want from me? If I get to ride you bareback you know I'll do almost anything. What do you want?'

She took hold of his hand and said, 'Come back to my house. I want you in the garage.'

Thirteen

4 Cedar View

Max opened the door. With a blink he acknowledged that the woman standing there wasn't Megan. Instantly his gaze darted across the road to number five. His brow furrowed as he scoured the illuminated windows for a silhouette that might belong to Megan.

'Mr McMurray?'

Still scowling at number five, not looking at the woman, he said, 'Call me Max.'

'Max. I've come to ask you a favour.'

For the first time he properly studied the redhead. It took him a moment to put a name to the face and, when he remembered who she was, he began to wonder why she was calling on him.

'It's Linda, isn't it? Linda from next door.'

'I'm here to ask a favour.'

She was blushing. Her gaze shifted from one side of the street to the other. Her fingers fumbled nervously with the buttons of the large coat she wore. Noticing her bare legs beneath the hem, Max wondered if everything under the coat might be bare too. The thought stirred a response in his loins and he regarded her with new and lascivious interest.

'A favour? What do you want?'

Her mouth twisted in indecision. Again, she cast a glance up and down the street, as though apprehensive at the thought of being seen on his doorstep. The crimson colouring on her cheeks turned a painful shade of purple.

'I want ...' Her voice trailed off. Her forehead creased with a puzzled frown.

Max drew a short, sharp breath. 'What favour do you want, Linda? You'll have to speak up and tell me. I'm not psychic.'

'I've been told you know how to dominate a woman,' she said quickly. 'Dominate and humiliate a woman. I mean *sexually*.' It was only with the final word that she dared to glance up at him. Her gaze lingered for a painful instant and then she lowered her eyes. Her eyes were glassy with threatened tears. Embarrassment coloured her décolletage and Max wondered how much further down her body the vibrant hue descended. He licked his lips and regarded her with a tight grin. As the silence stretched between them he said softly, 'That's not asking a favour. That's just repeating gossip. What do you want, Linda? Tell me what you want.'

'I want you to humiliate me,' she whispered.

'Say again.'

'I want –'

'Louder!'

She raised her head and glared at him. Her tears were now close to falling. He was surprised by the effect of his cruelty. He was used to teasing Megan until she glowered at him with the anger of a frustrated submissive. He was familiar with the triggers that took Megan's sister, Aliceon, to the point of infuriated loathing. But he hadn't expected to find his neighbour's Achilles' heel within seconds of her showing up on his doorstep. He stifled the urge to grin at his phenomenal abilities.

'I want you to humiliate me,' she hissed. 'I want you to dominate me and humiliate me. That's the favour I want.'

He considered his response without looking at her. His gaze trailed along Cedar View. There were more cars on the street than he was used to seeing. He had assumed the vehicles belonged to partygoers at Ted and Linda's house but, with Linda standing on his doorstep, that seemed unlikely. What sort of host would abandon her party and go next door to ask a neighbour to humiliate her?

Max's gaze came to rest on number five. He knew Tanya was still in that house and wondered what was keeping her so long. The property was similar to his: three bedrooms and a bathroom upstairs, two receptions and a kitchen downstairs. Max didn't know if Joanne had a cellar at number five but he felt fairly confident that the house wasn't large enough to merit Tanya spending so long inside, supposedly looking for Megan. The suspicion that she might be playing for time, trying to pretend she was doing more in her search for Megan than she really was, blackened his mood. When he turned back to face Linda, he was scowling.

'You want me to dominate you?'

'Yes.'

'Humiliate you?'

'Yes.'

'Take your coat off.'

She faltered only for a second, but it was long enough for him to make his authority felt. A glimmer of hesitation appeared in her eyes and her hands, reaching for the buttons of her coat, paused rather than unfastening them.

'Fine,' he snapped. 'If you don't want me to do this for you I'll say goodnight.' Briskly, he reached for the door handle and started to close it in her face.

'No,' Linda wailed. 'Please! No!'

* * *

'No,' Linda wailed. 'Please! No!'

It had taken such a magnificent effort of courage to approach Max McMurray that she couldn't believe the opportunity to learn from him was already being snatched from her grip. The door was closing. Max stepped out of the range of its arc with a grace that was almost feline. Linda pushed one hand against the glossy white door and cried again, 'No. Please! No!'

A cruel smile rested on Max's lips. He stopped the door closing and studied her with such intensity that she blushed again. He was a brooding, silent ogre of a man, dressed in faded denims and a brilliant white wife-beater. His brawny biceps were covered with an assortment of black and blue tattoos that looked like stylised bruises. Light from behind him made a halo round his shaved scalp. Linda felt intimidated and aroused in equal measure. If he had been a decade or two older, Linda thought, he would have looked like her idea of the ideal man.

She wrenched the coat open and shrugged it from her shoulders.

Common sense and the urgency of the situation had told her that there was no point in wearing anything beneath the coat. She was in a hurry to see if Max McMurray could provide all the wonderful illumination that Tom had intimated. It was true she had been admiring and envying Joanne's gimp at the party. If, as Tom had suggested, Max McMurray was able to teach her how to enjoy the pleasures of servility and humiliation, Linda believed it could be the revelatory experience that she needed to change her life.

She allowed the coat to fall to the doorstep and stood naked. She had thought Max's gaze had flicked over the road again, as though there was something at number five of more interest than her and her naked body. But when she dropped her coat his cruel smile was fixed directly on her. It didn't broaden with approval or fade with disappointment. It simply remained inscrutable.

'Very good,' he grunted. 'That should save us some time.' He licked his lips and, for the first time, Linda noticed that his smile didn't touch his eyes. 'Now get down on your knees,' he snapped. 'Get down on your knees and suck my cock. If you ask me to repeat that instruction I'll close the door now and no amount of begging from you will get me to open it again. Do you understand?'

A thousand questions sprang to the forefront of her mind. She wanted to ask him if he was comfortable with being blown on the front step, if he wasn't worried what the neighbours might think, and if his partner, Megan, would approve or understand. Not only that: she also wanted to ask herself if she was ready to subjugate herself to this uncouth bully. He was younger than any man she had ever been with – very close to her own age – and she wasn't sure it would be right to get intimate with someone who was only in their mid-twenties.

But she needed to find out if the experience of being servile was all that she had hoped it might be. Sure that Max wouldn't tolerate a moment's vacillation, she simply dropped to her knees and placed her mouth at the same level as the crotch of his jeans. Boldly reaching for the zipper, unfastening him and releasing his soft, stout length, she inhaled the scent of his sweat and arousal before putting her mouth around his cock.

Max sighed. Linda didn't dare look up at him. His flaccid cock began to thicken as she sucked on his flesh and lapped the sweat from his shaft. There were flavours of pre-come and pussy musk on his burgeoning erection. As he grew stiffer and filled her mouth with more of his thickness, drops of salty pre-come filled her mouth, collecting at the back of her throat and making her want to gag as she licked, lapped and swallowed.

The night's chill air swept over her bare body. A cool breeze teased her stiff nipples, caressed her thighs and froze her labia. Her heart pounded loudly. The slurp of her mouth against Max's shaft was deafening. She wondered if she should be listening for the sounds of approaching neighbours, or any other noise that might indicate someone was about to discover them, but she doubted she would hear anything over the sound of her own panic as she sucked Max's cock. She felt dangerously exposed but that sensation brought with it a feeling of intense and overwhelming excitement.

'Not bad,' Max allowed. He managed to sound supremely indifferent. 'It needs a little more sucking and a little less licking, I think. But, other than that, you're doing OK.'

Immediately, she tried to make sure that she was blowing him the way he wanted. Instead of drawing her tongue against his length in long, leisurely licks, Linda concentrated on taking the end in her mouth and sucking. She worked her lips around him, trying to make her mouth into a tight vagina as she bobbed her head vigorously up and down. His thickness made the position awkward but she had to admit it was exciting to be working to his instructions.

As the first trickle of pleasure teased her loins, Linda conceded that Tom had been right when he said Max McMurray knew how to dominate a woman. She couldn't remember a time when she had felt so much at risk of embarrassment and so unable to do anything about it. Ted would never have placed her in such an invidious situation and there had never been a boyfriend or partner before him who would have expected her to risk such humiliation. She tried to recall the last time she had put herself and her well-being entirely under someone else's control. She was naked, she was out in public, she had her neighbour's cock in her mouth and her safety and satisfaction were wholly reliant on the whim of a comparative stranger. The sense of her own vulnerability was exhilarating.

'Now that's too much sucking,' Max said dryly.

His tone was dispassionate, cool. He sounded so uninvolved in the intimacy that, if she hadn't been sucking his cock and had only heard his voice, Linda would have thought he was discussing a piece of machinery.

'A BJ should be a combination of sucking and licking,' Max informed her. 'There should be no fingers or hands involved. That's just cheating. And there should be a perfect balance of sucking and licking. Not an even balance: that would be wrong. The perfect balance would be about seventy per cent sucking and thirty per cent licking. Please do it properly or I'll simply take my cock out of your mouth and close the door.'

Frightened that he might act on the threat, Linda threw herself into the task of sucking and licking Max's cock with renewed fervour. Her lips were slippery against his flesh. She could feel him stiffening against her tongue, as though he was ready to explode. Taking him at his word, and believing he meant what he had said about a seventy-thirty balance, she licked him for three seconds, then sucked him for seven. Counting inside her head, anxious to do things just as he demanded, she realised that her own pleasure had been all but forgotten. Admittedly, it was a humiliating situation, and, when she reminded herself that she was being subjugated, the thought did stir a warm rush of responses. But she remained aware that she was giving Max far more pleasure than he was giving her.

'Carry on,' Max urged. 'You've just about got the balance right there.'

Daring to glance up at him, she wondered if she would see the telltale signs of his impending climax etched on his face. Because she didn't know Max very well, she wasn't sure what those signs might be. His jaw might grow tense, she thought, or his expression might become more focused. There was even the possibility that his austere features would be broken by a smile.

Instead, when she looked up at his face, she saw Max was still glowering across the road, his gaze dourly fixed on number five: Joanne Jackson's house. He seemed oblivious to her and what she was doing to his cock.

His length filled her mouth and she sucked harder on his glans.

'Don't make me come yet,' Max said. 'If I'm going to properly punish and humiliate you, I want to spank your arse and then fuck you.' He said the words absently, still staring at the windows of number five. Tanya had been in there too long now. Either she had found Megan and was talking with her or she was simply messing round in Joanne Jackson's house, wasting time and trying to make it look as if she was conducting the search, in order to claim her rent-free week.

Acknowledging the two options left him no wiser about the truth of the situation. He vowed, the next time Tanya was scheduled to clean his house, he would find some reason to cane her backside. It wouldn't matter if she cleaned the house perfectly from cellar to attic: he would find fault with something and stripe her broad buttocks until she begged for forgiveness.

Irritated by the impotence of his situation, he leant back into the house without moving his erection from

132

Linda's mouth. He had to concede that she was quite competent when it came to sucking cock. She had already taken him to the point of climax and the only thing stopping him from releasing his ejaculation and shooting into her mouth was a heroic effort of willpower. Determined that Linda wouldn't see how hard he was working to resist his climax, he kept his features a mask of indifference.

'Aliceon!' he bellowed, calling back into the house. 'Aliceon!'

Aliceon's voice came from the TV lounge. 'I'm watching the telly,' she complained. 'What do you want?'

'Fetch me a beer,' he called. 'And I'll need my crop. There's an arse out here that needs properly striping.'

His length stiffened as he said the words. Glancing down at Linda, admiring the sight of her ripe lips around his flesh, he contemplated simply letting go and spurting into her mouth. It would be satisfying to watch her gag and swallow. There would be a brutal pleasure in seeing a dribble of his white spend trailing from her lips. He could slam the door in her face once he had climaxed, telling her that his ejaculation ended the first lesson on humiliation. But he resisted the urge, sure he could have far more fun if he waited until Aliceon brought him his crop.

'Who's she?' Aliceon asked, handing him a beer. She hadn't bothered dressing since being in the cellar. She wore only the skimpiest of thongs. Her pert bare breasts swayed enticingly close to him. The crotch of her thong was pulled so tight he could make out the alluring shape of her labia. Even though the fabric was black, Max thought he could still see the telltale signs of wetness that made the gusset glossy. His erection twitched with more force and he made a renewed effort to stop himself climaxing in Linda's mouth.

Trying to appear cool and nonchalant, Max opened the tin of lager and drank a mouthful before replying. 'This is Linda. She's one of the neighbours.' He thought of offering fuller introductions. 'Linda, meet Aliceon, Megan's sister, who I found chained and ready to be striped and fucked in the cellar this evening. Aliceon, meet Linda, the next-door neighbour who's come here unexpectedly to suck my cock.' The words sounded too unreal inside his head and he simply said, 'Linda wants me to humiliate her.'

Aliceon cast a sneering glance in Linda's direction. 'What does Megan think about this?'

'It's difficult to know what Megan thinks about this,' he growled. 'Since Megan pissed off earlier this evening and didn't leave any word about where she was going or what she was doing, I have no way of knowing her thoughts about anything.'

Aliceon glared at him. Now she was no longer chained, he noticed, she could be defiant. It was a trait that he knew he could have thrashed out of her if he had devoted the necessary time to the project. But, because he loved Megan and adored Aliceon, Max preferred to see both women being characteristically rebellious.

'Don't you think Megan's going to be pissed off that you're getting a BJ from the next-door neighbour?'

Max shrugged. He kept the gesture economical so it didn't shift his cock from Linda's mouth. 'Megan and I have an understanding,' he reminded Aliceon. 'You should know about our understandings better than anyone else.' As he spoke he reached for the crop that she had brought for him.

Aliceon deliberately held it out of his reach. 'Megan's told me you both agreed not to have anyone else inside the house without the other's permission. Have you got Megan's permission for this?'

Max nodded down towards Linda, on the step. 'Look carefully,' he told Aliceon. 'She's not inside the house, is she?' While Aliceon was distracted Max snatched the crop from her fingers. It felt good to have the familiar stiff length in his hand. Glaring down at Linda, admiring the way she had accepted so much of his erection into her mouth and sucked and licked exactly as he commanded, he said, 'You can stand up now. You can stand up, turn round and bend over. I think it's time I began to teach you a little about punishment.'

Linda continued to suck his rigid cock as she stared uncertainly up at him. He had spent so long talking to the woman in the house that Linda wasn't sure if he was now talking to her.

'You can stand up,' Max repeated, 'turn round and bend over. I think it's time I began to teach you a little about punishment.'

She didn't dare hesitate. He had made it clear before that, if she showed any signs of hesitation, he would simply close the door and the opportunity to learn from him would be snatched from her for ever. For the first time she saw the near-naked woman behind Max and was amazed how strikingly similar Aliceon was to Megan. The woman was attractive – painfully attractive. Linda didn't think Max would be troubled by the prospect of closing the door on one willing female when another was so close to hand.

She took her mouth from Max's length and stood up. Acting quickly, not daring to make him repeat his instruction again, she turned round and bent over.

'Put your hands on your knees,' Max snapped.

Linda obeyed.

'Keep your back straight. Hold your arse as high as you can.'

Doing as he asked made the muscles in her back, thighs and calves ache like bruises. But, knowing she

135

had to obey him, Linda did as she was told. Night now held Cedar View in the folds of its black, oppressive cloak. The two lamps that illuminated the street shone liquid gold that dripped from the bonnets and windscreens of the parked cars. Linda couldn't resist glancing along the street, searching for movement, fearful that someone might see what she was doing and compound her embarrassment with discovery. The shifting of a shadow across the road made her inwardly cringe. But, with no time to peer into the darkness and try to work out who was there, she simply closed her eyes in shame and struggled to maintain the position that Max had requested.

'Ten stripes,' he said.

He made no attempt to lower his voice. His words echoed along the darkened street. It was almost as though he was shouting his command so it would be heard inside the party at her house next door.

'I'll teach you about punishment with ten stripes across your arse. If you think I've taught you properly, once you've had your ten stripes, I'll kindly let you take my cock up your arse afterwards. Do we understand each other, Linda?'

'Yes,' she whispered. She wondered if she should say the word louder, not sure if he had heard and worried he would think she was hesitating or ignoring him. 'Yes,' she answered more forcefully. 'Yes, we understand each other.'

As she was saying the words there was a whistle of air. A shock of blazing heat assaulted her buttock and Linda stiffened in pain. She was so surprised by the impact that she couldn't immediately tell how much it hurt. It happened in a sensory vacuum, void of sensation. Cocooned in an expectant silence, she waited for her body's reaction and wondered how pleasurable the pain might prove to be. She bit back an exclamation as she felt the raw anguish shriek through her rear.

Max landed a second slice with the crop. Again it whistled. For a second time the rusty razor of agony scored her buttocks. The force was severe enough to make her teeter on the verge of collapse. The pain was so shocking she wanted to scream.

Max struck a third blow. There was another vicious whistle, a bitter, brutal sting. This time Linda couldn't stop sobbing in protest. She kept the sound soft and low, not wanting to draw attention to herself or what she was doing.

Behind her she heard Max chuckle. Worse than Max's mirth, she was crushed to hear Aliceon's voice, lowered to a reverential whisper and edged with both awe and arousal. 'That's harsh, Max. You're really laying into that poor bitch.'

'You've had worse,' Max grunted.

'Not much,' Aliceon mumbled.

Another blow. This one scorched like a branding iron. The pain was too much, too intense, more than she could handle. Linda didn't know what sort of insanity had made her think she could suffer punishment like this, and she no longer cared to explore it. She was hurt, she was humiliated and she wasn't going to take any more. Her backside ached as though it had been scoured by a million needle-sharp shards. For her own safety, as well as for the remnants of her dignity, she had to escape the brutality of Max's punishment and get back to her party.

Movement over the road caught her attention. At first she wasn't sure if she was seeing a glimmer of light or a reflection of something through the tears that filled her eyes. When she turned her head slightly and concentrated, Linda realised that the movement came from outside the garden of number one. Although the shadows were at their densest in that part of the road, she could make out the silhouette of a figure holding something against its face. The reflection of the streetlights shone from the lenses of his binoculars.

With a broad smile, Linda held her body stiff. She renewed her grip on her knees and straightened her back. Deliberately, she raised her backside higher to meet the next blow from Max's crop. Staring towards the figure outside number one, Linda began to feel the delicious sexual warmth that was instilled with each kiss of Max's crop – a warmth enhanced by the knowledge that her humiliation was being watched and admired.

Fourteen

2 Cedar View

Tanya was still sneering with disgust when she returned home. There had been very little worth eating or drinking inside Joanne's house. The woman seemed to live off a diet of mineral water and some nasty-looking white paste labelled 'tofu'. There had been an anaemic lettuce in the bottom of the fridge but no real food she could enjoy as she pretended to continue her search. Even if she had discovered something edible, Tanya didn't think she would have been able to enjoy eating in Joanne's home. The vague smell of pee that lingered there had killed her appetite for everything except the tin of lager she'd found. But Tanya's sneer had nothing to do with Joanne's unwitting lack of hospitality or the disquieting fragrance.

It was the photographs that disgusted her. They weren't particularly explicit or shocking but she was appalled by their presence. It didn't trouble her too greatly that Joanne had photographs of other people. A couple of them showed faces, so Tanya guessed they had known she was taking their picture. But Tanya was repulsed by the idea that the woman had taken secret pictures of *her*, showing her private parts. She also felt sure that much of Joanne's photo collection had been obtained without permission, which was just wrong.

She wondered why Joanne would have such a collection. If she had wanted the pictures for the fun of having a private porn collection, she would have kept them in her bedroom, or somewhere else where she was likely to have a wank. Tanya had a collection of explicit novels and magazines that she kept in her own bedside cabinet, next to the cheap vibrator she had bought for herself at Christmas. She felt certain that all adults kept their porn close to the place where they were most easily able to wank. But since Joanne had stored the photographs in a drawer in the front room, she must be keeping them for another reason. It could only be blackmail.

Her desire to quit working for Joanne Jackson surged stronger than ever. As soon as Max had confirmed she had a week's reprieve from the rent – a month's reprieve if she could squeeze that much out of him – Tanya intended looking for a job that would replace the income she got by working at Joanne's. The thought should have made her smile but her mood remained black. Even when she went to the kitchen sink and burnt the Polaroids one by one in the stainless-steel bowl, her spirits refused to return. Her frown remained deep and she squeezed her nostrils shut against the smoke that threatened to prompt unwanted tears.

She sneaked out of the back door of Joanne's, aware that Max would be watching the street as she pretended to conduct her search for Megan, and stole through gardens and shadows in an attempt to return home without alerting him to her movements.

The lights remained bright at number six. The sounds of the party, the shrieks and bays of laughter, made her natural scowl turn even more sour. The unusual number of cars on Cedar View that evening made it easier for her to steal past Max's house. But at the same time they reminded her that everyone else on Cedar View was enjoying the night, while she was frustrated, alone and shunned.

Movement outside number one made her pause. Bitterly, she realised the seedy old voyeur who lived there was outside the house training his binoculars across the road. Instead of looking towards the house with the sex party, he was facing towards number four. She tried to catch a glimpse of what was happening that had caught Tom's interest, but the angle of the house and the large four-by-four filling Max's driveway prevented her from seeing the front door.

As Tanya watched, a couple ran from Ted and Linda's. They shrieked and giggled happily together, heading into the heart of the cul-de-sac. Tanya recognised Denise Shelby, but only when the woman took the burly stranger she was with up the path of number eight and into the garage.

Tanya's scowl of contempt tightened into a grimace. Seeing Denise with another man confirmed her suspicion that everyone on Cedar View was having some sort of fun this evening. 'Everyone,' she muttered, 'except me.'

With the last of the photographs transformed into an ashy memory, Tanya decided to pick up the phone. She was going to call Max and tell him to find his own missing wife. Everyone on the street was ignoring and excluding her. If they were all going to shun her, she could return the compliment and shun all of them. She no longer wanted to be a part of Max's games with Megan, or belong to a street that excluded her from their parties and fun.

Her decision made, Tanya walked over to the telephone beside the window. Snatching the receiver from its cradle, glowering through the curtains, she watched Joanne rush – panicked – from number six.

The woman was dressed like a leather slut and, to Tanya's irritation, it made her look very sexy. And yet, Tanya thought, regardless how good the woman looked in her provocative clothes, her house still smelled of piss. The pettiness of that thought made her smile with grim pleasure.

Joanne's features were briefly illuminated by a streetlight, her brows furrowed and her muscles taut. Tanya succumbed to a moment's happiness at her neighbour's upset. Then her gaze travelled up the street to number seven. Her cruel smile broadened as she realised that, even if none of her neighbours wanted to include her in their fun, it was still possible to get pleasure at their expense, and possibly a month's reprieve from her rent. Placing the receiver back in the cradle, not bothering to trouble Max with her call, Tanya went out of the back door and stole along the street to the Graftons'.

Fifteen

3 Cedar View

Everything happened so quickly that John was briefly disoriented.

He had sucked the Goddess's plastic cock until it was slathered with saliva. Kneeling at her feet, worshipping her with his actions, thoughts and tongue, he felt as though he had finally found his rightful place in the world. The Goddess had endured his adulation as the party continued around them. The Goddess had made him feel that his adoration was wanted and appreciated. She had excited him with her wickedly innovative domination. And then, brutally, she had torn the plastic cock from his mouth and stepped behind him.

She had pushed the round wet end of her cock against his anus, on the verge of penetrating his rear, of possessing him. And John had never wanted anything as much as he needed her to slide her strap-on phallus into his body.

His muscle had protested, but John was more than willing to submit. The Goddess's erection was unnaturally large, much bigger than he believed his body could accommodate. But the chance of having her inside him was so compelling he prayed for his body to relax and surrender. The eroticism of having a beautiful and dominant stranger about to take him was powerful enough to push John to the brink of climax. His anus was so lubricated he could almost taste the grease she had applied to his sphincter. His heart raced and his head pounded in anticipation of the thrust she was about to deliver.

And then the Goddess had pulled her hard length away from him.

'No,' she hissed. 'This isn't what I want.'

John had been struggling to understand what he had done wrong and how he could make amends when the Goddess dragged him by the collar to his feet. His mask slipped a little, covering his eyes and making it impossible to see where she was leading him. He stumbled in her wake, his failing erection cooled by a passing breeze, his orientation disturbed by the rise and fall of conversations, faraway grunts and nearby sighs. He didn't know what had caused the Goddess to change her mind about taking him in full view of the party, and he didn't really care. Wherever she wanted him, if she did still want him, he was determined to follow. Eagerly, he stumbled in the Goddess's wake.

The carpet beneath his feet gave way to something harder, like paving stones. The noise of the party dimmed and disappeared. The air outside his gimp suit was suddenly cooler, and the mild breeze that had flowed over his exposed cock became a bitter chill. He wanted to ask her where they were going and what she was doing with him, but he knew he couldn't question his Goddess. Trying to catch a glimpse of his surroundings but repeatedly thwarted by the mask, he heard the sound of a key in a lock and then was dragged inside another building.

'Shit!' the Goddess muttered. 'And still the bastard isn't here. Still down at the pub with his fucking mates. Well, fuck him. Fuck him right up the arse.'

The words made no sense, although they did remind him that there was something very familiar about the Goddess. Rather than dwell on those thoughts, he dismissed them as natural. He had found his soul-mate, a woman who inspired him more than any other he had ever met, a woman whom he had been destined to meet – so it wasn't surprising that he found certain aspects of her familiar.

She dragged him up a flight of stairs, then pulled him around a corner, banging his arm against a doorframe. Before he had time to acknowledge the brief, dull pain, she threw him on to a comfortable softness that he knew could only be a mattress.

The mask finally moved from his eyes. He took in his surroundings with a blink. The bedroom was identical to so many on Cedar View it could have been a room at Ted and Linda's, the main bedroom at Joanne Jackson's house or even the room where he slept with Jane. The only difference between this bedroom and every other one he had seen on Cedar View was that this room was made divine by the presence of the Goddess. His Goddess.

She looked magnificent. The plastic erection continued to protrude from her loins. He stared hungrily at the length, and her desirable body, and wondered if she was finally ready to take him.

'Suck me again,' the Goddess demanded. She climbed on to the bed and towered over him. 'I want my cock good and wet for when I fuck your arse. And I do like seeing you trying to swallow me.'

Without hesitating, John raised his mouth and began to suckle her huge plastic cock.

The decision to take the gimp home had been an impulsive one. Jane was suddenly struck by the idea that she didn't want to be the centre of attention when she fucked him. She hadn't minded the approving smiles and the suggestive leers while she had been wandering around Ted and Linda's party. She understood, because of her mask, she was being perceived as a woman of mystery and that was probably why everyone in the room found her interesting and desirable. Not wanting to spoil that image, sure that a woman of mystery wouldn't hump a gimp in full view of a crowd of partygoers, Jane had decided it would be more appropriate for her sophisticated image if she fucked the gimp in the privacy of her own home.

No one complained when she dragged the gimp away from his pedestal by the side of the pool. No one voiced any objection when Jane pushed her way out of the house and across the road. She had briefly feared that Joanne might suddenly appear and demand to know where she thought she was going with the gimp. But, because Joanne was clearly engaged elsewhere, Jane was able to escape the party without anyone stopping her.

At home she was only momentarily disappointed to discover no sign of John in the house. On reflection, his absence meant she could exploit the gimp the way she wanted, and if John came back while she was fucking the gimp . . .

She couldn't complete the thought without grinning broadly. Her upper lip curled into a wicked sneer as she pictured her husband's face in such a scenario. If John came back home while she was in bed with the gimp, it would be the ideal time for him to learn what she wanted from a man. The thought filled her with a triumphant rage that was almost orgasmic.

She glanced down at the leather-swathed figure on her bed and licked her lips. His waning erection hung loosely from the crotch of his bodysuit. She regarded the semi-soft length as a challenge. Once he had finished sucking her cock she intended to fuck him hard. She didn't know if that would be as pleasurable as she anticipated but she was determined to spend the night as an unknown dominatrix and enjoy every drop of satisfaction she could milk from the gimp. She was looking forward to the experience of having sex like a man and anxious to know what it would be like to have a man bucking and thrashing beneath her as she penetrated him again and again. The idea sent a shiver down her spine.

'Is it wet enough?' she barked.

With his mouth still around her length, the gimp nodded.

'Are you ready to take it up your arse?'

More eagerly this time, he nodded again.

She held his collar, keeping his head still, as she pulled the erection from his mouth. Manipulating him with ease she positioned him on all fours and then knelt behind him. She snaked her hand underneath his body, wound her fingers around his shaft and grinned as she stroked him to hardness. The end of her plastic cock nudged gently against the greasy hole of his anus.

'This is going to be fun,' Jane promised.

The gimp said nothing. He trembled beneath her touch. His erection was already as taut as a steel bar and she could feel the length tingling as though he was teetering on the verge of climax. Her smile grew broader as she realised she was solely responsible for taking him to such an apex of pleasure.

'This bedroom hasn't seen much in the way of sexual excitement up to now,' she murmured. Her wrist worked slowly back and forth as she spoke. 'But I think you and I will make up for that tonight, won't we?' She curled her fist tight around his cock and pulled back hard. At the same instant she pushed her hips forward and the length of her plastic cock slipped inside him.

* * *

John almost screamed when the Goddess penetrated his anus. The huge shaft was broader than he expected. It had been filling his mouth, and he had thought he knew something about its girth. But it still came as a shock to him when it plunged into his rectum. The sting of pain was harsh and acidic. But it was muted by the pleasure of knowing he was hers and she was using him in a way that they both wanted.

Unable to stop himself, John groaned.

'Good boy,' the Goddess whispered. 'Good boy.'

The hand that held his cock remained tight around the base of his shaft. She was holding him so firmly that he could feel her fingernails digging into his flesh. Even if he had wanted to ejaculate, John knew, the Goddess wasn't going to allow him the release. Her power over him was the most thrilling and total experience he had ever encountered and he began to wonder if she might be a real Goddess who had come to earth in response to his prayers.

'Good boy,' she said again. Her tone was breathless. She sounded as though she was receiving as much pleasure as she was giving. Her free hand, the hand that didn't hold his cock in a vice-like agonising grip, was clamped against his hip. She pulled him back to meet her penetration, urging him to accept her length as she pushed it deeper and deeper. 'That's a good boy,' she cooed. 'You're going to take all of this cock of mine. You're going to take every fucking inch.'

John's groan echoed loudly from the bedroom walls.

Jane didn't think she had ever seen a man enjoying sex with so much relish. In all the times she and John had gone through the Saturday-night ritual Jane had never seen her husband enjoy himself with the enthusiasm of the gimp. The man was moaning and groaning and wriggling and writhing and she knew his excessive pleasure could only be attributed to the efforts of one woman.

She smiled proudly and acknowledged that, as never happened in her Saturday-night sweat-exchanges with John, she too was consumed by passion. Her sex was flooded with a rush of warm, wet desire. The stimulation that came from dominating the gimp, and the pleasure she received from seeing his satisfaction, was almost enough to inspire a satisfying, if ordinary, orgasm. But Jane refused to allow the pleasure to take her in such a way.

Beneath her, the gimp's anus opened slowly to accept her plastic cock. She teased him the first few times, coaxing his lubricated sphincter wider before plunging inside, then pulling completely out, watching the muscle tighten and contract, then starting the whole glorious tease all over again. Finally, knowing she couldn't spend the whole night toying with the gimp, Jane forced herself to fill him.

'Oh! Yes!'

They said the words in unison. Jane wondered if that indicated a unity of spirit. Now she had discovered the gimp she wanted to believe that they were soul-mates and destined to be together. She couldn't tolerate the idea of ever giving him up and her mind was already working through ways for them to build a long-lasting relationship, even if it had to be one conducted behind her husband's back.

His back arched as she pushed the length deep inside him. She kept her hand wrapped tight around his shaft, determined she would feel his climax when it eventually came. Pulling slowly backwards, not letting her length spill out of him this time, and riding him with an implacable force, Jane licked her lips and savoured her authority.

'Thank you, Goddess,' the gimp muttered. 'Thank you, Goddess.'

Jane thought his words were going to push her beyond the brink of orgasm. She buried her fingernails deeper into the base of his shaft and rode him swiftly, until she felt sure one of them was going to scream.

The sense of impending euphoria built quickly. As she jerked her hips back and forth and drove the cock repeatedly into him, Jane knew the climax was going to come hard and fast and with devastating impact.

'GIMP! Where the hell are you, gimp?'

Jane and the gimp climaxed in the same instant.

John's length pulsed in a rush of orgasmic agony. The Goddess was buried deep in his rear, stretching his sphincter and filling his bowel. He trembled at the sensation of being used by her and wondered how he had been able to stave off his climax for so long. A roar of glorious satisfaction burst from his lips as he collapsed into the bed beneath her. The Goddess's length was wrenched from his rear, leaving him empty, hollow and painfully satisfied.

And again, as it had before, the angry, panicky call cried out for him. The words flew up from the street outside and fluttered in through the open bedroom window. 'Gimp! Where the hell are you, gimp?'

Jane tried to keep her grip tight around the gimp's cock as he climaxed but the force of his eruption was too strong. It didn't help that she was in the throes of her own orgasm. Her eruption was inspired by the thrill of fucking the gimp. Hearing his satisfaction, knowing she was responsible for every pleasure he enjoyed, Jane had been carried to a new realm of satisfaction by her own magnificence. She groaned, a soft hiss that barely expressed her total pleasure, and then she collapsed on top of the gimp's slumped, spent body.

150

'Gimp!'

Jane was infuriated to recognise Joanne's voice intruding on her pleasure.

'Gimp!' Joanne bellowed. 'Where the hell are you, gimp?'

Jane pulled herself away from the gimp and went to the window. She could see Joanne standing in the middle of the street, still in her short leather skirt, thigh-length boots and biker's jacket, looking incongruously sexual in the suburban haven of Cedar View. If she had been closer Jane would have thought about spitting on the woman's unsuspecting head.

She glanced back to the bed and sighed.

She supposed it would be sensible to return the gimp to the party before anyone discovered she was the one who had borrowed him without permission. It crossed her mind that kidnapping was probably a more accurate way of describing the situation but she elected to use the word *borrowed* because it seemed less provocative. She wasn't troubled by the fact that she had taken Joanne's gimp from the party, only worried that knowledge of her theft might cause some embarrassment. The temptation to keep him for a while longer was almost irresistible. She had enjoyed the thrill of fucking his arse and climaxed from the satisfaction of seeing the gimp come. Common sense told her there were a lot more pleasures to be had from the gimp if she simply put him to work in a manner that suited someone so submissive. But she fought against that urge, sure that it would be wiser to enjoy him once he was safely back at the party. Admittedly, if she took him back, she wouldn't have the pleasure of seeing John discovering her in the position of a dominatrix. But she supposed that pleasure could wait for another day. Coming to a decision, she stepped back to the bed and slapped the gimp's exposed buttocks.

He flinched, turned, and stared up at her. Although his face was masked she could see the nervousness in his eyes. The fact that he was intimidated by her made Jane's pussy drip with new arousal. She saw the puddle of semen he had released with his climax, a thick white dollop lying on top of her patterned cotton quilt cover.

'You spurted on my bed,' Jane told him. Her voice was hard and deliberately free from emotion. She pointed to the puddle of semen and said, 'Lick that clean.' Immediately he turned to lap up his own spend.

Jane's wetness grew warmer as she watched his grovelling response to her instructions. She contemplated playing with herself but doubted that there was sufficient time to satisfy herself properly again. Hearing Joanne shout again from outside, amazed the woman could be so brazen as to call for her gimp on a semi-lit street in suburbia, Jane realised she had to return her new friend to Ted and Linda's quickly and discreetly. She waited until the gimp had finished licking the bedspread clean before slapping his arse again.

'Come with me.'

'Where are we going, Goddess?'

Jane shivered when he called her by that name. It felt so good to be appreciated. Properly appreciated. 'We're going back to the party,' she told him. 'But I'm going to use you one last time before we have to separate for the evening. Do you understand that?'

Standing up, staring at her with a directness that was almost daunting, the gimp said, 'You can use me whenever you want, Goddess. I'm yours to command.'

Sixteen

5 Cedar View

Hearing footsteps in the shadows, Joanne whirled. She reached out for the large figure and, with vicious speed and natural strength, grasped at the person that had been trying to sneak past her. Her anger, already incensed by the gimp's insurrection, transformed into pure outrage when she discovered she held Tanya Maxwell.

'Where's my gimp?'

Tanya tried to pull away. Joanne's grip was firm and unrelenting. Her left hand held Tanya's right shoulder, her right a fistful of hair. Shorter and surprised by the attack, Tanya could only struggle weakly in Joanne's grasp.

'I haven't touched your pictures.'

Joanne frowned, not sure what that meant. How stupid could Tanya Maxwell be, hearing 'gimp' and thinking it meant 'pictures'? 'My gimp,' Joanne bellowed. 'Where is he? What have you done with him?'

'How the fuck should I know where he is?'

If anyone had been watching them grapple in the centre of the midnight street, Joanne thought, it would have looked like the strangest standoff imaginable: a fat peroxide blonde in the clutches of a leather-clad dominatrix, both infuriated and neither prepared to relent.

'You know everything that happens on this damned street,' Joanne hissed. 'You must know where my gimp is.'

'I don't know nothing,' Tanya squealed.

Her voice rose an octave as Joanne tugged hard on her hair. The two women moved as if in a slow dance. Tanya's expression was contorted into a grimace of pure loathing. Joanne tried to quell her disobedience with an expression of commanding authority. When that failed, she resorted to pulling harder on Tanya's hair.

'You know every damned thing,' Joanne sneered. 'And you were in my house earlier.' She grinned when she revealed that nugget of information, delighted to see Tanya blushing. Discovering her fridge was missing one of the four cans of lager she kept for guests, Joanne had suspected Tanya of the theft, although she had no real proof. The woman's embarrassment was as good as an admission of guilt.

'I didn't take nothing.'

'Liar!'

Joanne pulled Tanya's hair even harder, and Tanya shrieked. The two women continued their embarrassing dance, Joanne spitting vitriol and Tanya cursing and fuming with impotent outrage.

'You took a can of beer,' Joanne snorted. 'Admit it. You took a can of beer.'

'That's all I took,' Tanya hissed. 'And I haven't seen your damned gimp since I saw you walk him across the road to Ted and Linda's party. For all I know he's still there.'

'He's not there,' Joanne scowled.

'Maybe he went back to your place?'

Joanne yanked at Tanya's hair again.

'We both know he's not there. He wasn't there when you went searching through my house and he's not there now.'

154

She thought of forcing the woman to her knees and then properly dominating her. If Tanya had aroused any sort of sexual response, Joanne would have bullied her into submission in the middle of Cedar View's midnight darkness. But, because Tanya only inspired feelings of nuisance and revulsion, she curbed that thought and continued to hold the woman's head in an uncompromising lock. It was satisfying to spank Tanya's backside after she had cleaned her house, but that was the only time Joanne got any pleasure from dominating her. Forcing her to sexually surrender now would be counter-productive and it wasn't what Joanne wanted. She only wanted her gimp.

'He's not at the party and he's not at my house,' she hissed. 'So where is he, Tanya? Where the hell has he gone?'

'How the hell should I know?'

'I've told you the answer to that one before. You know everything that happens on this street.'

'But I don't know where your gimp is,' Tanya sobbed. 'Maybe he went home?'

Joanne paused and cast a doubtful glance in the direction of number three. Her eyes flickered in that direction for only an instant, but it was enough to show that there was a light in an upstairs room. She dismissed Tanya's suggestion as if it was the most ludicrous thing she had yet heard.

'He wouldn't have the balls to go home without changing,' she snapped. 'And he wouldn't dare leave without my permission. He knows I've got Polaroids that his wife would never want to see. And he knows she'll see them if he ever crosses me.'

Tanya staggered backwards, wrenching herself from Joanne's grasp. She lost a few hairs, and almost tumbled over with the effort, but Joanne could see that the woman had escaped her clutches and wouldn't let herself be caught so easily a second time.

'I don't know where your damned gimp is,' Tanya growled, pulling her tracksuit jacket back into shape. 'And I don't like demented lunatics jumping out at me from the shadows and pulling my hair and –'

'Find him,' Joanne broke in.

'What?'

'Find him. Find my gimp for me. If you find him, I might not press charges for you illegally entering my house this evening.'

Tanya stood dumbstruck. Her mouth hung open and she looked as though she had been slapped across the face. Eventually she spluttered, 'How could it be illegal? I'm your cleaner, aren't I?'

'Not any more. I won't employ a cleaner I can't trust.'

'But –'

'Find my gimp,' Joanne demanded. 'Find my gimp and I won't press charges. But if I'm not reunited with him by the end of this evening, the police will be on your doorstep in the morning asking why you took a midnight stroll through my property.'

The moment dragged out. Chill and empty, the night street was like a still photograph. From the brightly lit exterior of number six they could hear the sounds of Ted and Linda's party. Music thumped at a deafening volume, underscored by shrieks of laughter and cries of festive delight.

'Find my gimp,' Joanne insisted, 'and you might come out of this evening only losing your job as my cleaner.'

'What makes you think I can find him?'

'You seem to have access to every house on this street. If you're sufficiently motivated, I think you'll find him.'

'I've only got access to some houses on this street. He might not be here any more.'

Joanne shook her head. 'He won't have left this street.'

Tanya glowered for a moment. Joanne watched her in silence, confident that she had won the battle of wills and sure she was only waiting for Tanya to acknowledge it.

'Where will you be if I do find him?' Tanya asked.

Joanne nodded towards number six. 'When you find him, take him to Ted and Linda's. I'll be there.' Joanne waited until Tanya had grudgingly started in the direction of number seven, then headed back to the party.

Seventeen

7 Cedar View

Megan stepped into the kitchen wearing only hold-up stockings, ankle boots and a broad smile. Not for the first time in her life, she was grateful for the sunglasses that hid her eyes. If either Charlie or Rhona Grafton had seen the expression of contempt in her eyes they would have realised that she knew they had deceived her. But because she was naked neither of them was particularly concerned about her eyes or the sincerity of her smile and she re-entered the room apparently in the same playful spirit with which she had left.

Her image stared back at her from the opaque mirror of the kitchen window. With Charlie Grafton on one side of the room and Rhona on the other, Megan's reflection was framed between the couple. Her bare body, slender and lithe, seemed almost androgynous, the breasts small and pert, the thin line of pubic curls above her sex a smudged shadow in the reflection. The stark contrast of the black stockings and huge sunglasses against her pallid flesh made Megan look like a comic-book drawing of cheap and tawdry sexuality. It was an effect she had always been proud to cultivate.

'Don't you look lovely?' Charlie muttered.

'Beautiful,' Rhona agreed.

Megan stepped between the pair, first giving Rhona a kiss, then turning to place her freshly painted lips against Charlie's. 'I feel lovely and beautiful,' she murmured. Stroking the bulge at the front of Charlie's trousers, mildly surprised that he had put the thick, meaty erection back inside his pants, she lowered her voice to a suggestive drawl. 'And I hope I'm going to be feeling a lot more before the night's over.'

Being honest with herself, she wasn't entirely sure what she felt. She was still angry that the pair had orchestrated events so she would be coerced into having sex with them. Their plot to engineer her consent was devious and underhand. But acknowledging those faults in her hosts did nothing to lessen Megan's arousal. She remained excited by the idea of having both Charlie and Rhona. It had taken a long time in the bathroom, playing with Rhona's extensive and exclusive make-up collection, for her to reconcile her conflicting feelings. Once she accepted that the pair could be classified as both desirable and despicable, she realised her reaction could be framed in equally simple terms: the Graftons could be fucked – and then screwed.

'You're expecting me to undress you, aren't you?' she said with a grin, remembering Charlie had made the suggestion earlier. She didn't wait for his response, but placed her mouth over his and savoured a long, penetrating kiss. With their mouths joined, their tongues sliding and twisting together, she reached for his groin and pulled his zipper slowly down. Behind her, she heard Rhona's gasp of encouragement.

Megan remained focused on her task of exciting and enjoying Charlie. Even when Rhona's hands began to caress her buttocks, stroking appreciative circles on the bare cheeks and then gently pushing them apart, Megan concentrated on kissing Charlie and releasing his cock from the open fly of his trousers.

He was warm, thick and hard. He was also sticky against her palm and she guessed he had been playing with Rhona recently. Very recently. The feral scent of his excitement filled the kitchen. Behind her, Rhona still teased her rear, but now she was exacerbating the sensation with the heat of her breath. With her mouth still locked against Charlie's and her fingers encircling his cock, Megan realised that Rhona was kneeling on the kitchen floor and preparing to add kisses to her sensual massage.

'Do you two ever stop working as a team?' she giggled.

Charlie placed an arm around her back and used his free hand to cup one small breast. Urging her to bend forward so that her buttocks were more accessible to his wife, he asked innocently, 'What do you mean?'

The warm, wet muscle of Rhona's tongue brushed against the wrinkled flesh of Megan's sphincter. The intimate kiss added fresh fuel to the fire of her arousal. Her nipples were taut and receptive to Charlie's inquisitive fingers. Her body tingled with the adrenalin need that the Graftons inspired. She would have to concentrate if she wanted to have any hope of besting the couple. She shivered before she spoke again.

'What I'm asking is: are you two like this with every girl you get your hands on?'

'Like what?' Charlie asked, still feigning innocence.

If Rhona said anything it was lost as a slurping gurgle between the cheeks of Megan's buttocks. Her tongue delved deeper, forcing its way through the tight ring of muscle and making Megan quiver. Charlie pressed another kiss upon Megan's lips as his fingers lightly squeezed the stiff tips of her nipples. His erection was thick, hard and irresistible.

'It's like being in one of those wildlife documentaries,' Megan began. The words came out in a breathless whisper. She had thought she might have to pretend to be excited when she returned to the kitchen but, because the couple were so adept, attractive and insatiable, it was easy to give into the pleasure they inspired.

'I feel like a helpless gazelle,' she explained, 'and you two are like a pair of predatory lions, closing in, bringing me down and gobbling me up.'

The couple chuckled. 'I've got no problem bringing you down,' Rhona murmured behind her. Each word tickled Megan's buttocks. 'I've got no problem doing that at all.'

With a salacious laugh Charlie added, 'I thought you were the one who'd be gobbling me up.' Megan knew he wasn't just joking and she took the initiative. She urged him to sit down in one of the kitchen's comfortable captain's chairs, knelt in front of his exposed shaft and licked her lips. His erection was large enough to present a challenge. The thought of how wide she would have to open her mouth to accommodate him, and how exciting it was going to be when his monstrous cock finally pushed into her sex, was sufficiently powerful to make her pussy tingle. She kept her backside raised so Rhona could continue to lick at her rear. The three of them were briefly joined together, Megan sucking Charlie's shaft while Rhona's tongue slid through the forbidden ring of Megan's anus. To Megan it was like a milder version of the spit-roasting she occasionally enjoyed with Max and his friend Daniel. But, she reminded herself, there was nothing mild about Charlie and Rhona and she cautioned herself against underestimating the pair.

'We could take this up to the bedroom,' Charlie suggested.

Megan shook her head. She had one hand against the side of his cock and was licking along his shaft and

161

up to the glans. His foreskin had peeled back to reveal the swollen purple end. His pre-come coated her tongue as she lapped at him.

'Bedrooms are for sleeping in,' she said, dismissing the suggestion. 'And I don't think any of us are feeling sleepy. Kitchens are where you enjoy eating things. I'm happy here. I'm happy eating things.'

'I'm rather content too,' Rhona giggled. Her laughter made Megan's buttocks tremble.

'Lick my pussy,' Megan suggested. She spoke over her shoulder. 'You can taste how wet I'm getting at the thought of having this cock fill me up.'

Charlie sighed.

Obligingly, Rhona shifted her tongue to the moist folds of Megan's labia. The sensation of the warm, wet muscle was a velvet caress upon her flesh. A thrill of arousal spread through Megan's loins. She marvelled again that the couple could inspire such conflicting responses. She still thought they were hateful, but her body craved the satisfaction that she knew they could deliver.

Tilting her head to look at Charlie's face, she asked coyly, 'Do you think you can fit all this cock inside me?'

Charlie grinned down at her.

Rhona lapped sublime circles of bliss in the warmth of Megan's pussy. The sensations she evoked were delicious but distracting. Megan wanted to simply give into the pleasure but she didn't dare risk losing her focus on the evening's ultimate outcome. Determinedly, she refused to let her body be swayed by her excitement.

'I'm looking forward to trying,' Charlie admitted.

Megan gave the end of his shaft a final kiss and then stood up. Smiling down at him, glancing at Rhona so her grin included both Graftons, she said, 'I want you to do me on the kitchen table. I want to be fucked across the kitchen table before we do anything else. Can we do that?'

Rhona's eyes widened. 'Fucking across a kitchen table! How delightfully working class! Should I wear clogs or buy myself a whippet?'

Megan laughed at the woman's enthusiastic snobbery. She was still giggling as Charlie helped her on to the table. She lay with her back against the cool linen cloth and her legs hanging over the table's edge. Rhona helped maintain the arousal of the moment, kissing Megan's lips and teasing her breasts while Charlie shrugged off his clothes and shoes. Naked, his body looked surprisingly athletic for a man in his early fifties and Megan braced herself for a vigorous bout of passion.

'There's condoms in my coat pocket,' she remembered.

Glancing towards the empty kitchen chair where she had left her coat, Megan realised the long leather was no longer in sight. Her brows furrowed. She knew, if she concentrated on the missing coat any longer, her arousal would be smothered by suspicion and distrust. She shunned the thoughts, fearful her enjoyment of the moment might disappear altogether. As much as she was determined to fuck the Graftons and then screw them, Megan knew she wouldn't be able to take full pleasure in the experience if she was harbouring resentment for the couple.

'I've got one here,' Charlie said, rolling a sheath of rubber over his erection.

Megan nodded. With a concentrated effort she surrendered herself again to Rhona's kisses. The woman was gifted at exciting arousal and, each time her lips stole over Megan's mouth, throat and breasts, Megan could feel the prospect of an orgasm inching closer. She watched with interest as Rhona reached for Charlie's cock. The eroticism of the moment grew more intense when Megan realised Rhona was guiding Charlie's erection towards her pussy.

It was the sort of intimacy Megan wanted to share with Max. On those occasions when they had played sex games with others there had been a chasm between her and Max that Megan had never been able to bridge. Even when he was pushing his length into her, whether he was penetrating her mouth, pussy or anus, she didn't feel close to him while they were fucking with other people. She didn't like the Graftons – they were duplicitous and manipulative – but she envied them the fact that they could share their intimacy so easily in the presence of others.

Charlie grinned affectionately at his wife as she led his cock to the brink of Megan's sex. The rubber-sheathed tip slipped easily into the soft, yielding slit of Megan's labia. Rhona's fingers slid down his shaft, cupping his balls, while her grip around his length remained tight. As Charlie began to slide inside Megan, she realised that she was being fucked by both of the Graftons. It was Charlie's cock and Rhona's rhythm.

A tremor tore through her body. The pleasure was tainted by a headrush of jealousy but she refused to let the negative emotions triumph. Giving into the enjoyment, Megan groaned loudly.

Her cry was enough to stop Charlie and Rhona from staring misty-eyed at each other. They both gave their full attention to Megan. Charlie hesitated in his penetration and then Rhona pushed him deeper. In the same instant the woman shifted her fingers so she was both holding her husband and teasing Megan's clitoris. Charlie lowered his face to Megan's left breast while Rhona suckled her right. Hands and fingers slipped over the sweat-slick surface of her flesh, brushing hair from her forehead, stroking the sensitive length of her throat, touching her bare stomach. Every caress inspired excitement and thrilled her with the knowledge that she was the centre of their attention. Between her legs, Charlie's cock and Rhona's hand continued to spark bright flashes of blissful pleasure. The table beneath her rocked gently as Rhona urged Charlie to slide back and forth.

Megan could feel the orgasm swelling in her loins, but she resisted the urge to just let the climax tear through her body. Regardless of how much she disliked Charlie and Rhona, she had to concede that the pair knew how to pleasure a woman and she wasn't going to miss a single marvellous second of satisfaction. Relaxing, she concentrated on the playful teasing of Rhona's lips against her breasts and the more forceful pressure of Charlie nibbling at her nipples. His cock was so broad that under other circumstances it would have been uncomfortable, but, buoyed by the arousal of having them both trying to satisfy her, and encouraged by Rhona's playful teasing at her clit, Megan happily stretched to accommodate him.

She knew the experience would have been more fulfilling if there had been no thoughts of Max in her mind. But her worry that he would consider himself wronged nagged at her conscience. If it turned out that he was unhappy with her infidelity she knew the issue would be dealt with later. But she was convinced she hadn't broken any of the rules of their vaguely open relationship. Aliceon had been left with Max, so he had the opportunity to get laid. And Megan certainly wasn't doing anything to violate the sanctuary of their home. But, although those conditions were met, she still wasn't sure that would be enough to satisfy her husband and Master.

Rather than dwell on what Max might be thinking, she found it easier to direct her thoughts to the sensations of Charlie's thick cock sliding between her legs, Rhona's fingers teasing at her clitoris and toying with the folds of her pussy lips, and the orgasm that swelled in her loins. She needed to concentrate on Charlie and Rhona if she wanted to finish the evening to her own satisfaction.

'Straddle my face, Ronnie,' Megan begged.

Rhona gave her a curious look.

'I want to eat your pussy while your husband's fucking me.' Megan gasped the words in an adrenalin-fuelled rush. 'Get up here on the table with me. Squat over my face while he's riding me. Let me eat you while he's fucking me.'

Rhona responded with a haste that was almost embarrassing. 'Thank God we didn't buy the table from Ikea,' she giggled. She slipped out of her clothes to reveal a salon-kissed suntan and a surgically sculpted form.

Another surge of arousal flooded over Megan as she realised the woman's picture-perfect physique was hers to enjoy. She admired the modified breasts, the flat, flawless stomach and the smooth, freshly Brazilianed cleft. Her excitement continued to swell with each thrust of Charlie's cock, and it grew to an irresistible urge when Rhona climbed on to the table and lowered her slick, smooth sex over Megan's face. The scent of her musk was intoxicating.

Megan could see that Rhona's body was regularly pampered. Her skin had the smooth appearance that could only come from a lifetime of exfoliation and neurotically obsessive moisturising. The inner lips of her pussy barely protruded from the glistening slit of her sex. The little Megan could see was a gash of blood-red flesh with sweetly slender lips and she immediately thought: *labioplasty*. It was the most delectable specimen of a pussy she had ever faced, a credit to Charlie's investment funds and Rhona's surgeon.

But it was Rhona's musk that exacerbated her need for the woman. The scent of her sex was rich and tangy but so delicately fragranced that she could have worn it as a perfume. Megan wondered if Rhona had undergone some cosmetic procedure to make her pussy smell so sweet. Hungrily, she lifted her face to meet the approaching sex and then plunged her tongue neatly inside.

Rhona groaned. Charlie sighed. Megan buried her tongue deeper. Rhona's tight pussy clenched around the prize of Megan's tongue. The wetness of her arousal flooded Megan's lips and throat. She could feel the pulse of Rhona's mounting excitement and was thrilled to think she was contributing to such a moment of bliss. And then all rational thoughts were snatched from her mind when Rhona's lips kissed Megan's pussy.

Charlie continued to slide his thick length deep into Megan's sex. Megan willed herself to continue licking and lapping at Rhona. And somehow – Megan couldn't work out how Rhona was managing the position – Rhona had slipped her tongue against the over-stretched folds of Megan's hole.

The three of them climaxed in unison.

If there had been a way to slow down time and list the order of their climaxes, Megan thought, Rhona would have been shown to have orgasmed first. Her juices squirted freely over Megan's face, bubbling up her nostrils and almost choking her as they streamed into Megan's mouth and down to the back of her throat.

The thrill of that explosion pushed Megan beyond the brink of resistance. She gave into the ecstasy that rushed through her body and was immediately swathed in sweat, both hot and cold, as the climax convulsed her body. The inner muscles of her sex clenched tight around the mammoth grip of Charlie's cock and the power of her orgasm wrenched the climax from his shaft.

The couple pulled away while Megan was still trembling through the thrill of her orgasm. Her mouth was sticky with Rhona's wetness. Her sex felt sore, gaping and empty now that Charlie had withdrawn his huge shaft. The ache in her stomach – a dull pain borne from too much pleasure coming with far too much intensity – made her feel weak and light-headed.

'I knew you'd be good,' Rhona said with a laugh, and kissed Megan's cheek.

'You weren't so bad yourself,' Megan replied, climbing unsteadily from the table. She expected one of the couple to help her but they were busy embracing each other. Rhona gently removed Charlie's condom while Charlie put an affectionate arm around his wife's shoulder and bestowed occasional kisses. When Megan finally eased herself from the table and stood on trembling legs, the pair were embracing each other and staring expectantly at her.

'How was that?' Rhona asked.

'That was good,' Megan answered honestly. She hesitated for a second, wondering if she should still try to exact her revenge on the pair. The orgasm had been satisfying and the sex had been more than mere fun – it had been illuminating. Admittedly they had lured her there under false pretences and had shown themselves to be devious and manipulative. But the shared climax had released a lot of her animosity, the revelation of how they could be intimate with someone was something she was determined to try with Max, and Megan couldn't find the enthusiasm to harbour resentment or grudges. Then she glanced at the empty kitchen chair where her coat had been draped. Common sense told her that she should show them no mercy.

'That was *very* good,' she added with forced sincerity. She laughed self-consciously and said, 'It's just a shame you two . . .' Her voice trailed off. She shook her head as though dismissing the matter and reached for her glass of wine. The liquid was cool and welcome after the sweaty passion she had just enjoyed and it soothed her hot thirst. She took her time sipping from the glass, knowing that her uncompleted comment would be fuelling Charlie and Rhona's curiosity.

'There was something wrong with that?' Charlie sounded as though he was struggling to hide his incredulity.

'There was nothing wrong with that,' Rhona insisted. She glanced from Charlie, to Megan and then back to Charlie and then placed a reassuring hand on his chest. 'Honestly, darling. There was nothing wrong with that.' She switched her gaze back to Megan and said, 'You didn't really think there was something wrong with that, did you?'

Megan kept her features composed, delighted she had so easily found the couple's weakness. From the expression of disbelief on Rhona's face it was apparent that she thought, like Charlie, that the sex had been phenomenal – that she and her husband were exemplary lovers with abilities that were beyond reproof.

But the dismay was more obvious on Charlie's face. 'What could have possibly been wrong with that?' he asked. The pitch of his voice suggested he was ready to argue.

Megan shook her head. She placed a hand on his arm to reassure him. 'There was nothing *wrong* with that. It really was good. *Very* good. It's just, you two were so busy working as a team I don't think you got as much pleasure from the experience as you could have had.'

Charlie looked set to disagree but Rhona shushed him. 'What would you have done differently?'

Megan took another sip from her wine glass. 'It really was fantastic,' she began. 'It was great for me. But it would have been better for you two if you'd allowed me to take the lead. You two are so busy working together as a couple, I'll bet you've forgotten what it's like to have individual fun. The next time you find yourselves alone with a lucky woman like me, you should let her take control of what's happening. You'd get a lot more out of sex if you weren't constantly looking out for each other. I'm sure it would be better.'

Rhona and Charlie exchanged a glance.

It crossed Megan's mind that the couple were unnaturally cautious. She knew she would have to handle the situation carefully if she wanted a hope of getting her revenge on them. If they suspected she was trying to play them, Megan knew they would regroup and foil all her efforts to get her own back.

'Better?' Rhona asked.

Charlie said, 'What did you have in mind?'

Megan drew a deep breath. 'Charlie reminds me of Max,' she explained, speaking directly to Rhona. 'He enjoys dominating and being in control. But I think he'd like it better if we were in control.' She let the comment linger between them for a moment before telling Charlie, 'Max has always said, when the control's taken out of his hands, he has some of the best sex we've ever enjoyed.' She licked her lips, moistening the sultry pout of her smile before adding, 'You should try it.'

170

'Charlie does enjoy his control,' Rhona admitted. 'But I don't think he'd get a lot of pleasure without that.'

'No,' Charlie agreed. 'I can't see that being my thing.'

Megan could see that her opportunity was slipping away but she wouldn't allow herself to appear desperate. The couple were wary and would only be won over by a display of indifference. If she tried to press the point their suspicions would be roused. She shrugged off the subject as though it was a matter of no importance.

'I guess, if there's one couple on Cedar View who know what they enjoy, it's you two. I shouldn't have mentioned anything.' She stood up and flexed a lecherous grin. 'I'll get myself off home and see if Max is in the mood for giving up control this evening. Like I said, he always enjoys those games when we play them. He was the one who encouraged me to learn Shibari.'

Rhona shot a quick glance in Charlie's direction. 'We could give it a try,' she said, standing up quickly and placing an arm around Megan's waist. She fixed Charlie with a meaningful glare – an expression that Megan knew she wasn't meant to notice or understand – which she read as a silent warning for Charlie to play along with Megan's suggestion until they had heard more.

Megan tilted her head and gave Charlie an amused smile. '*Do* you want to give it a try?' she asked sweetly. 'You've paid a lot of money for my pleasure this evening. I'd like to make this an unforgettable experience for you – and I should have a black belt in kinbaku considering I'm so skilled.'

Charlie blushed, laughed and held up his hands in a gesture of surrender. 'Fair enough. I'm not going to

171

argue with both of you. What do you want to do with me?'

Rhona expectantly turned to Megan. Shrugging indifferently, Megan said, 'Just sit down in that chair, relax and close your eyes. We'll do all the work.'

'Work?' Rhona said the word as though it was a foreign concept. 'I don't do work, Meggy. I'm a lady of leisure.' Hearing that, Megan knew she had the couple's trust. Charlie didn't suspect that she was plotting revenge, and Rhona had no idea that Megan had overheard their conversation. It rankled that Rhona had now decided to call her Meggy, an epithet Megan found diminutive and insulting, but she could live with that for the next hour or so. Determined to teach the couple a lesson she believed they needed to learn, Megan felt her good mood soaring. She warned herself not to appear too confident and continued to study the pair carefully as she tried to manipulate the situation to her advantage.

Mentioning kinbaku meant that she might get the chance to tie the couple up later in the evening. But she knew that, if she asked for two lengths of rope now and simply tied the couple to the kitchen chairs, they would suspect something was amiss and she wouldn't get an opportunity to exact her revenge.

Smiling easily, not letting her thoughts move so far ahead, she encouraged Rhona to kneel at one side of Charlie's chair while she took the other. 'Keep your eyes closed, Charlie,' she whispered. 'You've got to guess which one of us is kissing your cock.' Nodding in Rhona's direction, she wordlessly encouraged the other woman to make the first move.

Rhona shifted her head forward, curling one hand in her hair so it didn't brush against her husband's bare leg. Extending her tongue, she licked gently against the semi-soft shaft of his spent length, a lazy lap against the semen-sticky skin.

172

Charlie shivered and said, 'That's Ronnie.'

Rhona sat back, grinning.

'You looked!' Megan exclaimed. She sat back on her haunches and glared at Rhona. 'He looked. That's cheating.'

'I didn't.'

'He didn't.'

'You had to have looked to get that so quickly.'

'I didn't,' Charlie insisted.

'We should do this blindfold until you've got the hang of it,' Megan decided.

At Charlie's nod of consent Rhona disappeared from the room and returned moments later brandishing two lengths of black silk. She tied one of them over Charlie's eyes as he remained in the kitchen chair.

The thrill of fresh excitement stole through Megan's body. It had been exciting to be fucked by the couple but now, slowly putting her plan into action, she could feel her arousal reaching a new level of subversive excitement.

Rhona saw her sly smile.

'He looks good in the blindfold, don't you think?' Megan asked.

'Yes,' Rhona agreed. 'He looks vulnerable.'

Megan shrugged and wondered if she dared to risk suggesting bondage again. If she mentioned it too often, the intuitive couple would pick up on her enthusiasm and possibly back away. But, if she left it too long, there was always the chance that another opportunity might never occur.

'He'd look properly vulnerable if we tied his hands behind his back,' Megan explained. 'And, if we did that we could really enjoy this game.'

'What do you mean?'

Megan leaned close and whispered in her ear. Her wrist accidentally brushed Rhona's breast as she

173

reached for her shoulder. The stiff nipple pulsed with the prospect of sexual excitement. When Megan had finished explaining her proposed variation on the game Rhona shifted away. Her eyes were wide and sparkled.

'We have to do that,' Rhona insisted. 'I'll go and fetch cuffs and rope.'

Minutes later Charlie was secured to the chair. His thighs were spread wide apart, his ankles were tied to the chair's legs, and cuffs held his hands behind his back. His erection had grown stiffer as Megan and Rhona secured him in place and Megan had to admit that his bound body looked incredibly appealing.

'This better be a fun game,' Charlie growled. 'Because right now I just feel like a hostage.'

'It's the same game as before,' Megan assured him. 'Only this time you don't guess whose mouth is around your cock. You have to guess which pussy is fucking you.'

Rhona shivered. Charlie's length twitched like a divining rod.

Megan could sense that the atmosphere in the room was again charged with electrical chemistry. Taking a condom from the set Rhona had tossed down, she rolled it over Charlie's stiff cock. Touching him, aware that the shaft was already thick and stiff enough to take her to another plateau of pleasure, she wondered if she dared risk fucking the couple again before putting her revenge plans into action. The only danger with that option was that she might be tempted to simply fuck them and then forget about retribution.

'You're aware of the rules, Charlie?'

'I think I've just about followed them,' he said with a grin.

'We're both going to ride you,' Megan explained. 'Then you have to say which of us was the first and which of us was the second. Do you think you can do that?'

'Do I get a prize if I get it right?'

She pressed her mouth close to his ear. Still holding his sheathed cock, and saying the words loudly enough for Rhona to overhear, Megan said, 'If you guess right, I'll let you put this thick cock of yours into my tight little anus.'

A broad grin stretched across Charlie's lips.

Megan kept her hand around the base of his shaft while nodding to Rhona to go first. In silence she guided Charlie's cock towards the slit of Rhona's sex. Watching closely, enjoying the sight of the woman's pussy lips yielding to the pressure of his thickness, Megan knew she would have to have one more orgasm before she completed her revenge.

Charlie trembled as Megan gripped his shaft. Rhona slipped her sex against him, teasing the end of his length inside and holding him there for a moment. Megan saw how Rhona tensed her muscles three times before letting Charlie's cock fall free from her slit. Megan caught every intoxicating sound of the couple sliding together. She was able to breathe in the sweet and succulent perfume of Rhona's arousal. It took a huge effort of willpower to stifle her own moan of excitement. Watching the pair, and being so intimately involved as Rhona teased Charlie, was a far greater aphrodisiac than she had anticipated.

'I don't know who that is,' Charlie murmured. 'But it feels good.'

Megan motioned to Rhona to stay silent and move aside. Taking Rhona's place, she pressed her own pussy lips over Charlie's erection. While she had been laid on the kitchen table his erection had felt large, but she had been just about able to accommodate him. Her sex still felt sore and overused but there had been no pain sliding his enormous length inside. This time, in the unusual position of trying to sit on him, she thought it would be nearly impossible to fit him into her tight wet hole. Guiding him back and forth, trembling as the contact inspired ripples of electric excitement, Megan couldn't decide whether sliding on to Charlie would be too much to tolerate or the perfect end to the evening. She lowered herself on to him, allowed the length to fill and stretch her and mimicked Rhona's subtle clenching. Then slowly, while Charlie was still gasping beneath her, Megan pulled herself away from him. The temptation to remain on his length and simply ride him until he climaxed was almost irresistible.

'Can you work out which is which yet?' Megan asked. 'Or do you want to try it for a second time?'

Charlie said he needed to feel the experience a second time, and then he insisted on a third, and a fourth. Each time Rhona and Megan kept the same order. Rhona slid the lips of her sex over him first, then stepped aside and allowed Megan to ease his thick length into her hole. The atmosphere in the kitchen was thick with tension and excitement, and the scent of sexual musk was rich everywhere. Megan knew that, if she didn't start getting her revenge on the couple soon, she was only going to fuck them again before returning home to face the inevitable confrontation with Max.

'You've just been inside two pussies,' Megan told Charlie. 'We want to know which one of us was first and which you thought was second.'

'I think I need to try them again.'

'You've been inside each of us four times,' Megan sighed. 'Give us an answer.'

'I'm bored with this game,' Rhona announced. 'Charlie is getting all the fun and I'm doing all the work. I don't do work. I want him to just guess so we can get on with doing something that satisfies me.'

Megan moved closer to her. 'You want satisfaction?' she whispered.

Pushing her into a chair, Megan urged Rhona's legs apart and placed her mouth against the woman's sex. She devoured the slender lips, sucking and drinking and plunging her tongue deep inside. Rhona groaned and buried her fingers in Megan's hair. The muscles in her thighs tensed and she arched her back. Megan pulled her face away and shook her head. Gesturing to Rhona to keep her hands by her side, she pushed her face back against the woman's pussy and gently suckled her clitoris. Her fingers trailed over the soft, flat surface of the woman's stomach. She slid her hand down to Rhona's inner thigh, tracing the shape of the well-defined muscles while she continued to taste, tease and titillate her pussy.

'What are you doing?' Charlie asked.

'Megan's eating my pussy,' Rhona panted. 'And she's doing a damned fine job of it.' Her voice was breathless. She sounded as though her boredom had been thoroughly vanquished.

'I want to watch,' Charlie protested.

Megan lifted her head from Rhona's sex and whispered in her ear. As soon as she had finished speaking she moved her mouth back to Rhona's pussy lips and continued to drink the woman's wetness. Repeating what Megan had said, Rhona told Charlie, 'You can watch later. For now, you need to work out which pussy was mine and which one was Meggy's. Until you've made your decision you can just sit there like a good boy while we have our fun.' As she spoke, Rhona's fingers reached again for Megan's hair.

Megan pulled away with a frown. She still didn't like the name Meggy. Reaching for one of the spare lengths of rope, she tied one end around Rhona's wrist and then encouraged her to put her hands behind her back.

She didn't know if she wanted to go through with her plan to avenge herself on the Graftons or simply play with them as she intimated. However, getting the pair of them tied to chairs in the kitchen was a necessary step towards revenge, if that proved to be what she wanted. When Rhona put both hands behind her back and allowed her wrists to be secured to the chair, Megan realised she could progress with either option. The freedom of choice was exhilarating. She was in a position of absolute control over the couple and she relished the authority.

'I'm ready to make my decision,' Charlie announced.

'You can tell us in a minute,' Megan assured him. 'I want to hear Ronnie come before I hear what you've got to say.' Not bothered whether the answer satisfied him, she wrapped the spare silk scarf around Rhona's eyes and then returned to the delicious chore of drinking the woman's pussy. Rhona's sex remained sweetly flavoured with arousal. The musk was flowing in a constant, warm stream. The more Megan lapped at her, the wetter the hole seemed to become. Feeling Rhona's responsiveness grow with each sultry kiss, aware that she was trembling with the onset of climactic pleasure, Megan finally moved her lips away and turned her attention back to Charlie.

'I want more,' Rhona whispered.

'You'll have more later,' Megan assured her.

'But I want more now, Meggy!'

Megan grabbed the base of Charlie's shaft and felt his length stiffen beneath her fingers. Deciding she had to feel him fill her from this position, aware that her teasing game hadn't come close to giving her the fulfilment she needed, Megan stroked his sheathed glans twice against her labia and then held him against the centre of her hole. Bracing herself for penetration, knowing it would combine pleasure and some degree

178

of pain, she urged herself to sit down on his thick, stiff length.

Charlie groaned. Megan barely heard the sound as her body was instantly convulsed with a rush of sheer animal excitement. Ordinarily she didn't take a great deal of pleasure in penetration – she preferred Max's cruel domination and her own sexual servitude – but with the thickness of Charlie's cock, and the control she had over the couple, Megan couldn't imagine a more arousing scene.

It crossed her mind that she would have liked to share this experience with Max. Charlie and Rhona clearly got a lot of their satisfaction from sharing things with each other, and she wished she and Max had a similar attitude. Depending on how he reacted when she told him what she had been doing this evening, she might be able to convince him that they needed the Graftons' honesty and openness to complete their own relationship.

Then that thought was pushed aside as the tidal wave of satisfaction convulsed her body. She teetered on the brink of collapse, then the ripples of her climax undulated through her frame. She had to bite her lower lip to stop herself from shrieking with joy.

'That was you, Megan? Am I right?'

Megan ignored him.

'Megan?' Rhona called. Her blindfolded head twisted from one side to the other. 'Have you just fucked Charlie?'

'Why are you asking that?' Charlie demanded. 'You can see what she's doing, can't you?'

Megan said nothing. Finally pulling herself away from Charlie, she collapsed on to her knees and took a long, lingering kiss at Rhona's sex. Wearily she stood up, drained the contents of her glass and stared at the bound and blindfold couple.

'Where's my duster?' she asked quietly.

'Where's your what?'

'You want a duster? What are you going to do? Clean the house?'

'My coat,' she said patiently. 'My duster. I left it in here when I went to the bathroom. It's gone. Where is it?'

'Ronnie hung it up in the kitchen cupboard.'

'That's right,' Rhona added quickly. 'I put it in there while you went to the loo. But you don't need to get it now.'

Megan glanced around the room and saw the kitchen cupboard Charlie had mentioned. Like the rest of the cupboards and units in the Graftons' spotless kitchen, it was designed to be unobtrusive. She retrieved her coat, reached inside the pocket and was not surprised to find her money was no longer there. Shaking her head with disappointment, she retrieved her tobacco pouch and cigarette papers. Then she shrugged the coat back over her shoulders and sat down at the kitchen table.

Rhona and Charlie sat in restless silence as she rolled a cigarette. Neither of them spoke until she lit it.

'What's happening?' Rhona asked.

'What are you doing?' Charlie demanded.

'My money's missing,' Megan said quietly. 'And I don't want either of you insulting my intelligence by pretending you don't know what's happened to it.'

'You cheap shit, Charles,' Rhona spat viciously. 'Did you have to take her money back? That was very mean of you.'

'Climb down from your high horse, Ronnie,' Charlie grumbled. 'It was your idea.'

'You lying . . .'

' . . . greedy . . .'

' . . . told you . . .'

180

'... going too far –'

'Enough!'

Megan said the word loudly, silencing them both. She drew thoughtfully on her cigarette and regarded the bound and blindfold figures in front of her. Glancing at the kitchen window she saw Tanya Maxwell staring avidly into the room, watching the three of them. A smile of marvelling appreciation split the woman's lips.

Megan grinned back at her. She dropped a heavy, conspiratorial wink, placed a finger over her lips in a shushing gesture and beckoned for Tanya to come in. Tanya crept stealthily into the room.

Megan stood up, went to Charlie's discarded trousers and retrieved them from the floor. She found his wallet in a back pocket and removed the money he had given her earlier in the evening. Shaking her head in disappointment at his greed, she stuffed the notes back into her coat.

Tanya stared at the wallet with wide-eyed wonder.

'What's happening?' Charlie demanded. 'Everything's gone quiet. And it's cold, as though the kitchen door has been opened. What's happening, Megan? What are you doing?'

'Untie us,' Rhona insisted. 'Untie us and take these stupid blindfolds off. Once you've done that Charlie can sort out giving you your money back.'

'Yes,' Charlie agreed. 'That's what we should do. Untie us.'

Beneath the stiffness of his tone Megan could detect a rising note of panic. 'There's no need for you to give me my money back,' Megan said softly. 'I've just taken it out of Charlie's wallet.'

Charlie groaned. Rhona released an impatient sigh through her nostrils. 'If you've been through his wallet then you should untie us now, Meggy.' Despite the fact

181

that she was naked, bound and blindfold she still spoke with the authority of a woman used to having her orders obeyed. 'It sounds like we've all exploited each other enough for one evening, don't you think?'

Megan glanced at Tanya. They shared a knowing smile.

'It's not quite over,' Megan began carefully. The tone of her voice made them both respond with suspicion.

'What else do you want?' Charlie growled.

'This is no longer funny, Meggy. Untie us both. Untie us now.'

'I had thought of leaving you both tied up here,' Megan admitted. She took a final draw on her cigarette and then tossed it into the Graftons' stainless-steel sink. 'After the way you two got me here through manipulation and deceit . . .'

'There was no deceit in getting you here,' Charlie insisted.

'We didn't manipulate anything,' Rhona protested.

'That was just a genuine mistake,' Charlie agreed.

'A misunderstanding.'

Megan ignored them. 'After the way you two manipulated me, I would be justified in walking away and leaving you both tied naked to your chairs.'

'Come on, Megan.'

'Don't you think you're being a little bit silly?'

Megan ignored their interruptions. 'After the way you stole that money back from my coat, I should have just stormed out of here and left you to work your own way out of the blindfolds and bondage. But I'm not such a vindictive person. I'm going to forgive you. And I've even arranged to do you both a favour.'

'What favour?' Charlie's voice was sharp with suspicion.

'You wanted to employ Tanya Maxwell as a cleaner, didn't you?'

Guardedly, Rhona said, 'Yes.'

'Well, she's here now,' Megan said brightly. 'She's here now and I think she'd be quite interested in giving you her services for a couple of nights each week.' Megan snatched another fifty-pound note from Charlie's wallet and pushed it into Tanya's hand. 'I've just given her fifty quid for tonight's work,' she explained. 'I'll leave Tanya to clean round now and she might think about untying you before she leaves for the evening – unless there's anything else you want her to do for you?'

Megan didn't bother to wait for their response. She made a quick gesture to Tanya, signifying that they would talk later, and then rushed out of the kitchen and into the night. She was trying to hold in a splutter of laughter, amazed that she had come out of the Graftons' house one thousand pounds richer, having triumphed over their duplicity and theft. But, when she saw what was happening outside her own house, her mirth instantly vanished.

Eighteen

'What do you think?' Denise asked, pointing. 'Do you think you can do anything with it?'

Phil frowned. For the first time since they had met, Denise thought he looked preoccupied, even sombre. At the party he had been cheerful, constantly making jokes and encouraging her to smile. Now his expression was solemn and businesslike.

'It's a pretty big gash,' he mumbled.

Glancing round the garage, staring at the shelves packed with tins, labelled boxes and her husband's tools, he said, 'I should be able to repair it, but it's going to take me a couple of hours or more. And that's only if your husband has got all the stuff I need in here.' His gaze shifted back towards the garage doors, as though he was looking through them towards his brother's house at number six.

Denise jumped into his arms and kissed him. At the party she had fucked two men and one woman. She had been involved in a group daisy chain, had played a little with Joanne's gimp and, before the party, had spent two hours with her tongue in Jane's pussy. But none of those experiences had filled her with the thrill of hearing Phil say he could repair the scratch on the door panel of Derek's car.

'I can't wait to have your bare cock inside me,' she whispered. Pressing her lips close to his ear, determined to distract him from the notion that there might be other pleasures available at the party – other pleasures that weren't so hard won – she said, 'I'm hot for you now. Slide a finger inside me and see how eager I am to have your bare cock.'

She had her legs around his hips and her arms over his shoulders. It was a clement night and she hadn't bothered dressing to walk the paltry distance from Ted and Linda's back to her own garage. When his hand moved to her buttocks and then slipped closer to her sex, she knew he would have no problem penetrating the exposed flesh of her pussy. His thick middle finger slid against her wetness before pushing easily inside.

'Damn,' Phil marvelled. 'You really are ready for me, aren't you?'

She kissed him. The bulge at the front of his pants had already been firm but she felt it thrust into eager hardness as her tongue slipped into his mouth.

'I think we're ready for each other.'

He turned her around and laid her across the bonnet of the car.

It took him only a few seconds to shrug his clothes off. At the same time Denise wondered if she should make him wait for his prize until he had finished the repair. She knew such bartering was more suited to Jane's temperament than her own but she had vowed to follow her friend's advice and become more forceful in her interactions with men. Jane had said Denise should just tell Derek what she wanted and continue telling him until he relented. If she had been in the garage with them now, Denise knew that Jane would have told her to make Phil wait for his reward until he had finished repairing the car. And, being honest about it, Denise thought Jane's advice would make good, sound sense.

But as soon as she saw Phil naked, Denise told him to take her across the bonnet of Derek's Rover. She needed him badly and she was desperate to feel his cock inside her.

Across the bonnet was an awkward position. The metal beneath her back was hard and uncomfortable. If not for the layer of sweat that oiled her body, Denise would have slipped to the floor. Her legs kicked air until Phil was between them, holding her calves and pressing his erection against her cleft. Staring up at the cobweb-covered ceiling, Denise thought it was an awful place and position to have sex. But she stopped thinking about that when Phil's length slid into her pussy.

She didn't know how long it had been since Phil had last ridden anyone bareback, but she knew it had been too long since *she* last enjoyed the pleasure. Feeling the solid, warm flesh fill her hole, basking in the knowledge that she was being properly fucked by an unsheathed cock, Denise forgot about the discomfort of the bonnet beneath her shoulder blades and gave herself completely to the moment, focusing entirely on her wet sex, aware only of his thick erection sliding into her and the greedy palpitations of her inner muscles.

'You really are ready for this,' he grunted, as he thrust into her.

A gurgle of satisfaction welled in her chest but she suppressed the sound, not wanting to spoil his rhythm or mood. Squeezing her sex around him, she yearned for the rush of a climax to hurtle towards her.

'Fill me, Phil,' she whispered.

The words sounded ridiculous and she could no longer contain the burst of satisfied laughter inside her chest. Squeezing hard as she chuckled, wrapping her arms around him in a passionate embrace, she laughed as he came quickly and spurted deep inside her. His cock pulsed and pulsed. The hot jet of his semen douched her inner muscles. Denise's own climax felt small in comparison to the blatant power of Phil's ejaculation. But she didn't think a short, quick fuck had ever been so satisfying. Rising gingerly from the bonnet, she let his length slip from her, but continued to kiss him.

'I'm sorry that was so quick,' he muttered. The rose of a blush coloured his cheeks. 'I'd forgotten how good bareback could be.'

She drew her fingers down his chest to his stomach, then wrapped her hand around the spent, sticky flesh of his cock. The smell of his ejaculate was heady and intoxicating. 'I'd forgotten too,' she admitted. 'But if you get this repair done quickly, we can both have another reminder before we go back to the party.'

Immediately, and to her surprise, Phil became coolly professional after his climax. He found a pair of Derek's old overalls in a corner of the garage and wore them over his naked body as he worked on the car. The neck was open to the torso, revealing a long, exciting V of his manly, hairy chest. Manoeuvring briskly around the car, accepting Denise's offer of a drink, he started to prepare the gash in readiness for masking and filling.

Denise had time to glance around the garage – a place she seldom looked at, even when she was parking her bike – and was amazed by the orderliness Derek had imposed on the room. The shelves were lined with cardboard boxes, all clean and uniform and each neatly labelled. Her first thought, a thought that was cruel enough to have come from Jane, was that her husband clearly spent too much time in the garage and this was the damning proof. If Jane had been with her, Denise knew her friend would be saying this wasn't a hobby, it was an obsession.

But Denise couldn't help feeling a tug of affectionate gratitude for her husband. The garage was the only room in the house that was considered Derek's responsibility and he clearly kept the place punctiliously tidy. But as she dwelt on that notion, her mood began to spiral downwards. It was a shame that Derek didn't pay her the same amount of attention as he devoted to the gloomy garage and his beloved car. If he had shown a modicum of sexual interest in her, her life would have been complete. It would only take the slightest suggestion of carnal curiosity from her husband and Denise knew she could introduce him to her passion for a wealth of sexual pleasures. They could enjoy the fulfilment of a normal and satisfying love life. He could give her the family she craved. And they could grow old and happy together like every other normal couple she had ever envied.

There would still probably be affairs. If Derek ever did come round to her way of thinking, she would have to make time for lovers like Jane and Joanne and Linda and the others she occasionally played with. But she would happily give up a lot of the extra-marital relationships if her husband stopped devoting his life to his car and give her some of the physical affection she craved.

'We have to wait twenty minutes for that to dry,' Phil told her. He dusted his hands against the thighs of his overalls and peeled off a pair of latex gloves.

She glanced at the tidy repair that now covered the gash in the paintwork. Her low spirits were instantly forgotten as she happily embraced Phil and smothered him with kisses. Knowing she would not have to sell

188

her bike, realising there would be no bitter and punitive argument with Derek, she hugged Phil with genuine gratitude.

'Tell me what you want,' she panted. She pressed her bare body against his, enjoying the scratch of the overalls against her breasts. 'I don't care how kinky or depraved it is. I'm making you a serious offer here. I owe you big time for this and I'll do anything you want.'

Phil's hands were stroking her back and bare buttocks. His stirring erection nudged from the loins of his overalls and pressed into her stomach. 'You must think a lot of your husband,' he murmured.

'I like to keep my man happy,' she admitted. She wanted to say more but this wasn't the time or the place to tell Phil that she wished Derek felt the same about her. Pressing urgently against him she said, 'I like to keep any man happy if he does something good for me. Now, tell me what you want to do, and we'll do it. It doesn't matter how depraved it is.'

Her thighs were wrapped around his waist. His hands cupped her buttocks. When he flexed his fingers she could feel their tips brushing against the moist flesh of her pussy.

'I'm not a kinky person,' Phil confessed as he squeezed her into his embrace. He paused for a moment and then said, 'Well, no kinkier than most.'

Wriggling her sex against him to encourage him, Denise breathed, 'Anything you want, Phil. I'll do it for you if you can complete that repair tonight.'

He pressed a kiss against her throat. The intimacy was maddening. Her gratitude for him had been transformed into a greedy need. She had promised she would do anything he wanted, and now that prospect filled her with a carnal urgency that was frightening. Writhing against him, delighting in his muscular masculinity, she breathed in the aged and dusty scents of the garage as well as the sweaty vitality of Phil's nearness.

'I'll need some sandpaper,' he told her. 'Another pair of latex gloves, meths, a few rags, and a couple of dust masks.'

Denise stiffened. She pulled her face away from his throat and stared at him in horror. 'Jesus, Phil,' she breathed. 'That sounds a lot kinkier than I expected.'

He laughed and released her from his arms. 'Those are the things I'll need for finishing the car,' he explained. 'And you can get them once I've finished fucking you.' A moment later he was inside her again as she bent over the bonnet, his bare flesh thrusting into her warm, wet pussy. Denise pressed herself against the bonnet of Derek's Rover, allowing Phil to enter her from behind. Her breasts were squashed against the cool, glossy paintwork, her stomach chilled by the icy skin of the car. But the heat of her sex warmed her, and the frisson of his bare cock sliding smoothly into her. Phil's hands fell to her hips and he gripped her hard as he thrust himself into her again and again.

A glance through the garage window told Denise that Ted and Linda's party was still going strong. She wondered if Phil was disappointed that he wasn't there, and then decided that the hardness of his erection, and his murmurs of satisfaction, suggested he was content with the way things were progressing in the garage.

It took him longer to reach his second climax, and he had pushed Denise through two orgasms before she reached between her spread legs and grasped his balls with one hand. Clutching him lightly, kneading his sac with delicate fingers, she said a silent prayer of gratitude, and squeezed him.

For the second time that evening – for the second time in years of barren disappointment – Denise felt her womb being sprayed by the hot rush of semen. Her orgasm was strong and provoked a grateful scream. She had to physically resist the impulse to scratch her nails down the bonnet of the car as the force of the pleasure buffeted her body.

Phil staggered away from her, clearly drained by the experience.

Denise turned, found her legs and grinned dizzily at him. 'We can do that again when you've finished.'

He laughed. 'You're insatiable.'

'Does that mean you want to?'

'Do you really need to ask?'

Denise gave Phil paint sprays and masking tape. In the kitchen she found gloves and rags and made them fresh drinks. Phil took his and started his final work on the car.

Denise watched him for a while and then saw that a clutter of boxes circled Phil's feet. Off their shelves, they made the garage look surprisingly untidy. Anxious to hide the fact that a repair had been effected on the car, she started to move the boxes back to where they belonged. As she passed the garage window, she heard something that sounded suspiciously like a footstep.

Her heartbeat raced at the idea that Derek might be nearby and that she might be in danger of being discovered with another man. The thought inspired a chill of apprehension that shivered down her spine. Denise had never made a big secret out of the fact that she slept with other men, but her serial infidelities weren't something she had gone out of her way to share with Derek either. While Jane clearly craved the thrill of John discovering that she had lovers, Denise preferred the simplicity of a life where she could believe that Derek was oblivious to her habits – even if that meant he seemed oblivious to her.

She stepped closer to the window, trying to peer through the dirty glass and see if someone, hopefully not Derek, was outside spying on them. She caught the shape of a silhouette. It might, she thought, be Derek, or it might be the outline of one of the shrubs that grew near the garage door. She took a tentative step closer.

Music suddenly filled the garage. It was deafeningly loud and wholly unexpected. Denise flinched as though she had been struck. She turned and saw that Phil had switched on the Rover's radio. He stood by the door panel, grinning at her as he pulled the latex gloves from his palms.

'Finished,' he said simply. 'What do you think we could do to celebrate?'

As she stepped to his side she brushed away her worry about the noise she had heard outside the window. His hands were warm and sweat-slick from being inside the latex gloves. When his fingers curved around her backside she trembled at their oily touch. Their mouths met in a slow, passionate kiss.

As her tongue entwined with his, Denise felt Phil's fingers creeping to the lips of her sex. She caught an excited breath as his hand moved towards the centre of her pussy, then released a sigh when he pushed one finger inside. He opened the car's rear door, lay her down on the back seat and, for the third time that evening, Denise was treated to the glorious pleasure of having him ride her to orgasm and then pump his ejaculate deep into her pussy. It was fast, vigorous and deeply exciting. She caught the scent of her own overused pussy and its fragrance, as much as his passionate and furious rhythm, impelled her to her climax.

She lay exhausted on the back seat of the car as he climbed out.

'I'd best get back to the party,' Phil muttered. 'Ted will be wondering where I am.'

She nodded and found the strength to reach to the dashboard and switch off the radio. Wearily getting out of the car, wishing she could just go to bed and not bother with the remainder of the party, she said, 'I'll be over there myself in a few minutes. I'll just tidy round here so Derek doesn't notice anything out of place when he gets back.'

She glanced at the repaired door panel and tried to remember where the gash had been. Phil had expertly removed all trace of the scratch and it was now no more than a memory. Her gratitude made her feel weak and humble. 'You did a good job.'

He was stepping back into his trousers and pulling on his shirt. Treating her to a cheeky grin he asked, 'On you, or the car?'

Denise laughed and kissed him, then went back to replacing the boxes on the shelves. She had just put away the last when she turned and saw her husband. She placed a hand over her mouth. He didn't seem to have noticed she was there. As long as she remained concealed by shadows, Denise thought it unlikely he would see her.

But then she realised what had happened. Derek had been watching while she fucked Phil. And, seeing the familiar jerking motion at his groin, she knew Derek had been doing more than watching. In the dim light of the garage his wrist moved quickly back and forth and Denise gazed open-mouthed at her husband masturbating.

Derek was a good husband and she loved him dearly, but she had never known him to be interested in her sexual antics. The thought that she might have misjudged him filled her with dismay. If he was suddenly interested in watching her, she didn't think it would be long before he might want to join her, and possibly provide the family she so longed for.

Excited, she continued to watch as Derek tugged himself to climax. A trickle of Phil's semen seeped from her pussy lips, the wetness like an unexpected tear. Denise clutched her stomach, nauseated by the thought that she might have wronged her husband by getting pregnant with another man.

Continuing to wank himself, Derek stepped closer to the car. He pulled on his length with one hand while the fingers of the other hovered over the freshly repaired scratch.

Denise wondered what was going through his mind. Most likely he was remembering how she had looked when Phil took her over the bonnet, or when the mechanic's fingers had been inside her sex, or that climactic moment when Phil had thrust into her pussy and filled her with spunk. Thinking back on those moments, and remembering the raw excitement of each incident, she supposed her husband could be recollecting any of those private moments as he pulled himself to orgasm.

Derek groaned. A spatter of his semen shot across the door panel of the car. He fell to his knees as he continued to milk himself. Pulling a handkerchief from his pocket he wiped the ejaculate from the paintwork while sighing contentedly.

'Beautiful,' he murmured, allowing his fingers to linger over the freshly restored surface. 'Absolutely beautiful.'

Denise waited until her husband had left the garage before going back to the party. The evening had offered the small hope that Derek might have some sexual interest in her and she was determined to use that to full advantage. She only hoped that Phil hadn't spoilt things by giving her the pregnancy she had so desperately craved at the start of the evening.

Nineteen

6 Cedar View

Light from the conservatory splashed on to the garden
and its furniture. Jane could just make out the
shadowy shape of her gimp in the darkness. The
insatiable thrill of arousal swept over her again. She
had thought, approaching the house from the rear,
they were less likely to be seen by any of the other
guests at the party. It had been an effective plan,
bringing them back to the party with no one realising
that she had stolen the gimp in the first place.

But she still needed to use him again. Her body
craved the satisfaction of having the gimp's cock inside
her, filling her and satisfying her need for climax. She
still didn't warm to the idea of taking him in full view
of a cheering crowd of swingers and swappers. But she
was determined that, before the party was over, she
was going to have the gimp once more. And she was
going to have him on her terms.

'Lie down on that bench,' she said, gesturing behind
him towards the garden furniture. 'I want to fuck you
again.'

He adjusted his mask – the head covering of his
gimp suit was too large and kept falling over his eyes,
effectively blindfolding him – and studied her silently.
For a moment she feared that he had grown weary of

her domination and incessant commands and was no longer in her thrall. It was only when he whispered, 'Yes, Goddess,' that she realised he truly was her devoted slave.

'Lie on your back,' she told him. 'I want to ride that thick cock of yours this time. I want to feel you buried deep in my pussy.' Not sure he could hear through the thick mask, which covered his ears, and taking a delightful satisfaction from expressing her needs so boldly, she said, 'Lie down, gimp. You're going to fuck me.'

The gimp gasped. 'How would that be possible, Goddess?'

She frowned, not sure what the question meant. He was a gimp and, if he didn't know how a man and a woman were supposed to fuck, Jane thought there was a serious deficit in his knowledge.

'Your cock,' he explained, nodding towards her crotch. His gaze was fixed on the huge dildo that protruded from her loins. 'Won't that get in the way if I'm going to *fuck* you?'

He whispered the expletive, almost as though he was too timid to say the word. His coyness made her feel as though she was exploiting him and the cruelty of that idea added to her growing wetness. Jane reached down and unsnapped the strap-on with an elegant flick of her wrist.

'I can take it off while we *fuck*.' She tried to mimic his coquettishness. Holding the girth of the dildo in one hand she asked innocently, 'But I can't think where I should put this dildo for safety while we *fuck*. Do you have any ideas?'

The gimp chuckled as he lay across the top of the garden table.

John chuckled as he lay on top of the garden table. The Goddess had a wicked sense of humour and a

196

devious sense of fun. He didn't think he had ever encountered a woman who embodied everything he ever wanted and was so in tune with his own thoughts and desires. He watched as she stepped closer with the dildo in her hand. She grinned as she rubbed an oily palm along the length and he squirmed with mounting excitement. His arousal reached a new peak when she unzipped his suit and pressed the end of the rubber length hard against him.

His erection immediately twitched into life and again he marvelled at his good fortune in finding himself under the domination of this incomparable woman. She pressed a hand on his stomach as she straddled his body. He admired her long, slender legs and the shapeliness of her buttocks. Earlier in the evening he had been admiring Joanne's backside and revering it for its size and shape. But Joanne was a mere amateur compared to the perfection of John's newfound Goddess. When she pushed her backside over his face, forcing him to taste the sweet musk of her sex, he realised that this was the woman he had always wanted, the woman he had always needed.

'Lick my pussy while I slide this into you.'

He could have climaxed on hearing the words. Even without the pressure of her fingers spreading his buttocks, even without the scent and sensation of her sex slipping closer to his mouth, even without the seductive shape of her silhouette poised over him, the force of her words was enough to thrust him to the point of no return. Steeling himself against the urge to ejaculate, John tried to relax and allow his body to accept the fat girth of the dildo.

'Stop holding yourself so tight,' she complained. 'I gave you a direct command, didn't I?'

He grinned on hearing the irritation in her voice. There was a playful edge to her tone that made her

seem irresistible. Trying to obey – desperate to obey –
John released the tension in his muscles. Immediately
the fat dildo began to slide into his rear.

'Fuck! Yes!' he gasped.

The Goddess chuckled. She pushed her pussy closer
to his face and rubbed the moist lips against him. His
nose and chin were instantly lathered with her wetness.
The succulent scent of her sex – ripe, gamey and
overpowering – was exhilarating. He basked in her
nearness and pushed his tongue hungrily against her
labia. Drinking the rich flavour, savouring her bitter-
sweetness, he let the dildo slide deeper and tried to
concentrate on lapping and licking.

It was hard. His erection throbbed with the need to
climax and the sensation only grew stronger with every
inch of the dildo that she forced into his anus. His
backside felt full to the point of bursting and his
responses buzzed from the thrill of so much mental
and physical stimulation. It had to be the most
satisfying experience of his entire life – but he wanted
to make it better.

'Goddess,' he spluttered. 'Please! Goddess.'

She turned to sneer at him. 'What is it?'

'Piss on me,' he mumbled.

'Do what?'

'Piss on me. Please, Goddess. Please. I'm begging
you. Piss on me. Piss in my mouth.'

There was a moment's silence. It was an agonising
instant that stretched to infinity in the darkness. John
held his breath, wondering if she was going to respond
by simply spraying pee in his face. The sound of flesh
smacking flesh was so loud and unexpected he didn't
feel the pain of the blow until his mistress was roaring
at him in outrage.

'How dare you beg your Goddess to do anything?'
she demanded. She slapped his backside a second time.

198

The shock of the first blow hadn't properly registered on his senses but the impact of the second more than made up for that. A burning tattoo of agony branded his buttock. His muscles automatically stiffened and he was made punishingly aware of the dildo that filled his rear. The Goddess's outrage, the pain in his rear, and the sensation of being filled by her cock, all combined to make a powerful blend. He fought so hard to resist his orgasm he believed he could feel internal muscles tearing from the effort. The extremes of pain and pleasure were so severe he didn't know whether his body was racked by delight or devastation. He sobbed when she slapped him for a third time.

'You don't beg your Goddess for anything except mercy,' she snapped. She threw another slap against his backside. Each time she struck him her open palm landed with the force of a whip crack. Every blow smacked against the same mark, making the skin sensitive, the pain more intense.

John's sob turned into a wail.

'You don't beg your Goddess for anything,' she repeated. Another slap. This one forced him to rock his head back. His head smacked hard against the garden table. He could see bright stars exploding even with eyes tightly shut.

'You don't ask for sick and twisted things like piss in your mouth.'

Another slap. The sound was louder than the music and laughter that rang from Ted and Linda's conservatory. The pain was wonderful, immense. He could imagine the flourish of bright red palm prints that would be decorating his pale buttocks.

'And you stay still while I'm trying to slide a dildo up your arse.'

Another slap. His entire body trembled with the effort of holding back his orgasm. He had never invested so much effort in the act of resisting a climax. His need to come, and his absolute commitment to waiting for her command, placed him in the centre of an impossible dilemma. His wailing trailed off to a soft and grateful weeping.

'Stay still,' the Goddess insisted. This time there was no slap. There was only the sensation of her hands returning to his backside as she tried to urge the dildo deeper. 'Stay still and eat my pussy.'

He held his breath and did as she asked. At the back of his mind he was worried that her reluctance to pee on him might suggest that she wasn't the deity or the soul-mate he had believed she was. If she was truly worthy of his servitude, he believed, she would leap at an invitation to piss in his mouth. But the way she had dismissed his request, almost as though she was speaking with distaste, left John wondering if she had a revulsion for watersports. Not sure that such a fundamental difference could ever be reconciled, he pushed the worry from his thoughts and pressed his mouth against her pussy. Licking her wetness and wishing he could provide her with the same satisfaction that she had given him, he slurped hungrily at her hole.

'That's more like it,' Jane gasped.

John didn't know if she was complimenting him on his abilities or simply pleased that she had forced the last few inches of the dildo into his rear. The full length was a magnificent weight inside his bowel. Its presence made his erection stiff and sensitive.

'Get me good and wet,' she demanded. 'I'm going to slide myself on to your cock now.'

He held himself rigid and gave her pussy a farewell kiss. She slid the wet lips of her labia away from his face and down over his stomach. Keeping her back to him, only allowing him to see her from behind, she squatted over his erection.

Guiding him into her pussy, accepting him into her wet velvet, the Goddess moaned as his cock filled her. Her fingers went to the tight sac of his scrotum and clutched. The nails bit hard into the delicate flesh. He could feel his balls being brutally squeezed in her hard grip.

'Don't you dare come yet,' she insisted. She flexed her wrist a little as she spoke, reminding him that she was in absolute control. The skin of his sac was pulled and stretched in a crushing agony. The combination of pleasure and pain was devastating.

'You can't come until I've given you permission,' the Goddess reminded him. 'Do you understand that?'

'I'll try.'

'No.' Now there was real steel in her voice. She clutched his balls with more force and he almost shrieked at the sudden delicious sting of pain. Instead of tugging at his skin her hand closed into a tight, powerful fist. He whimpered and pressed himself hard against the table.

'No,' the Goddess insisted. 'You won't *try* and do as I've told you. You *will* do as I told you. Is that clear?'

He struggled for air before replying. The pain was so severe he knew that the slightest lapse in concentration would allow a climax to rip through his body. 'Yes, Goddess,' he managed eventually. The words took a gargantuan effort and came out in a whisper-soft mewl. 'Yes, Goddess.'

She released her punitive hold on his scrotum. The relief from pain was so immense he almost ejaculated. Remembering his adoration for the woman above him, and wondering if her lack of interest in watersports might not be the big problem he had expected, John savoured the experience of being beneath his Goddess.

This, Jane decided, was the sex she had always wanted. The faceless man beneath her revered her as though she had genuinely been sent from heaven. The pleasure of exciting him to the point of no return, and then demanding he stay on that point as she satisfied herself, was thrilling and fulfilling. His length felt good inside her. She guessed he was not much larger than her husband. But because he was lying beneath her, moving only in response to her explicit commands, Jane thought he was a far more gifted lover. Delighting in the silky sensation, urging his shaft to ride in and out of her wet pussy, she decided that while they were having sex was the ideal time to pressurise him into making a commitment.

'I want to see you again.'

He hesitated for a beat. His cock remained hard as she slid down on him.

'I'm married.' He said the words quietly, almost as though the fact shamed him.

Jane shrugged and began to urge herself upwards.

'So am I. I'm married to a useless pathetic specimen of a man. I assume you're married to a silly bitch who doesn't know how to treat you in the bedroom.'

She paused, allowing herself a moment to slide down and then up his length. The gimp was so close to his climax she could feel the electric throb pulsing from his shaft. Her own orgasm was no more than a breath away but she resisted its tempting call, determined to bend him completely to her will before either of them was allowed to come.

'Since we're both hitched to idiots who don't know how to satisfy us, why don't we arrange to satisfy each other on a regular basis?'

There was another pause. Jane took advantage of the moment to slide down and then up again. Her inner muscles were warm and sopping with moisture. The gimp's cock promised to give her the rush of satisfaction that her body now craved. Each time she impaled herself on him, Jane could feel a devastating orgasm inching closer and closer. With growing impatience, she waited to hear how the gimp would respond.

She wondered if her words had lacked subtlety. The only thing she knew about the man beneath her was that his submissiveness excited her beyond anything she had encountered before. He had a respectable body that she longed to use and a servile disposition that allowed her to dominate him without mercy. But she knew nothing about the man inside the gimp suit and wondered if her suggestion might have offended his moral code. The fear that she could have jeopardised her future relationship with the gimp made her aware of the night's chill as her bare flesh turned prickly with goosebumps.

'Well?' she prompted. Glancing back over her shoulder, staring down at the shadows where his face was hidden she asked, 'Will you see me again?'

He lifted his head to stare at her. His mask and the darkness made his expression unreadable. There was something annoyingly familiar about his posture but she supposed all men would probably look similar if they were wearing a full gimp suit. His body language and the heavy shadows meant it wasn't until he spoke that Jane had any idea of how he might respond to her proposition.

The gimp asked, 'How could I refuse the direct command of my deity?'

She grinned. Even though his words had a stiffness that reminded her of her husband's pedantic vocabulary, Jane was warmed by the idea that she would have the pleasure of the gimp for as long and as often as she wanted. The thought that he genuinely wanted to worship as her subordinate fired a glorious need in the centre of her pussy. She twisted herself round and, desperate to preserve the sensation of his cock filling her, held him tightly with her inner muscles, feeling every delicious ripple of his erection as it turned against the muscles of her pussy. Greedily, she devoured his mouth. The kiss was passionate enough to take them both to the brink of climax.

'My husband goes to the pub with his friends every Tuesday and Thursday night,' she said quickly. 'We could meet up on either of those nights.'

'I usually see Joanne on Tuesday and Thursday nights,' he began. He laughed softly and said, 'My wife thinks I go to the pub with my friends. But I'd be happy to stop seeing Joanne and start seeing you instead. You're divine. You really are a Goddess. My Goddess.'

The thrill of power swept through her. She had found her sexual soul-mate, secured sexual satisfaction for the foreseeable future and managed to convince Joanne's gimp to turn his back on his mistress and commit himself to pleasuring her. The conviction of her own superiority was enormous and, when she pushed herself fully on to the gimp's erection, she could feel the climax starting to ripple through her stomach.

Beneath her, he bucked and shivered and thrashed through an unavoidable release. Jane held him, relishing the enormous thrill of knowing she had given the gimp such a rush of satisfaction. Her own orgasm, a satisfying burst that erupted through her stomach and ended in dull, aching tremors in her loins, was only a shadow of the pleasure she felt from having caused his cock to pump repeatedly inside her pussy.

'The next time we fuck,' she whispered. 'I think I *will* piss on you first. I'm going to piss on your face, piss in your open mouth, and make you drink every last drop. That's what's going to happen the next time we fuck.'

He howled. His climax had been hard and fast. But, as she spat the words in his ear, Jane realised another surge of pleasure had ripped through his body. As his cry tapered off to a muffled sob, he whispered, 'Thank you, Goddess. Thank you.'

It was, Jane thought, a perfect moment, one that couldn't be spoilt by anything.

'Gimp!'

Jane lifted her head from the gimp's when she heard Joanne's voice. Instantaneously all her feelings of warmth and happiness disappeared. Adjusting her mask, to make sure her identity remained a secret, she gave the woman her coolest smile.

'What the hell are you doing?' Joanne demanded. She kept her gaze fixed somewhere between Jane and the gimp so it wasn't immediately apparent which of them she was addressing. Speaking before the gimp had a chance to respond, Jane said, 'He's servicing me. Isn't that obvious?'

The frosty gaze lifted to meet Jane's. 'I told him to stay by the pool.'

'I brought him out here to fuck me.'

'He should have told you that I'd given him an order.'

'He couldn't speak,' Jane returned. 'Because he had my cock in his mouth.' She paused for a moment, smiled contentedly to herself and then shook her head apologetically. 'I'm sorry, Joanne. It was thoughtless of me to take your gimp when I could have had any man at this party. You must have felt terribly neglected being all on your own and not being able to attract anyone. I'll send this one back to you as soon as I've finished with him.'

Even in the dark Jane could see a thunderous expression cloud Joanne's features. She grinned at the woman's obvious fury and wondered if she should tell

Joanne that the gimp had just consented to become her regular illicit lover and would never be seeing her again. Deciding that would probably cause more disharmony than was necessary, she dismissed Joanne and her animosity with a wave before turning her attention back to the waning length of the gimp's cock that filled her hole.

'That felt good,' she confided. She wasn't sure if she meant the orgasm he had provided or the satisfaction of snubbing and insulting Joanne. 'How was it for you?'

With a satisfied sigh he murmured, 'You really are a Goddess.'

Joanne snorted impatiently. 'Send him back in as soon as you can,' she snapped. 'And make sure you come back in too. I'm sure you'll love to see what I can do to that gimp when I've got the right audience.'

She said something else under her breath. Because she was heading back into the house, Jane wasn't sure she caught all of the words. It sounded as though Joanne was saying, 'Let's see how smug you can be when I've taken his mask off.' It struck Jane as a peculiar thing for the woman to say because she didn't think the sight of the gimp without his mask would stop her knowing that she had found her ideal man.

She made swift plans with the gimp while she eased the dildo from his rear, telling him that they would always meet in costume for their illicit Tuesday and Thursday trysts at a local motel. And, although the gimp's return to Joanne would be the ideal time for her to leave the party, Jane thought she might stay around long enough to see Joanne unmask him.

John stumbled wearily back into the conservatory, squinting against the bright lights and shying from the excess of noise. He spotted Joanne immediately and, while he knew he had to obey her orders and go to her

206

side, the prospect left him cold with dread. After spending so much of his evening with the Goddess, he expected Joanne to be furious with him. Deservedly furious. And, while he had previously looked forward to suffering the full brunt of her ire when she was angry with him, he knew it would no longer be the pleasurable experience he had once enjoyed.

'Come with me.'

He didn't get a chance to see who had spoken. The dog leash attached to his collar was yanked and, before he had a chance to let Joanne know he was back in the party, John was pulled through a doorway into another room. The lights seemed muted after the brightness of the pool area. His mask had fallen over his eyes again and when he pulled it away he found himself alone with three women.

He recognised Denise Shelby standing in front of him. The evening had been a revelation in discovering so many of his neighbours attending the sex party. Obviously he had expected to find Ted and Linda present, as well as Joanne, who had brought him to the party. But so far he had encountered Denise, and Ted's brother Phil, the street's favoured mechanic, and he had heard people talking about the Graftons and the McMurrays. It made him wonder if he and Jane were the only normal people who lived on Cedar View.

On either side of Denise were two women he remembered seeing earlier at the party, both dark-skinned, one with long black hair that flowed down to her shapely buttocks, the other sporting a short crop that mirrored her neatly trimmed pubic bush. Their bodies, exotic and available, inspired a sudden rush of sexual interest. Even though he had spent the entire party being taken to extremes of arousal by his newfound Goddess, John could feel the familiar stirrings of an erection between his legs.

207

'These ladies have always wanted to play with a gimp,' Denise explained. 'But they didn't fancy begging permission from Joanne or being part of the evening's floor show. That's why we've brought you in here.'

John glanced around and realised he had been led into the pool's changing room. The Spartan surroundings did not hold his interest as much as the three glamorous naked women. He looked at them in turn, appraising the splendour of their bare flesh. His erection grew more noticeable. The stiffness of his shaft made him blush.

'Can we touch him?'

'Can we play with him?'

'You're a greedy pair of bitches,' Denise said, laughing. 'But you can do what you want with him. He's a gimp. He's here to be enjoyed.'

John's cock twitched again.

'He doesn't look very aroused,' the long-haired woman complained.

'I thought gimps were supposed to be permanently erect,' her friend agreed. 'Has someone broken him?'

Denise rolled her eyes. 'Jesus, girls. It's just a man in a suit,' she told them. 'If you want him hard you've got to make him hard. Excite him. And then have your fun with him.'

John listened to her words, squirming with embarrassment at being spoken about as though he wasn't able to respond. Denise's dismissive tone made him feel small and inadequate. The exposition of his inadequacies inspired another surge of excitement to stiffen his shaft.

The short-haired woman stepped closer to him. His head was clutched from behind and his buttocks were clasped by a large, firm hand. Pulled into her embrace, he was kissed by her hungry mouth. The woman's tongue slipped between his lips. Her bare breasts pressed against the thin sheath of his gimp suit. Through the leather that covered his legs he could feel her pussy kissing his thigh.

'Don't you want him to lick you?' Denise asked.

'He's only a man.' The long-haired woman sniffed in disdain. 'He's not going to eat my pussy as well as you or Connie could.'

'Corinne's got a point,' the other woman agreed. 'What can a man do that we can't do ourselves?' She grabbed his semi-soft length and laughed cruelly. 'Especially when he can't get properly hard.'

Both of the dark-skinned women chuckled. John's cock shrivelled beneath their amusement. If not for the gimp suit, and the fact that Denise was holding the leash attached to his collar, John would have fled from their disdain and either rushed home or at least returned to the party and Joanne.

'Jesus, girls,' Denise exclaimed.

She pushed Corinne away from embracing John and glared at them both. John felt Denise's fingers encircle his exposed length. The contact was surprisingly light and sensitive enough to make his body respond eagerly.

'I thought you wanted to play with this gimp?' Denise demanded. 'I didn't think you wanted to just whine about the fact that he's a mere man.'

'He's not getting hard,' Corinne argued. 'Can you blame us for whining?'

Denise rolled her eyes. John felt her fingers stiffen around his shaft. He trembled excitedly beneath her touch.

'You've made every man in here rock-hard so far this evening,' Denise told them. 'Why don't you try exciting the gimp in the same way and see if you can play with him then?'

John watched the two women exchange a glance. They gave each other slow, suggestive smiles and then nodded eager consent. He didn't know what they were going to do but, when he saw them fall into each other's arms in an intimate embrace, his cock immediately began to thicken.

They shared a passionate kiss, stroking each other's bodies, touching breasts and hips. Corinne insinuated a thigh between her friend's legs and the two women melded against each other. John couldn't tear his gaze from the scene to look at Denise but he could feel her hand working slowly up and down his stiff shaft. Steadying his breathing he watched the other two women sink to the floor as their mouths continued to explore each other's body.

It was furiously erotic. They slid together with practised ease. He watched tongues flicking at nipples, heard the heady chuckles of their arousals, drank in the scent of their mounting excitement. As the two women twisted around one slid her tongue against the flushed pink slit of the other's pussy.

Denise's hand moved faster round his length. His balls grew tight with the anticipation of another climax. It was the perfect end to the evening, he thought. He had been the humiliated gimp for most of the party, and then he had met a Goddess whom he revered and who wanted him to satisfy all her sexual demands. Watching the two dark-skinned women writhe together, gasping softly and slyly encouraging further intimacy, he knew he was superfluous to their pleasure. The knowledge of his own irrelevance made his erection grow to its full length and hardness. As Denise stroked him more swiftly, he wondered how long it was likely to be before his erection twitched and pulsed for a final time this evening.

As he watched, Corinne's slender fingers disappeared inside a velvet wet cleft. Connie arched her

back as her lover doubled over in a groan of ecstasy.
Their words were whispered in dark, feral grunts.

'. . . fuck me . . .'

'. . . drink me . . .'

'. . . harder, you bitch . . .'

'. . . deeper, you slut . . .'

Listening to them, watching and inhaling and living
through the experience, John fought the threat of a
premature ejaculation. He had come so many times
this evening that his shaft ached from the excess of
pleasure. But that dull pain didn't stop him from
wanting to feel the orgasmic pulse of release one last
time before the evening was over.

'Well done, girls,' Denise laughed. 'You've got the
gimp hard.'

Corinne raised her head and glanced in John's
direction. When her gaze fell on his erection she flexed
a brief smile before dismissing him with a sniff and
turning her attention back to Connie. 'Who needs a
hard gimp when you've got a wet pussy?' she said with
a laugh. Beneath her, Connie chuckled as though
Corinne's question was the funniest thing she had ever
heard. Then the sounds of their shared laughter
merged into a wet slurp as each woman returned her
mouths to the moist haven of her friend's vagina.

'Don't you want to play with him?' Denise asked.

'You play with him, if you want,' Corinne suggested.
'Or you can send him back to Joanne,' Connie allowed
magnanimously. Her voice was smug with satisfaction
as she said, 'We're going to keep each other enter-
tained for the rest of the party.'

As they became an entangled mass of arms and legs,
John realised they had no interest in him as either a
potential partner or a frustrated observer. He was
satisfied to think his humiliation could not be more
complete. If Denise had continued to stroke his cock,

John knew he would have climaxed from the wonderful, crushing shame. But she chose that moment to release him, leaving him frustrated and unsatisfied.

Gently, Denise tugged on his leash and led him towards the door.

'They say they don't want you,' she said quietly. 'And I've had enough of men for one night.' There was a sadness in her voice, despite her attempt to sound pleasant and cheerful. 'All of which means you're superfluous to our requirements, so you'd better go.'

He wanted to ask her if she was OK. He supposed it wasn't a gimp's place to offer emotional support at a sex party but he didn't like to think of his pretty neighbour sounding so upset and struggling to hide the emotion. Before he could speak she had shoved him through the doorway and out of the pool's changing room.

John sighed, sorry he hadn't been able to offer Denise any comfort or reassurance and disappointed he wasn't able to watch Connie and Corinne as they continued to lick and suck each other. He wondered if he should take Denise's dismissal as a sign that he wasn't meant to stay at the party and that he really should go home. He had arranged to meet his Goddess on Tuesday and again on Thursday. He had just witnessed an exceptionally erotic exchange between two beautiful, exotic women. He didn't think it would be possible for the party to end on a better note. Joanne no longer held any interest for him: he would be happy to put her and her malicious bullying out of his life forever. Telling himself this would be the ideal time to leave, he braced his shoulders and started towards the conservatory door.

Someone tugged on his leash. The collar pulled hard at his neck.

'There you are, gimp,' Joanne laughed. 'I'm so glad I found you again. Come with me.' Not waiting for his reply, Joanne dragged John with her and started calling for everyone's attention. His mask didn't shift this time and he was able to see everything with horrifying clarity. He watched Joanne glance towards the Goddess, who stood by the conservatory door. Under her breath, in a whisper just loud enough for John to hear, Joanne muttered, 'This will be fun. I'm really going to wipe the smug grin off that bitch's face.'

She tugged the gimp to the head of the pool. Few people bothered to look in her direction but Joanne could ignore their indifference for the moment. She wanted things to be perfect before she executed the gimp's final humiliation of the night. She could wait for people to watch rather than force them.

'Look at you,' Joanne marvelled. 'You're sporting another erection.'

The gimp glanced down at himself and seemed surprised to notice his arousal. He also seemed uncharacteristically eager to pull away from her, as though he no longer wanted her company. Joanne smiled tightly at that thought. After this evening the gimp would have a damned good reason to avoid her company.

'I'm tired, mistress,' he whispered. 'I just want to go home.'

'I don't care whether you're tired. I don't care what you want.' She forced him to stand with his shoulders back and his legs apart. Because the servility was ingrained in him, he responded to her orders even though he obviously wanted to disobey. Taking pleasure from his discomfort, Joanne decided to unsettle the gimp completely by taking him in an unexpected embrace. She pressed her body close to his and rubbed at the stiff length of his cock. 'I'm going to do something for you that I've never done for any gimp before,' she murmured. 'How does that sound?'

'You don't have to do anything . . .' he began.

Joanne wasn't listening. She wanted the gimp's cock to be soft before she brought about his final humiliation. Also, she wanted Jane to watch the gimp being exceptionally intimate with her. Telling the gimp to hold his position, slowly lowering herself to her haunches, she took the gimp's thick cock in one hand and began to work her mouth round him. He groaned and tried to pull away, but she still held his lead.

He was desperately hard. She could sense his need for climax as soon as she placed her lips around the ruddy end of his length. Slurping greedily at him, trying to coax the climax from him, she teased his balls with her fingers and urged him to climax.

'Come in my mouth, gimp,' she muttered. 'Obey me now and come in my mouth.'

'Please, mistress,' John hissed. 'Just let me go home.'

Joanne sucked harder. She wasn't comfortable on her haunches, and she didn't like having the gimp's cock in her mouth. Making the small daisy-chain in Ted's bedroom, Joanne had not minded licking and sucking Ted's cock. Ted was neither superior nor subordinate – simply a neighbour and the party's host. Swallowing his cock had not been a power exchange between a servile gimp and his superior mistress. That had been a mutually satisfying exchange of pleasure.

But blowing a gimp in front of a crowd of partygoers was something she had never done before. The entire action screamed of servility and she wished there was a different way to do this. But, knowing that time was against her, sure that the party would be winding down soon, Joanne hurried to urge the climax from the gimp's length while there were enough people remaining to see what she had planned.

'Come,' she insisted. 'Come in my mouth, now.'

'Mistress!'

'Now!'

The gimp sighed. His sibilant whisper seemed to say, 'Yes.' But his shaft remained frustratingly rigid and his climax refused to come. Joanne kneaded his balls with more force. She worked her lips backwards and forwards along his shaft, slurping at him and willing his muscle to erupt. As the seconds passed into minutes and he still refused to ejaculate, her feeling of annoyance turned to outright anger.

Behind her she heard someone giggle. From the corner of her eye Joanne saw Connie and Corinne emerge from the pool's changing room. One of them pointed at her and the other laughed.

'She's blowing the gimp?' Corinne chuckled. 'I had no idea Joanne was such a cock monster.'

Her frustration turning to fury, determined to find some way of coaxing his climax, Joanne wriggled a finger against the gimp's anus. The flesh was wet and open from a night of too much use. He stiffened as soon as she touched the sphincter. 'Come,' she urged him, raising her head from his cock. 'Do it now.'

'I can't come in your mouth,' the gimp protested. 'You've always said I was never allowed to do that. You've always said you'd punish me more severely than ever if I dared to come inside any part of your body.'

'And now I'm telling you to do it,' Joanne growled. 'Come in my mouth, gimp. Come in my mouth.'

She squirmed a finger deep into his bowels and placed her mouth over the end of his length. When she sucked firmly on the swollen end and kneaded his balls at the same time, she was rewarded with the pulse of the gimp's ejaculation. Her mouth was filled with the salty flavour of his spend. The length of his cock juddered against her tongue.

Joanne stood up, pressed her lips to his and spat his spunk into his mouth as she kissed him. She felt him trying to pull away from the exchange but it was easy to hold him in place. When the last of the semen had been transferred from her mouth to his, she pulled her face away and wiped her mouth with the back of her hand. She felt satisfied and triumphant. There was only one more thing she needed to make the evening complete. She forced him to his knees.

'You came in my mouth, gimp,' she growled.

'You told me to.'

'You came in my mouth, and I've always told you that you're not allowed to come inside any part of my body.'

The gimp started shaking his head. If his face hadn't been covered Joanne knew she would have seen an expression of panic on his features.

'I was only doing what you told me,' he stammered. 'I was only doing . . .'

'I'm going to have to punish you for that,' Joanne advised him solemnly. 'I hope you're ready for this.' She stepped back and watched the gimp stare up at her with wary resignation. Turning her attention to the rest of the room Joanne shrieked, 'Quiet! Right now! All of you! I want some quiet!'

Jane stepped to the nearby CD player and turned the music off. The house fell quiet in expectancy. The only sounds were the clatter of heels on the poolside tiles and the lap of water echoing in the conservatory. Joanne stood at the head of the pool with the gimp kneeling by her boots.

Jane stood by the conservatory door, watching the scene with an air of cool detachment. She could see, from the way Joanne kept glancing in her direction, the woman was trying to make a point, a point intended exclusively for her. But Jane had no idea what that point might be. The woman had just blown the gimp and, although Jane would be the first to admit that she didn't know much about the exchange of power-play that was expected between a gimp and his mistress, she felt sure that getting down on your knees and blowing a gimp was not something a competent dominatrix should do. It crossed her mind that she should mention as much to Joanne and then she decided that wouldn't be the first point she needed to make. Clearly Joanne wasn't very good at oral sex and ought to practise more. The gimp had seemed distinctly uncomfortable while the woman was gobbling him and his climax looked painful and unpleasant. Jane also didn't think it was becoming for a supposedly dominant woman to have a gimp's come trickling from her lips. But, because she had decided that Joanne wasn't worth the trouble of her animosity, Jane simply relaxed against the wall and watched the impromptu show that Joanne was providing.

'You all know this is my gimp, don't you?' Joanne called out.

There was a polite murmur of assent. Joanne's interruption of the party's activities was obviously unprecedented and Jane could see that no one was sure how to respond.

'Has everyone who wants to use him had an ample opportunity?' She glanced pointedly at Jane and added, 'I know some people have had more than ample opportunity. But I wanted to make sure everyone else – everyone who wanted to play with my gimp – has had that chance.'

No one spoke.

Jane sensed a shift in the atmosphere. The fun and pleasantness of the party had evaporated. The sound of laughter had been replaced by Joanne's grating voice. The mood of sexual playfulness had been dispelled by the chill of impending disaster.

'How many pussies have you eaten this evening, gimp?' Joanne demanded. 'A dozen? More? How many women have played with your cock? What would your wife think if she discovered what a naughty little boy you've been?'

Jane leaned forward, wondering why Joanne was labouring this point and where she was going with it. Denise appeared by Jane's side, looking uninterested in Joanne and clearly anxious to say something about her evening, but when she started to whisper in her ear Jane pulled away and indicated Joanne and the gimp.

'I want to hear what this bitch has to say,' she murmured.

Nodding agreement, Denise fell silent and watched.

'We've all had a lot of fun with this gimp tonight,' Joanne said loudly. She glanced in Jane's direction and added, 'Some of us have had more fun with him than is decent.'

Jane pursed her lips and said nothing.

'And so,' Joanne went on. 'So that we can all properly thank him whenever we see him out on the street, I think I should take his mask off and reveal his identity.'

'What a bitch,' Denise murmured.

Her words were lost in the uneasy whispering that echoed round the conservatory. Ted and Phil both shook their heads and gestured to Joanne, shouting that it was inappropriate, not right. But Joanne was clearly lost in the moment of her own power.

'I'm doing it,' she declared.

Jane thought it should have been impossible to know what the gimp was thinking. He was encased in a sheath of black leather that hid his features completely. But his body language revealed a man who desperately did not want the domineering woman above him to expose his identity.

'I'm doing it,' Joanne insisted, pulling the zip at the back of the gimp's neck and exposing a layer of pale flesh. 'I'll show you all who my gimp is!'

She wrenched the mask from his face as a piercing scream came from the street outside.

Twenty

4 Cedar View

Linda screamed when Max pushed into her.

She had spent so much time holding back her orgasm that when it finally tore through her the pleasure was infinitely worse than the punishment Max had inflicted. Her buttocks were ablaze with heat. If she concentrated, she would be able to feel each individual line of the criss-cross pattern that now tattooed her cheeks. Her anus felt sore and stretched and overfull. But it was the sensation of having Max push his length into her, and the subsequent superlative orgasm, that ignited the scream. The sound of her joy ricocheted from the walls of the facing buildings.

'That's it,' Max grunted. 'Take every damned inch.'

'Yes,' she gasped. 'Give it to me. Make me take it all.'

He laughed. 'You're a greedy bitch, aren't you?'

'I'm greedy for cock,' she told him. 'Greedy for your cock.'

As she said the words, Linda was aware of footsteps and conversation. She looked up and saw that the party guests were coming out of her house and glancing curiously – concernedly – in her direction. Max, clearly untroubled by two dozen scantily dressed onlookers, continued to slide his thick cock in and out of her bowel. Linda stiffened, uncertain if she wanted everyone from the party to see her being used by her uncouth and rather menacing neighbour. At the party, she supposed, any of the guests could have seen her doing all manner of sexual things, if they had bothered to notice her. She had joined in the daisy-chain with Phil, Denise, Ted and Joanne. She had pumped up her pussy lips and paraded them round the party for everyone to admire or ignore. Until she stole away on Tom's advice, the party had not been dissimilar to any other she had hosted or attended. But never before had she been watched by a crowd while she was brutally serviced by a domineering bit of rough. The rush of satisfaction was enormous.

She glanced towards number one and tried to make out Tom's silhouette in the shadows. She could see only darkness there but she fervently hoped that he was watching, with the appreciation he seemed to reserve specially for her, and admiring the show she was putting on for him.

Savouring the sensation that Max had awoken inside her, basking in the interest and attention of so many people as they pointed and exclaimed, Linda clenched her anus round the length of his shaft and screamed as another wave of joy ripped through her body. Fireworks flashed at the back of her eyes. The inner muscles of her sex contracted in a spasm of pure bliss. His erection remained hard as it pushed in and out of her anus and she wallowed in the rush of the orgasm.

Slowly, as the world round her crept back into her consciousness, Linda became aware of approaching footsteps. Unlike the guests from the party, this person was close and moving swiftly. She stiffened and glanced up to see Megan walking down the path.

As usual, Max's young wife looked stylish in her desirable gothic fashion. The long leather coat made her appear tall and graceful. The sound of her boot heels was almost hypnotic as she strode rhythmically up the path towards them. It was close to midnight but her eyes still remained hidden behind her ludicrously large dark glasses.

Linda had the impression that Megan gave her no more than a brief, uninterested glance. If asked, she would have guessed that Megan looked at her long enough to recognise her and to note that Max's erection was buried deep into her. Realising that she now craved the attention of being noticed, Linda found Megan's lack of interest in her strangely exciting.

As Megan briskly approached, Linda wondered if she was going to bring the evening to an unpleasant end by being upset at finding her husband having sex with a neighbour. The thought made her stomach churn with mounting dread. It was bad enough to hear the sounds of raised voices coming from the direction of her own house. Phil and Ted seemed to be shouting at someone but Linda couldn't tell who or why. Whatever unpleasantness had happened at number six, Linda was glad she had missed it. She didn't enjoy argumentative confrontations and she hoped that wasn't what Megan intended now, as she strode purposefully up her front path. Linda could easily imagine the woman bursting on to the scene with the fury of an apocalyptic explosion.

Joanne burst on to the scene with the fury of an apocalyptic explosion. 'Where did everyone go?' she demanded.

Ted flinched as she stepped closer and Joanne wasn't surprised by his reaction. She had barked the question in his ear. Even if she hadn't been shouting she supposed her furious mood was obvious: her hair was in disarray, she brandished a riding crop as though she was ready to flail anyone who met with her disapproval, and she suspected her eyes were wide and staring with maniacal outrage.

'Where the hell did everyone go?'

'We came outside to see what the noise was,' Ted explained. 'Linda's scream brought everyone running.' He nodded towards the doorway of number four.

Joanne could see Max McMurray riding Linda from behind. It wasn't something she had ever seen on a quiet suburban street before. The sight made her nose wrinkle and her upper lip curl. 'That's disgusting,' she hissed. 'Aren't you going to go over there and stop her?'

Ted laughed.

'What's so fucking funny?' Joanne snapped.

'Why on earth should I stop my partner having fun?' He sounded incredulous that Joanne could even think of such an idea. 'Linda tries her hardest to enjoy the parties but she never seems to get the full benefit from them. This is the first time I've heard her scream through an orgasm at one of our evenings. Why would I go over there and stop her enjoying herself?'

'You're sick,' Joanne told him.

Ted stared at her solemnly. 'What you were trying to do with that gimp was sick,' he said quietly. 'You shouldn't have been trying to publicly unmask him. If that poor boy wanted to keep his identity secret you should have respected it.'

Joanne came close to striking him. She lifted the crop and was about to slash it down hard against his face when her wrist was clasped in a powerful grip. She turned around and saw that Ted's brother held her arm. He plucked the crop from her fingers and threw it aside before releasing his hold on her. His smile was frustratingly genial as he said, 'Denise has just untied your gimp and sent him home. Perhaps it's time you went home too?'

Joanne shifted her glare from Ted to Phil and then back to Ted. She had never known such pure outrage as the fury that now flooded her system. 'Sick, am I?' she sniffed, remembering Ted's insult. 'Let's see how sick you think I am when I start to hand out my Polaroid collection.'

Ted shook his head. 'There are two reasons why I don't think you'll do that,' he said quietly. He took her to one side, away from Phil, guiding her with a firm grip on her arm, and lowered his voice. 'I don't think you'll do that because you know it would be wrong,' he began. 'And I don't think you'll do that because I'm sure you're not really that stupid.'

Joanne pulled her arm from his grip. This time the urge to strike him was almost irresistible. Seeing that Phil was watching them carefully, she realised she would be overpowered before she had a chance to vent her frustrations properly, and her inability to control the two men would no doubt make a humiliating spectacle. 'I'll show you how really stupid I am,' she growled. Then, realising the words probably weren't the best way to conclude an argument, she rushed away from him. She couldn't decide if she should head for the sanctuary of her home or try to cause some more upset before ending the day. But she was determined to get her revenge on someone.

'What's happening, Max?'

Megan managed to ask the question with a cooler delivery than she had expected. Standing by her husband's side – at midnight, in sunglasses, her coat slightly open to expose her stockings and much more bare flesh – Megan thought she looked like a parody of sexual chic. And somehow, she thought, the innocence of her question worked.

Max, she conceded, managed to respond with equal poise. A crowd of neighbours stood on the lawn before him, watching his sexual antics with avid interest. His wife had returned to find him naked on the step, butt-fucking Linda from number six. Yet the only expression he chose to show was a genuine yet understated pleasure at seeing his wife.

'Megan,' he exclaimed cheerfully. 'It's so good to see you. I was just playing with Linda.'

He thrust himself deeper into the redhead and then pulled back a little. She moaned in response. Her hands were on her knees, the nails buried into her flesh. Her face was twisted with bitter satisfaction.

'You'd gone out,' Max continued. 'Aliceon didn't know where you were. So I thought I should take advantage of the opportunity to become a good neighbour and do some suburban socialising.'

Megan nodded. Inside her stomach she felt a thrill of urgent need for him. His innate coolness, the way he was able to act as though he had mastery over every situation, these were the reasons she thought him her ideal man. The sight of him casually fucking Linda, while he spoke to her about being a good neighbour, lit a blaze of desire in her loins.

'Suburban socialising,' she repeated.

He nodded, grinned and thrust himself into Linda again. She moaned.

'And,' Megan started carefully, 'you're doing your suburban socialising on the doorstep because . . .'

'. . . because we have an agreement that nothing happens inside the house,' Max concluded for her. He continued to ride Linda as he spoke, his head tilted politely towards Megan. In an offhand tone he asked, 'Have you been anywhere nice?'

Megan thought for a moment before saying, 'I've been doing some suburban socialising of my own.' She stepped closer, kissed him lightly on the cheek and reached for his erection. He was buried so deep into Linda's anus that she could only just touch the base of his cock. But it was enough for Megan to hold. She saw he was studying her with a concerned frown and brushed his obvious worries aside. 'This is a trick I just learned whilst I was suburban socialising with the Graftons. You'll love this, Max. You'll absolutely love it.'

Max remained still and silent. Megan got a firmer grip on his cock and slowly eased it back and forth into Linda's backside. She placed her free hand on her husband's rear, encouraging him to sway his hips backwards and forwards as she helped him fuck Linda.

'The Graftons taught you this trick?'

'Do you like it?'

'I should really want to punish you for learning something like this,' Max admitted. 'But I have to be honest and say I'm impressed.' He was grinning as he added, 'It's pretty damned good.'

Megan bit back a rush of adoration for her husband. She didn't want to spoil their understated exchange by being the first to display excitement or affection, but she longed to embrace him and tell him how much she loved him.

He was right to describe her new trick as being pretty damned good. It was an incredible sensation: feeling Max's sticky stiffness in her hand, working it in and out of their grateful neighbour's warmth, knowing she was involved in the pleasure of both people and that they were all contributing to each other's satisfaction. In the background she could hear Linda's mounting sighs and the murmur of their neighbours behind them. But the main thing she listened to was Max's deepening groans as she worked him more swiftly in and out of Linda's body.

'That's such an intimate sensation,' Max told her. He placed an arm around his wife's shoulder and kissed her hungrily on the mouth.

'I knew you'd like it,' Megan grinned as she continued to thrust his cock into Linda.

'We're going to have to do this more often,' Max insisted. 'But I still think I need to punish you. You seem to have forgotten who the master of our house is.'

Megan searched his face to see if he was joking. With a quickening heartbeat she realised Max was deadly serious. His muscles bulged and his face wore a flint-hard expression she only ever saw in the moments before he treated her to the cruellest discipline.

'Janey?'

Jane turned sharply at the sound of the voice and then sighed with relief when she realised it was only Denise. Laughing at her own paranoia, fairly sure that no one else at the party had recognised her beneath her disguise, she embraced her friend and said, 'Thank you for inviting me to the party. I had no idea it would be so much fun.'

Denise grinned. 'You had a good time?'

'The best ever,' Jane assured her. Deciding it would be polite to ask about Denise's evening, trying not to dwell on the fact that she had happily parted company with her early in the evening and made no attempt to hook up with her afterwards, she asked, 'Did you enjoy yourself?'

'I had an informative night,' Denise said enigmatically. 'I found out what excites my husband and I now know what I need to do if I want him to get me pregnant.'

Jane raised her eyebrows. 'Derek's agreed to get you pregnant? I didn't even know he was at the party.'

'That's not exactly how it's worked out,' Denise said carefully. 'Derek wasn't here. I popped home briefly. And I now know, once he sees me polishing his car while I'm wearing a thong and a pair of heels, he's going to be willing to give me what I want.'

Jane laughed. 'You're learning how to get your own way.'

Denise kissed her gently on the cheek. 'I've been taught by the best, Janey.' With only a slight bitterness in her tone, she said, 'I just wish I hadn't spent my night with Phil. That might have prevented things working out perfectly.'

Jane didn't understand the comment. 'Phil is Ted's brother, isn't he? The mechanic?'

Denise nodded.

'A couple of the people I spoke with said they were surprised to see him at the party this evening. They didn't think he'd be fully functional after his recent vasectomy. Is that what's spoilt things for you?'

Denise didn't answer at first. She digested Jane's words with a stunned expression. A slow smile blossomed on her lips and, before Jane saw it coming, Denise grabbed her in a crushing embrace and smothered her face with grateful kisses.

'Jesus, Janey! I am so going to satisfy you the next time you're in my bed.' She giggled briefly, then returned to kissing her friend. 'I'll make you come so hard you'll explode. I mean it. I promise. I really do.'

'Jesus yourself, Denise,' Jane gasped. She pulled herself from her friend's embrace and studied her with a wary smile. 'I don't know what I've done to deserve your gratitude, but you know I'll be happy to exploit it. What did I say that's got you so fired up?'

Denise shook her head and said, 'I might tell you when we next get together.' Brushing the subject aside, belatedly embarrassed by her display of effusiveness, she said, 'Joanne's gimp asked me to pass on a message.'

Jane glanced over her shoulder as though she expected to see the gimp standing there. The rest of the party crowd were disappearing to their homes on Cedar View, but she was disappointed to note that the gimp wasn't visible.

'He had to get home,' Denise explained. 'He said his wife would be wondering where he was if he didn't get back soon. But he wanted me to tell you that he'll see you on Tuesday, like you agreed.'

Jane closed her lips to stifle a triumphant grin. Trying to appear nonchalant, she glanced towards her house and noticed a light in the bedroom. 'I suppose it's just as well that he's gone for the night,' she conceded. 'It looks like John's back home and there would probably be questions if I stayed out much later.'

She paused, remembering that Joanne had been on the verge of exposing the gimp's identity before they had all fled from the party to investigate Linda's screams.

'What did he look like? Under the mask, I mean? Did you see?'

Denise shrugged. 'I suppose he looked a little bit like your husband, only without glasses.'

Jane smiled at the idea of the gimp resembling her husband. It was so absurd it was almost plausible.

'Are you going to tell John that you've found another man?'

Jane considered this for a moment and then laughed. 'Imagine me telling John I'd met a gimp at a sex party,' she giggled. 'He wouldn't understand what I was talking about. He'd think I was speaking in tongues.' Shaking her head she said, 'I think I'll keep this secret from John for as long as I possibly can.'

* * *

Linda couldn't believe the couple had been able to sustain her pleasure for so long. Max had striped her with consummate skill and taken her to an extreme of ecstasy as he rode her on his front step. The appearance of the party guests had satisfied an urge inside her to be noticed and watched, and then Megan's intimate involvement in her climax had made the moment complete. But now, as he stiffened inside her and prepared to explode, she realised that her best climax of the evening was still to come. Her anus was obscenely wet from his penetration. Her backside still throbbed from the punishment earlier, and she knew that some of the partygoers were continuing to watch the impromptu show she was providing.

The encroaching climax built with a menacing force. She tried to steady her breathing, frightened that the power of this orgasm would render her unconscious. She could feel the pleasure welling like the threat of an explosion and she knew, when it did tear through her, the force would be devastating.

When Max's erection finally pulsed inside her, Linda screamed with pleasure. Megan held his length, her warm, sticky fingers tracing circles on the sensitive flesh of Linda's sex and anus. The sensory overload left Linda gasping and shrieking as the waves of delight rolled through her again and again and again.

As her thoughts came back from the misty red euphoria of her climax, Linda could hear the shrill ring of a telephone. Her muscles ached and trembled and she tried to pull away from the cock that remained buried in her anus. But Max and Megan refused to let her go.

'How was that, Master?' Megan asked.

'That was good,' Max allowed. 'But not so good that you can forgo your punishment.'

Linda looked back over her shoulder and saw that Megan was frowning. 'Why should you need to punish

230

me?' she pouted. 'I haven't broken any of our rules. I haven't reneged on any of our agreements. I didn't do anything in our home. I organised for you to get laid while I was involved in my own suburban socialising. And I've even shown you that new trick that we're going to use again and again at various parties.'

Max nodded. 'Yes,' he agreed. 'You've done all those things. But I'm still going to punish you.'

'But why?'

Linda strained to hear Max's response, as anxious to know the answer as Megan clearly was. She was pained when he pulled out of her. She shivered as a final ripple of pleasure tickled through her body, then felt a sense of emptiness. Megan distractedly helped her to her feet.

'Why are you still going to punish me?' Megan asked Max.

'Because you know we're both going to enjoy it.' He kissed his wife chastely on the cheek and turned to slap Linda good-naturedly. 'I'd stay and chat,' he told Linda, 'but my phone's ringing. Maybe I'll see you again some time?' Without waiting for a reply, he turned and disappeared into the house.

Megan placed a hand on her arm. 'It's Linda, isn't it?'

'Yes.'

'I'm sorry I came back so late. It would have been nice to make your acquaintance properly. I'd best go and join my husband if you're leaving now.'

Watching Megan follow Max into the house, Linda realised she had been dismissed. She hadn't even reached down to retrieve her coat from the floor when the door was closed on her. Shocked by the abrupt end to the evening, she tried to make sense of what had happened and work out whether there would be any consequences from the folly of the evening. She

231

glanced towards the lawn, where the guests from her party had been gathered. They had all gone. There were fewer cars on the street than when she first called on Max and she suspected that some of the partygoers had gone home, while the others were in her house saying their goodbyes.

The idea of returning to the party didn't hold any interest. Sore, satisfied and still charged from the climactic experience of suffering Max's domination, Linda only wanted to find someone with whom she could relive the whole experience.

A figure emerged from the shadows, picked up her coat and gallantly draped it over her shoulders. 'Let me walk you back home,' Tom murmured.

She fell gratefully against him. A giddy smile split her lips when she realised Tom had seen everything that happened. She privately wondered if it had given him as much pleasure as she had experienced. Taking him in a light embrace, telling herself she was only using him for support as she staggered down the path away from Max and Megan's, Linda let her hand brush against the front of Tom's trousers. She smiled with satisfaction, sure that he had enjoyed the evening.

Twenty-one

2 Cedar View

'Two evenings a week,' Tanya muttered into the telephone. 'And will you be wanting the same sort of services from me that you got tonight?' She paused, swigged from the night's last can of lager and tried not to laugh when she heard the hurried refusal. 'That was just a one-off for this evening, was it? Oh! Well, you never know what we might get up to next time. I'll leave it open as a potential alternative for future nights.' She paused for a beat, struggling to suppress her smile and taking a bitter satisfaction from hearing Rhona Grafton trying not to show distaste in her voice.

'The money's going to be the same as it was tonight, yeah?' Again, another pause, but only a brief one. She didn't give Rhona a chance to respond properly. 'Then that's settled. I'll see you in a couple of days.'

She severed the call before Rhona could think of an argument against employing her. Still riding high from the conversation, Tanya picked up the phone and dialled Joanne's number. The telephone rang more than a dozen times before Joanne picked it up. Her voice was slurred with tiredness, but she still sounded angry.

'I don't know who this is, but it had better be important.'

233

'It's your former cleaner,' Tanya spat. 'You fired me earlier this evening and I'm just calling to say, you can't fire me, cos I quit.'

'Thank you, Tanya.' Joanne's voice dripped with cool disdain. 'I'm glad we've got that cleared up. Now could you please fuck off and never call me again?'

'Do you know why I quit?' Tanya asked.

'I neither know nor care,' Joanne sneered. 'I'm hanging up now. I'll be changing my telephone number tomorrow. And I'll be leaving the telephone off the hook for the remainder of the night. Goodnight, Tanya, and –'

'I'm not just quitting because I've got another job,' Tanya broke in. 'I'm quitting because your house stinks of piss.'

'You were the one cleaning the house, Tanya,' Joanne drawled. 'What does that say about your abilities?'

Tanya winced, stung by the blow to her professional pride. 'You threatened me with the police earlier this evening,' she remembered. 'They'd better not come here. I'm warning you of that now.'

'And if the police do turn up at your house,' Joanne asked smugly, 'what do you propose to do by way of retaliation?'

Tanya glanced across the room to the open door of the kitchen. The sink was black with the sooty remains of the photographs she had burnt. 'If the police turn up here, I'll show them the Polaroids I stole from your drawer.'

'You bitch!'

Sensing she had struck a nerve, and wanting to make sure she caused the maximum upset with this last phone call to her former employer, Tanya said quickly, 'And I won't be feeding Mister Tiddles again until he's eaten your fucking koi carp.' She slammed the receiver back into its cradle, only to pick it up again and dial Max's number.

'Megan got back OK?'

'Yes.'

'I told her you were looking for her.'

'I know.'

'So that means you won't be wanting any rent for the next five weeks.'

'Five weeks!'

'Like we agreed,' Tanya said patiently. She lifted her can of beer and drained the last of its contents. 'One week's rent in exchange for me going to look for her. One month's rent as my finder's fee. I looked and I found, therefore I get five weeks rent-free.'

'You're pushing this too far,' Max growled.

Behind him, Tanya could hear Megan's voice.

'Is that Tanya?'

'Yeah.' Max's voice became muffled as he placed his hand over the mouthpiece but Tanya could still hear his words. 'The cheeky bitch is trying to squirm out of her rent for the next five weeks.'

'Pay her what you owe her,' Megan told him. 'And then come back to the dungeon so you can finish my punishment.'

There was a long, sullen pause before Max said, 'You and Aliceon are getting six extra stripes each for this.' Then he took his hand away from the mouthpiece and resumed speaking to Tanya. She heard excited giggles tinkling in the background. 'I'll let you off five weeks' rent,' he agreed. 'But I'll be watching you while you're cleaning our house and, if there's one thing done wrong, I'll stripe your arse until it glows in the dark.'

Tanya laughed and listened to him seethe in silence for a moment. Remembering the way Max had seemed so capable of pleasing Linda with his cruel discipline, and hearing the eager laughter of Megan and Aliceon, she reminded herself that he was far better at administering punishment than Joanne had been. 'I'll look forward to seeing you tomorrow,' she said sweetly, and wished him goodnight.

Epilogue

Like I said before, an aerial photograph of Cedar View would show that the cul-de-sac looks like an enormous keyhole. The short, straight entrance to the road is lined by two houses on either side. The curve at the road's bulbous end looks like the hole where the barrel of the key would be inserted. And maybe now you understand why I enjoy looking through keyholes.

Especially this keyhole.

Of course, I've just been relating the events of one evening on Cedar View, and I could only show you the things I saw. No doubt a lot more went on that I missed completely. But, whatever might have happened that I didn't get to see, I expect there'll be a repeat perform-ance for me to catch tomorrow night. And the night after that.

Are you wondering what I get out of watching these antics?

I'm a people-person by nature. I love watching people. I particularly love watching my neighbours when they're playing together. But that's not all I get out of it. I'd tell you more but Linda's still with me. She's been back home and retrieved that clever little pussy pump of hers. And, now that she's fully pumped up and looking ripe, swollen and wet, it looks like she wants to do more than talk.

Like I said before, my neighbours on Cedar View are a set of immoral, amoral bastards. They're constantly hopping in and out of each other's beds and they're at it like rabbits all the time. Tonight, because I think it's what Linda wants, I'm going to stop watching. I might just participate.

But only for tonight.

nexus

The leading publisher of fetish and adult fiction

TELL US WHAT YOU THINK!

Readers' ideas and opinions matter to us so please take a few minutes to fill in the questionnaire below.

1. Sex: Are you male ☐ female ☐ a couple ☐?

2. Age: Under 21 ☐ 21–30 ☐ 31–40 ☐ 41–50 ☐ 51–60 ☐ over 60 ☐

3. Where do you buy your Nexus books from?

☐ A chain book shop. If so, which one(s)?

_____

☐ An independent book shop. If so, which one(s)?

_____

☐ A used book shop/charity shop
☐ Online book store. If so, which one(s)?

_____

4. How did you find out about Nexus books?

☐ Browsing in a book shop
☐ A review in a magazine
☐ Online
☐ Recommendation
☐ Other _____

5. In terms of settings, which do you prefer? (Tick as many as you like.)

☐ Down to earth and as realistic as possible
☐ Historical settings. If so, which period do you prefer?

_____

☐ Fantasy settings – barbarian worlds
☐ Completely escapist/surreal fantasy

- ☐ Institutional or secret academy
- ☐ Futuristic/sci fi
- ☐ Escapist but still believable
- ☐ Any settings you dislike?

  _____

- ☐ Where would you like to see an adult novel set?

  _____

6. In terms of storylines, would you prefer:

- ☐ Simple stories that concentrate on adult interests?
- ☐ More plot and character-driven stories with less explicit adult activity?
- ☐ We value your ideas, so give us your opinion of this book:

  _____

  _____

  _____

7. In terms of your adult interests, what do you like to read about? (Tick as many as you like.)

- ☐ Traditional corporal punishment (CP)
- ☐ Modern corporal punishment
- ☐ Spanking
- ☐ Restraint/bondage
- ☐ Rope bondage
- ☐ Latex/rubber
- ☐ Leather
- ☐ Female domination and male submission
- ☐ Female domination and female submission
- ☐ Male domination and female submission
- ☐ Willing captivity
- ☐ Uniforms
- ☐ Lingerie/underwear/hosiery/footwear (boots and high heels)
- ☐ Sex rituals
- ☐ Vanilla sex
- ☐ Swinging

☐ Cross-dressing/TV
☐ Enforced feminisation
☐ Others – tell us what you don't see enough of in adult fiction:

_____

_____

_____

8. Would you prefer books with a more specialised approach to your interests, i.e. a novel specifically about uniforms? If so, which subject(s) would you like to read a Nexus novel about?

_____

_____

_____

9. Would you like to read true stories in Nexus books? For instance, the true story of a submissive woman, or a male slave? Tell us which true revelations you would most like to read about:

_____

_____

_____

10. What do you like best about Nexus books?

_____

_____

11. What do you like least about Nexus books?

_____

_____

12. Which are your favourite titles?

_____

_____

13. Who are your favourite authors?

_____

_____

14. **Which covers do you prefer? Those featuring:**
   (Tick as many as you like.)

☐ Fetish outfits
☐ More nudity
☐ Two models
☐ Unusual models or settings
☐ Classic erotic photography
☐ More contemporary images and poses
☐ A blank/non-erotic cover
☐ What would your ideal cover look like?

_____

15. **Describe your ideal Nexus novel in the space provided:**

_____
_____
_____
_____

16. **Which celebrity would feature in one of your Nexus-style fantasies? We'll post the best suggestions on our website – anonymously!**

_____

THANKS FOR YOUR TIME

Now simply write the title of this book in the space below and cut out the questionnaire pages. Post to: Nexus, Marketing Dept., Thames Wharf Studios, Rainville Rd, London W6 9HA

Book title: _____

NEXUS NEW BOOKS

NEXUS CONFESSIONS VOLUME 4
Various

Swinging, dogging, group sex, cross-dressing, spanking, female domination, corporal punishment, and extreme fetishes . . . Nexus Confessions explores the length and breadth of erotic obsession, real experience and sexual fantasy. This is an encyclopaedic collection of the bizarre, the extreme, the utterly inappropriate, the daring and the shocking experiences of ordinary men and women driven by their extraordinary desires. Collected by the world's leading publisher of fetish fiction, these are true stories and shameful confessions, never-before-told or published.

£7.99   ISBN 978 0 352 34136 5

To be published in August 2008

INDECENT PURSUIT
Ray Gordon

When young and sexually vivacious Sheena is dumped by her snobbish older boyfriend, she decides to get her revenge. So using her sexual prowess she sets out to seduce his three brothers. Her lewd language and loose behaviour prove irresistible to the men and before long she has bedded them all. But her goal of marrying into the wealthy family remains as distant as ever. In desperation, Sheena sets her sights on the father; but 'the Boss', as he is known by his sons, is determined to regain his family's honour and at the same time teach the wanton young woman a lesson in respect.

£7.99   ISBN 978 0 352 34196 9

To be published in September 2008

THE INDULGENCES OF ISABELLE
Penny Birch

In her third year at Oxford, Isabelle Colraine is still indulging her private obsession with dominating girls. Unfortunately for her, others are aware of her predilection and are determined to spoil her fun. There's Portia, an upper-class brat who refuses to accept Isabelle's dominance, and Sarah, a mature woman who believes the right to dominate has to be earned with age and experience. But worst of all is Stan Tierney, an older man, who wants to take advantage of her and won't take no for an answer.

£7.99   ISBN 978 0 352 34198 3

If you would like more information about Nexus titles, please visit our website at www.nexus-books.co.uk, or send a large stamped addressed envelope to:
  Nexus, Thames Wharf Studios,
  Rainville Road, London W6 9HA

NEXUS BOOKLIST

Information is correct at time of printing. To avoid disappointment, check availability before ordering. Go to www.nexus-books.co.uk.

All books are priced at £6.99 unless another price is given.

NEXUS

☐ ABANDONED ALICE	Adriana Arden	ISBN 978 0 352 33969 0
☐ ALICE IN CHAINS	Adriana Arden	ISBN 978 0 352 33908 9
☐ AMERICAN BLUE	Penny Birch	ISBN 978 0 352 34169 3
☐ AQUA DOMINATION	William Doughty	ISBN 978 0 352 34020 7
☐ THE ART OF CORRECTION	Tara Black	ISBN 978 0 352 33895 2
☐ THE ART OF SURRENDER	Madeline Bastinado	ISBN 978 0 352 34013 9
☐ BEASTLY BEHAVIOUR	Aishling Morgan	ISBN 978 0 352 34095 5
☐ BEING A GIRL	Chloë Thurlow	ISBN 978 0 352 34139 6
☐ BELINDA BARES UP	Yolanda Celbridge	ISBN 978 0 352 33926 3
☐ BIDDING TO SIN	Rosita Varón	ISBN 978 0 352 34063 4
☐ BLUSHING AT BOTH ENDS	Philip Kemp	ISBN 978 0 352 34107 5
☐ THE BOOK OF PUNISHMENT	Cat Scarlett	ISBN 978 0 352 33975 1
☐ BRUSH STROKES	Penny Birch	ISBN 978 0 352 34072 6
☐ CALLED TO THE WILD	Angel Blake	ISBN 978 0 352 34067 2
☐ CAPTIVES OF CHEYNER CLOSE	Adriana Arden	ISBN 978 0 352 34028 3
☐ CARNAL POSSESSION	Yvonne Strickland	ISBN 978 0 352 34062 7
☐ CITY MAID	Amelia Evangeline	ISBN 978 0 352 34096 2
☐ COLLEGE GIRLS	Cat Scarlett	ISBN 978 0 352 33942 3
☐ COMPANY OF SLAVES	Christina Shelly	ISBN 978 0 352 33887 7
☐ CONCEIT AND CONSEQUENCE	Aishling Morgan	ISBN 978 0 352 33965 2
☐ CORRECTIVE THERAPY	Jacqueline Masterson	ISBN 978 0 352 33917 1
☐ CORRUPTION	Virginia Crowley	ISBN 978 0 352 34073 3
☐ CRUEL SHADOW	Aishling Morgan	ISBN 978 0 352 33886 0
☐ DARK MISCHIEF	Lady Alice McCloud	ISBN 978 0 352 33998 0

- - - - - - ✂ -

Please send me the books I have ticked above.

Name ....

Address ....

....

....

.... Post code ....

Send to: Virgin Books Cash Sales, Thames Wharf Studios, Rainville Road, London W6 9HA

US customers: for prices and details of how to order books for delivery by mail, call 888-330-8477.

Please enclose a cheque or postal order, made payable to **Nexus Books Ltd**, to the value of the books you have ordered plus postage and packing costs as follows:

UK and BFPO – £1.00 for the first book, 50p for each subsequent book.

Overseas (including Republic of Ireland) – £2.00 for the first book, £1.00 for each subsequent book.

If you would prefer to pay by VISA, ACCESS/MASTERCARD, AMEX, DINERS CLUB or SWITCH, please write your card number and expiry date here:

....

Please allow up to 28 days for delivery.

Signature ....

Our privacy policy

We will not disclose information you supply us to any other parties. We will not disclose any information which identifies you personally to any person without your express consent.

From time to time we may send out information about Nexus books and special offers. Please tick here if you do *not* wish to receive Nexus information. ☐

- - - - - - ✂ -

NEXUS ENTHUSIAST

NEXUS NON FICTION